# ALERON

BOOK ONE OF

THE STRIGOI SERIES

8/22/12

## KANE

GREENLEAF
BOOK GROUP PRESS

Published by Greenleaf Book Group Press
Austin, TX
www.gbgpress.com

Distributed by Greenleaf Book Group

For ordering information or special discounts for bulk purchases, please contact Greenleaf Book Group at PO Box 91869, Austin, TX 78709, 512.891.6100.

Design and composition by Greenleaf Book Group LLC
Cover design by Greenleaf Book Group LLC

Publisher's Cataloging-In-Publication Data
(Prepared by The Donohue Group, Inc.)

Kane.
   Aleron / Kane.

      p. ; cm. -- (The strigoi series ; bk. 1)

   ISBN: 978-1-60832-382-1

   1. Immortality--Fiction.  2. Imaginary creatures--Fiction.  3. Vampires--Fiction.  4. Fantasy fiction.
I. Title.

PS3611.A64 A54 2012
813/.6                                                                   2012933705

   ISBN 13:  978-1-60832-382-1

Part of the Tree Neutral® program, which offsets the number of trees consumed in the production and printing of this book by taking proactive steps, such as planting trees in direct proportion to the number of trees used: www.treeneutral.com

Printed in the United States of America on acid-free paper

12  13  14  15  16   10 9 8 7 6 5 4 3 2 1

First Edition

*To Octavia, for your smile, for your laugh, for your loving kindness, I write. For your love, for your support, for your approval, I write. For your touch, for your dedication to us, I write. Thank you. I promise to keep writing.*

# PREFACE

In my mind's eye, I can see.

I can see heaven. I can see hell.

The angels. And, the Darkness alike.

And I've grown quite fond of the Darkness, for in it, I'm all powerful.

Without it, I'm nothing.

Come to a place which lies far beyond your mind.

A place that fantastical creatures thrive.

A place where We live.

A place where many perish at our hands.

Some call us demons. Some say we are spawn of Cain.

Some say we are undead.

I can assure you, we are alive!

For We are Vampyre.

—Aleron

# CHAPTER 1

y name is Aleron, and I was once human. Indeed, I still resemble a human, but I feel, smell, move, and even taste like something completely out of the ordinary, or should I say, extraordinary. I'm flesh and blood but not much more. I have tremendous power and strength, far beyond that of ordinary men. However, I didn't always have these qualities. They had an origin. And as time passed, they developed beyond my hopes, far surpassing the abilities possessed by others of my kind. I had a mentor-mother, who encouraged me and helped me explore the boundaries of my supernatural abilities. Who else would be better to teach a child about himself than the one who gave him life?

Camilia and Aknon welcomed me, the first of their two children, on the seventh day of January in the year 1791 in the Greco-Roman city of Alexandria, Egypt. My father held no significant political or religious office, no positions of prestige, but he was an artisan, crafting furniture out of anything he could get his skillful hands on.

Alexandria was growing at the time, and his art became known to many. My mother and sister, Shani, devoted their lives to religion. Day after day, night after night, they walked from home to home, village to village, preaching the word of God. My father urged my mother to cease, for the path of Christ wasn't well received by many in Alexandria. My mother's family originated from the southern region of the Carpathians. There the influence of Christ was prevalent. My father was born in Egypt, where Islam was the dominant religion. My father defied his faith and family to marry my mother. He brought her to Alexandria, for he recognized their safety wouldn't be assured if he chose anywhere else in the region.

Despite my father's numerous requests, my mother continued to do what she knew to be right. My sister, albeit reluctant in the beginning, gradually became as enthusiastic as my mother. My father gave up the battle, for the conviction of my mother proved to be unflinching.

Life for me as a boy was anything but common. Virtually every piece of gold my father earned and what was donated to my mother and sister was spent on my education. It was recognized early on that I had an unnaturally acute understanding of mathematics and science. My intuitive understanding of trade led to an apprenticeship with a banker. However, it was my love for history that led me to become an assistant to historian Davila of Grotius.

After I had spent several months under the tutelage of Davila, he recognized my yearning for knowledge of civilizations that were on the verge of being forgotten. His confidence in me eventually grew, and I was charged with assisting him with his research on the ancient Greek philosopher Epicurus, the most important research Davila had been commissioned for. My responsibilities included preparing Davila's presentation on Epicurus for our benefactor. This required much work, which often led me to spend every waking moment at the library and Davila's office in al-Montaza.

On March 22, 1817, I left the library for a short walk to al-Montaza Square. The night sky was clear, the air crisp, and the streets seemingly lifeless. I remember that night well, because it was the first time I felt Her presence. It was an unnerving feeling that became more intense as I approached the square, prompting me to steal glances over my shoulder a few times along the way. The moment I entered the square, a dream state fell over me. I wasn't asleep, but I wasn't entirely awake, either. My vision began to blur, and my breathing became quick and shallow. Suddenly lethargic, I stopped and leaned against the exterior wall of a building. I forced a deep breath and squeezed my eyes shut. When I opened them, I saw what I thought was a specter of a woman. I blinked and squinted to focus my vision, but it evaporated as quickly as it had appeared.

I ascribed the vision to fatigue. I gave it no further thought until the following evening, when I saw it again while working at my home. A slight noise interrupted my concentration on *Epicureanism*, a Hellenistic book I had been studying. I turned my head in the direction of the clamor, and an abrupt chill withered the candle flame, extinguishing it. I felt the hairs on my arms come to life, as the chill brushed past me. I stood and walked in the direction of the disturbance, hoping to see what I had felt. But I couldn't. And before I knew it the flame had rekindled, and I was standing in the middle of the room—alone.

I was convinced that I had been truly shaken by the unknown, and for days, even weeks afterward, I became more and more cautious. Day after day I became more withdrawn from my friends. The incident in my home consumed me entirely. I felt its presence, but I was not able to lay my eyes on it. As time passed, I looked over my shoulder less and less. Within a few weeks, the presence only lived in my dreams, and then I finally relinquished my recollection of its existence altogether.

On May fourteenth in Cairo, Egypt, I was attending the most prestigious social ball of the year, the Promethium. The ball was held at the Cairo Citadel just north of the Great Pyramids and the Valley of the Kings. Once a year, men of wealth and influence gathered to meet and socialize with their peers. It was an effort to make new acquaintances that would result in more wealth and influence. Kings, lords, landowners, and politicians were always among the many businessmen present.

A sudden and unexplainable illness had befallen Davila, leaving him bedridden, and I had come to the ball in his stead. I wasn't a man of wealth and had little to no influence, but as Davila's personal assistant, I was charged with tending to his affairs in his absence.

Though the men were more economically sound and politically connected than I, I didn't feel the slightest bit intimidated or awkward among them. No one there knew my true social status, so often when I was speaking to one or two, a small crowd would gather to hear what I was sharing with the others. While in the midst of a conversation with a rather large group, I felt that strange uneasiness that I had almost forgotten. Though I continued participating in the conversation, I was no longer as engrossed as I had been. I found myself looking at the silhouette of a woman standing in the arch of the long corridor that led to the adjacent rooms where the concubines awaited their duty.

The only women allowed inside were maids, servants, and concubines. Concubines were confined to the adjacent rooms and never allowed in the main hall during or immediately following an event because they were often used for persuasive negotiations.

She was watching me, and I couldn't take my eyes off her. In my mind I began to hear faint sounds and words spoken in a voice that wasn't mine. The men chattered around me, though I could no longer make out their conversation. But I was unconcerned with it or with the men. My thoughts were only of the woman. I turned my attention back to the group for just an instant so that I could extricate myself from the conversation. I searched for her through the corner of my eye, but I could not find her. I quickly turned back, and she was gone.

I wondered if she had disappeared into the darkness of the corridor, and I walked toward it in search of her. I entered the first room to the left, where a naked lady was sitting in a chair, waiting. She watched me as I took in the room and then closed the door. I then opened the next door. A woman stood in the middle of the room. She motioned for me to enter and take her. I closed that door as well. The unknown voice in my head began calling out to me as I continued looking into the rooms in the corridor.

When I came to the last room, I was certain she had to be inside, for no doors remained and there was no other way out without passing the guards, whose job was to prevent the women from leaving. I swung open the door, but to my surprise, I saw no one. The room was empty. One of the guards had been observing my curious behavior, and from the doorway I shouted, "Where did the concubine go who was occupying this room?"

"No one has left the room, my lord," he replied.

How strange, I thought, and reentered to investigate. A women's nightgown lay on the floor in a heap in the far corner of the room. I reached down to pick it up. It was sheer and white with a few scarlet drops resembling red wine smudged on it. Nothing else was in the room. Suddenly the door slammed shut. Startled, I swiftly turned around, only to see the hanging mirror on the inside of the door reflecting me standing in the empty room. I sprang to the door and tried in vain to open it, but it had somehow locked when it shut. I turned, hoping to find something I could use to pry open the door. Instead, standing in the middle of the room was the woman I'd seen in the corridor. She watched me, silently.

"Hello, my sweet," I said.

"Hello, Aleron," she replied in a sultry voice.

As soon as I heard her speak, I recognized hers as the voice that had been in my head those many nights as I slept, and the voice speaking the words I had heard moments before, while I was searching for her.

Strange. Women didn't speak in this manner to men. Furthermore, how did she know my name? I walked closer to her and found myself immersed in her gaze. I couldn't speak. I don't know if it was her perfectly proportioned body or her stunning brown eyes that seemed to change hues reflecting the candlelight, but I was utterly consumed by the beautiful goddess who stood before me. She had a petite stature, one I imagined an Egyptian princess might possess. Her face seemed absolutely innocent, accentuated by large, childlike eyes, even though I could sense that her intentions were anything but. Her lips were the perfect complement to her beautiful face. Her skin, an unblemished olive, seemed almost to glow. She held her head completely motionless as she moved gracefully across the room with perfect posture and preternatural precision, like a feline fixed on her prey.

Her dress was of another time, and it was made from the finest and most expensive silk that I'd ever seen. Clearly, this woman had known wealth. She couldn't be more than twenty years old, five years my junior. She was perfect. Inhumanly perfect. Heavenly perfect. Instantly I was drawn to her.

*Come to me, my love. Don't fear me. I've chosen you above all others. Come to me, Aleron.*

She was at least six feet from me, but in the blink of an eye, I was in her tender yet powerful embrace. What happened next, I couldn't quite comprehend at the time. Before I knew it, we were soaring over the building and then high above the neighboring rooftops. Closer and closer to the moonlight we flew. I was frightened, yet her embrace made me feel secure and calm, like the calmness a child must feel after he has been separated from his mother but is reunited as she guides him to safety.

"Close your eyes," she whispered and pulled me closer to her. I didn't know what was more chilling, the brisk night air or her hardened body that felt as if it were made of stone. Nevertheless, I drew closer as she guided us to our distant and obscure destination.

After some time, we began to slow and then to descend. I kept my eyes closed for I was uncertain of what was to become of me. I wondered where she was taking me and why I could not resist her. I finally gathered enough strength to utter, "Put me down at once." Before I knew it, I was free-falling on what seemed a bottomless journey into darkness. Screaming, I pleaded with God to spare my life, promising to do only His bidding from that point on. The ground was drawing closer, and I could see it plainly. Memories and thoughts of my family, friends, loved ones, and the various women I knew flashed through my mind.

I felt I was going to die, until something abruptly stopped my fall. I opened my eyes and saw her holding my leg from one arm as easily as if I weighed nothing at all. I dangled upside down, suspended in the air. I looked up at her and saw that she was amused by my cries and prayers for forgiveness. Then, she dropped me! My heart almost burst with fright, but before I was able to scream, my body hit the ground.

And with a smirk she inquired, "Why do you pray for God even though God doesn't care about you nor your prayers?"

Completely ignoring her question, I demanded, "What manner of being are you? Why did you bring me here?"

"Because I chose you," she replied. "You will be my king. You will give me what he refuses to. You will be mine for all eternity."

Instantly she had me in her powerful embrace again. I struggled this time, even though I wanted to be near her. My desire for her was over-whelmingly strong.

"Calm yourself, my love. I know how you long for me. I know what you desire from me."

She was right. I did long for her. Her voice was soothing and irresist-ible. I wanted whatever she brought me there for. I resisted no more and was soon calm again, wanting only to hold her close, to embrace and love her.

As I looked into her brown eyes, I closed mine and began to kiss her lips. Unnaturally cold they were, yet soothing and satisfying. It seemed my body heat had no bearing on her freezing touch. But however cold, I couldn't stop, and I didn't want to stop. I felt as if I were in a beauti-ful dream. I couldn't remember a dream so vivid in its interpretation of human senses and desires.

I forced my eyes open to capture the moment. To my surprise, she was staring at me. The rich brown of her eyes became a metallic copper. I tried feebly to continue the passionate kiss, but she slowly pulled her lips away, revealing sharp, elongated canines.

Before I could gasp she punctured my neck, and I felt pain like noth-ing I had ever felt before. I tried to scream, but no sound came out. I began to feel tears gather and fall. I used my remaining strength to push myself away from her grasp. Then she was on me again, and darkness fell over me. I began to lose consciousness, and I could sense only cold-ness and silence, save the beating of my heart. And just before the eclipse of death, I heard her voice for the last time through my human ears. "Be still, my love. You're safe with me."

# CHAPTER 2

awoke engulfed in a malodor that unmistakably arose from decaying flesh. I tried to move, but I could hardly persuade my arms and legs into motion. I lay help-less, in agonizing pain. I felt as if my insides were an inferno and rigor mortis were setting into my limbs. I felt something warm on my skin, and I struggled to raise my head. When I was finally able to see myself, I realized I was completely naked. I then noticed a bloody mass around my buttocks. I was no medical scholar, but I could tell the bloody mass was made of organs. My organs! I could see my own liver, kidneys, and a bloody pouch, which I soon came to realize was my stomach. My internal organs were outside of my body, lying in a fleshy soup. How could this be? How could I live without the very organs that keep me alive? I uttered a scream that echoed through-out the room I was lying in. The vibrating sounds danced off the nearby walls, mocking my withering existence.

I screamed over and over again, "Why have you brought me here? What have you done to me?" When I realized that I had raised my arms into the air reaching for an explanation, I instantly stopped screaming and looked down at my torso again. I could no longer trust my eyes so I began running my hands over my body, starting with my torso, searching for the apparent gaping wound I had seen.

My body was now intact, but I felt the warm, fleshy, almost rubbery substances that were my organs rotting near my buttocks and under my legs. My mind told my body to move. I reclaimed mastery over my limbs. My neck also obeyed my commands. The stiffness I felt just moments before was gone. As I stood, I felt the things that should be inside of me slide down the back of my legs onto the floor below. I stepped away from the mess and realized that my legs suddenly felt strong. My entire body was reanimated.

I surveyed the room. Candles burning around the room illuminated coarse walls made of a dark, clay-like material. The damp floor was made of the same material, as was the arched ceiling. There were no windows. The oversized, stone-framed door seemed fit for a giant, not a man. I walked over to the door, stepping over rusted chains and shackles. I put my hands flat on the door's warm metal surface. Just from my touch, I could tell the door was thick. I ran my hands up and down along its carved surface, trying to decipher the unfamiliar story depicting the cast of demons and monsters engraved in the metal. I turned around and leaned my back against the door and looked around the room.

*This is a dungeon!* I thought. This is where someone is brought who has wronged another and who will thus receive unspeakable torment. Despite what I had been through and where I now found myself, I felt no fear. Though I was naked, I didn't feel the slightest chill. I reached out to feel the warmth offered by one of the burning candles, and I felt nothing. I began to feel rage. "Why am I here?" I screamed. "What have you done to me? Show yourself!" I demanded.

My voice sounded as if I were speaking through an amplifier, greater than anything my lungs had ever produced. I realized that my sense of smell was extraordinarily keen. The different scents in the air assaulted my nostrils, and I wondered if even a bloodhound had a sense of smell so powerful. Suddenly, I felt an excruciating hunger of the likes I've never known and have yet to feel again. I was completely consumed by this unknown craving. It began to drive me mad; I felt I was going to die if I didn't find immediate nourishment, something to make the yearning subside. Food wasn't my desire. I wanted something different from what I had ever known. I couldn't figure out what it was, but I had to find and consume it!

I turned around and faced the grand door. I looked for a handle. There was none. I began pushing on it. It didn't budge. I tried once again with both hands, and it still didn't move. I then pressed my back against it, planted my feet firmly, and used my legs to push and propel myself backward. Though it seemed impossibly heavy, the door began to move, and I was able to push it open enough to allow me to slip through.

I found myself in a long dark corridor. There was a faint flicker of light from the dungeon I'd managed to escape, and even though this hallway lacked the candles afforded in the previous room, I could see everything in it as if it were illuminated by thousands of tiny metallic light-reflecting particles. The walls were consistent with the dungeon. I began to walk away from the slightly open door, and as I walked, I heard something familiar, yet I was unable to determine what it was. It had a steady rhythm that was faint at first and grew louder until it thundered, which is when I came to know it. It was indeed the sound a heart makes while circulating blood throughout a body. But whose heartbeat was it? Were it mine, I would have heard it all along. Someone else was here with me.

I followed the sound of the beating heart as it grew louder and more distinct. I hadn't realized my pace had quickened until I noticed that each of my steps brought me five yards closer to a candle that had once seemed thirty yards away. The heartbeat grew louder, and the smell filled my nostrils, intensifying my hunger. I stopped outside the room from which the heartbeat emanated. I heard a low moan. I was even able to hear each breath. The thick stone walls should have prevented the flight of these sounds. Logic and reason seemed to no longer exist.

I felt a presence, and I wondered if it could feel mine. I flattened a hand against the door. It was identical to the one that had held me captive moments before. I knew it would challenge my strength yet again to break through the door, but I was ravenous. Facing it, I pushed on it with both hands, and to my surprise, it nearly broke off the hinges as it flung open.

The room was smaller than my cradle. I didn't have the patience to examine its details, for the hunger in me was consuming. Instantly I affixed my eyes on a man stretched out on the floor. There was no light in the room, but I could see him clearly. At once I was upon him. I didn't quite understand why I was so drawn to him, but I knew it had to do with his scent and his heartbeat.

I blinked to focus, my mind trying to comprehend what my eyes were seeing. It was as if I were staring at an illuminated depiction of the body's circulatory system. I could see every intricate pathway from the farthest minute vein to the largest blood-filled artery, and I could hear the faint sound of blood slowly pulsing through his arteries and veins.

With one hand, I picked the man up by his neck. I grabbed his arm with my other hand and plunged my teeth into it, just below the wrist, and began sucking his blood. It was an indescribable feeling of pleasure and satisfaction. After a moment, my previously numbing, insatiable hunger was starting to subside. My knees began to feel weak as I greedily drained as much of his blood as I could take. I let his body fall lifelessly to the floor. I, too, felt lifeless as I struggled to maintain my balance. I dropped to one knee, breaking an unavoidable clumsy fall. What sweet nectar! Within him was the answer to everything. My mind began to swim in ecstasy, drunk from the most delicious wine I'd ever known, satisfied and settled within myself.

I knew no answers to why I felt this way. My eyes wandered about the room, while visions of the dead man circled me. Everything began to spin as my mind entered orbit, where gravity granted me freedom. No. I knew nothing of these things I could do. I knew less than nothing of what I'd just done. I was certain of little, but one thing I was certain of was that human I was not!

*What have I become? What type of beast am I?* I wondered. My head was filled with visions of latent yet vivid memories of things I could not possibly have experienced. *I'm dreaming while awake,* I rationalized. I felt a euphoric, comforting warmth. It was a blissful moment, each second feeling like an eternity.

I was weak, almost numb. I wanted to lie on the floor, but I didn't want to sleep. I simply needed to rest. It was as if my body willed itself to the damp, unyielding stone floor. I couldn't resist the call of gravity as the muscles in my legs were no longer under my command. The famine that had once ruled me had been replaced by paralyzing fatigue. I could barely move. It was as if my brain was failing to send messages to my muscles. My eyelids grew heavy. I tried to force them open, but I couldn't. Channeling all of my strength and will, I made an infant's cry for help.

"I'm sorry, my love," she answered softly. "Rest now. When the sun sleeps, you'll know more. I'll show you."

I slipped into unconsciousness.

I couldn't tell how much time had passed before my eyes opened. And when I awoke, I was fully aware but clumsy, as if I had partaken of too much brandy wine the night before. However, I had all of my mental faculties. My mind was sharp, my hearing keen. I detected a familiar and delightful scent, her fragrance. She was with me.

"Take my hand, my child," she said in a caring voice. I complied, and she lifted me to my feet. Though I still felt weak, her strength more than made up for my unsteady legs. She took me into her arms as we seemingly floated swiftly across the stone floor, out of the room, and into a grand room filled with vibrant, contrasting colors. Brilliant velvet drapes hung from the twenty-foot ceiling to the intricately designed white-stone floor. A painted portrait of an aristocratic figure stretched across the domed ceiling. I couldn't help noticing the striking resemblance the figure bore to me. The windows were vast and plentiful, as were the larger-than-life marble statues around the room that depicted men and women with beatific features. The artwork on the walls depicted surreal landscapes: beautifully captured bodies of water reflecting castles that were monuments to the architectural prowess of the most sophisticated designers of their time.

The room's furnishings were fit for a king: linens and rugs made from the finest silks, cotton, and animal furs. Unmatched luxury! Obviously, no expense had been spared in the creation of this magnificent place where the exquisite princess undoubtedly lived. Candles burned along the walls next to every door and windowsill, releasing the faint aroma of cinnamon and spice and casting dancing shadows about the room. Carefully designed floral arrangements sat in each windowsill, emitting their exotic scents. I wanted desperately to know where I was.

"You're with me, Aleron"—her reply to a question I didn't ask aloud. She walked over to me. With every step and every touch, I was bewitched. She continued, "Even though your thoughts are known to me as if my own, you do not have full access to my thoughts. It's in your nature to be inquisitive, so I grant you this now. Ask what you wish, and I promise to answer in such a way that you'll have complete understanding."

So many questions flooded my mind, but I chose the one that burned the brightest and eclipsed the others. "Who are you?"

"My name is Mynea," she replied softly.

"Where am I?"

"You're in my home. My castle."

"Why am I here?"

"You have been chosen."

"Chosen? For what?"

"It's not the time to reveal the answer to that question. Though I'm always certain of my choice, one's strengths and weaknesses after transformation are often unpredictable."

*Transformation,* I thought.

"Yes, my child, transformation."

"*What* am I?"

"That, my child, is why I've returned after your slumber."

*Slumber?* I thought.

"Yes, you were resting for nearly eleven moons during your transformation."

"What am I?" I repeated.

"I'll tell you what you are in due time. Now I must teach you the most basic and most important lesson of your survival. Your strength is waning, and your mind and senses are not as keen as they should be. The hunger awakened you. You just didn't know how to feed."

Before I could respond, I heard a door open, and I turned to see who was entering the room. It was a young woman dressed in garments not as elegant as the clothing worn by Mynea. She guided into the room, by a chain, a younger woman, a girl really, in a tattered robe. The chained girl seemed dazed and befuddled; however, she wasn't struggling. The young woman led her directly to Mynea.

"As you requested, my lady," she said while hesitating to look Mynea in the eyes.

"Thank you, Eliza. You can go now."

"As you wish, my lady."

Eliza left the room. Suddenly the captive girl lifted her eyes and affixed them on me. Without moving her lips she spoke to me. I could hear her thoughts in my mind. *Demons!*

I felt uneasy. Dizzy. How could I hear her thoughts as if she were speaking them directly to me? I thought of Mynea speaking to me at the Promethium without opening her mouth. I was confused.

Sensing my apprehensiveness, Mynea spoke, "Be still, my love. She's been brought here with purpose. You have much to learn about the hunger that awakened you. An appetite you'll feel every night until the end."

I've never forgotten the first hunger. It was excruciatingly painful. Mynea continued to tell me about the longing for blood that drove me to the edge of sanity. "You didn't know what you craved, but instinct led you to the meal prepared for you in the dungeon. The first door you struggled to open was the same as the one you seemingly tossed off the hinges. The difference was in the hunger-induced strength," Mynea explained. The taste of the blood rushed back into my mouth.

"You drank the blood. It quenched and satisfied your hunger, but it made you weak. Pay close attention to what I'm about to tell you, for it can mean life or death to our kind if not abided by."

"What you are now is far more than you've ever been as a human. In the eyes of man, you'll seem no different from them. No different from what you once were. However, you infinitely differ from your former self. I'm here to reveal what that difference is, starting with how we survive." Mynea left my side and walked a few feet away, never taking her eyes off of me.

"We are predators. We survive under the guise of our prey and the darkness that brings the shadows. Just like any other animal, we must know our food. Understanding their anatomy is essential for this most important lesson. The human blood system is simple. However, misunderstanding it can be fatal. The center of the blood system is the heart. It receives unclean blood from the veins and cleans it, then pushes the clean blood through the arteries to all the essential organs of the body. Though we can feed from any one of these organs or drink from any vein or artery, we must use caution in our choice. We can realize our true selves only with the consumption of clean blood. Unclean blood may quench the thirst, but it paralyzes our muscles and can render us vulnerable."

"I drank dirty blood."

"Yes, my love," Mynea confirmed. "Dirty blood filled you and arrested your movements with warm, swift, blissful judgment. The forbidden nectar. You must now learn to feed properly."

She fixed her eyes on the girl Eliza had brought in. Her body jolted straight and stiff, her fingers and toes outstretched, with her eyes opened wide. Her feet were no longer touching the ground. Mynea had her under total control. Her pupils fixed on me once more. I could hear her thoughts, but they were all jumbled, incoherent. I only made out what seemed to be a prayer.

"Look at her, my child." I did Mynea's bidding. I saw an ordinary female human. She was noticeably commonplace. There was nothing special about her, and just as I began to turn my attention back to Mynea, I began to see the girl's blood. I saw a beating mass of red muscle depicting a young and healthy heart. From the heart I saw thousands of tiny glowing conduits. My eyes felt strange as the picture became more vivid. And from the heart I heard its symphony, low and distinct, hastened in its rhythm, feeding her body.

"See the difference between the vein and artery, my love?" Mynea continued. I noticed a slight difference in the size of certain pathways and the direction of blood flow. Indeed, I now saw distinct differences between the arteries and veins.

"Good. Now do what comes naturally to you. Feed and feel revived."

Yes, I could hear her heart quickening as I opened my mouth to kiss her neck just above the shoulder. Mynea watched with a mother's grace and a father's expectation. My lips were now on her neck. She was in my arms, completely frightened and overwhelmed in my grasp. I bit down and felt my teeth pierce the skin. The girl opened her lips but only a whimper escaped. Next, I heard the crackling sound of my jaw crushing the bone. She withdrew from the pain but never did she scream.

"Gently, my love," Mynea said. "You needn't even try to break the skin. Simply kiss her with care, and you'll draw out her blood."

It was entirely too late. The blood from the artery filled my mouth and throat. The first meal paled in comparison to this cuisine. I felt invigorated. Her blood tasted like liquid fire. I was completely and utterly hypnotized by the visions of her thoughts and memories. With every passing second, a year of her life was told to me in disjointed little chapters. I pulled her closer as I fed from her throat as an animal might. It was as if my salvation depended on this child-woman giving her life to me, her blood in exchange for my mercy in hurrying her passage into whatever lay ahead, after death.

I opened my eyes and stared at her. She was no longer the young girl I'd had in my arms. She had become something else entirely. She was my nourishment, the source of my new strength and thus, inherently, my weakness. I continued to drink as her heartbeat grew more and more lethargic, until it was gone. Her body went limp as I struggled to remove my mouth from the open wound I inflicted upon her. The deed was done. All signs of life that had once danced in the eyes of this young woman were gone from her pale, withered body. She was no more. I, however, was forever more than I'd ever been! Everything she once was, I had taken into me.

"You see, my love. You feel stronger. Absolutely powerful. Therein lies the difference. The artery is the key to quench the crippling thirst you shall forever feel every night. The blood is your life force and shall revitalize all that you are every time you answer the call of your most basic and natural instinct, to feed."

Indeed, this was the single most important lesson she ever taught me. "Your basic instinct is necessary for your survival," she continued. "It's also through this understanding that you leave yourself vulnerable to others who may want to do you harm. You must not allow your hunger to control you. You must control it. It's fundamental that you discern how often you need to feed, for it will change as you grow older. It will also fluctuate depending on what you drink."

"What I drink?" I questioned. "Patience, my love. Patience. You have as many lessons to learn as I've lessons to teach, and we both have all the time in the world. For now, I will return to a question you asked me before your meal. You wanted to know what you are. What we are. We have been known by many names, my love: Undead, Nosferatu, Vrykolakas, Upir, Kyuketsuki, Reapers of death, God's hand, and many more that you'll hear from the distant shadows and moonless nights. To the children of Christ we're spawn of 'Those who were banished.' To the unflinching followers of Mohammed, we're hoseti. To this world we are life everlasting. We are vampire!"

# CHAPTER 3

 *ampire*, I spoke under my breath in astonishment. I was familiar with the legend and the folklore; however, I didn't believe in the undead. Until now!

"Now let us go into the night, into the moonlight, and discover the world through your vampire eyes."

Mynea took hold of me, affixed me to her side, and we swiftly moved through the house into the cool night air. This time I kept my eyes open. We were traveling much faster than before. We glided across a lake just over the surface. The water was still, a dark mirror reflecting the night sky. I looked into the heavens. It was spectacularly brilliant and filled with hundreds, no, thousands of stars. I couldn't remember a time when I had seen so many stars in one night. The moon seemed brighter, larger, and closer than ever. It seemed to illuminate the darkness with a soft and soothing blanket of light.

Mynea's curly hair was pressed against my face by the force of the wind. It smelled like the essence of the room where I had taken my first proper meal. Her silk gown flailed and opened from her breast down to her feet. I couldn't help noticing her darkened nipples, revealed slightly by a pearl necklace. She tightened her grip on my waist. I peered through the curly elegant locks to see our surroundings. The land drew nearer rapidly; I was sure we'd stumble and fall upon our arrival. However, we didn't. Instead, we came to an abrupt pause in our momentum, which would have surely caused any human to topple over. It seemed gravity had forgotten us over the water, yet remembered us on land.

I still didn't know where we were or how far we had traveled. I turned around and was amazed at the vastness of the lake we crossed. The castle was but a small spot in the distance. I turned to Mynea, who was staring at me, smiling, her eyes glowing like those of a cat. She seemed even more beautiful now than before.

"Look, my love. Look through your vampire eyes and see the world as you've never seen it."

Indeed, she was right. Everything was much more vivid. It was as if I had opened my eyes for the very first time. I was again a child. I could hear insects and tiny vermin scurry about. Mice stomping nearby sounded like elephants. The gentle breeze whispered through the trees and brush that surrounded the area in an infinite blanket of brilliant dark greens. The moonlight seemed to make inanimate objects come to life. All of these sensations and sounds filled my head at once. It became more and more difficult to distinguish one sound from the next, one scent from another. My vision blurred from the numerous objects moving. I closed my eyes for a moment when I felt a cold hand gently caress my cheek.

"Try to open your mind and take in nature's beauty. The vampire blood in your veins has awakened your once-human senses and made them sharp. In time they'll guide you."

I tried to open my mind, but I must admit, I didn't know what she meant at the time. Nevertheless, the noises became distinct once more. I was able to focus.

"You, my love, now walk between life and death. We're God's perfect predator, and we remain children of the devil. Even though we can be as gentle as angels, we possess strength beyond measure."

Mynea turned and looked at me, her eyes studying me from head to toe. Then suddenly her gaze turned into a staunch stare. She was now looking at me as if she could see through me.

The thought of being a vampire plagued my mind. "Am I dead?"

"No, my love. We're very much alive. But merely being alive is not why I've brought you here. I'll teach you how to live. Our way of life is not what you're accustomed to. We're beautiful, alluring creatures who must use all of our abilities to maintain our immortal gift."

*Abilities*, I thought. *Yes, abilities*, she replied without moving her lips. "Let me show you."

We began to move swiftly through the trees, traveling like cheetahs, without making the slightest sounds, save the whistling winds. We saw candles burning in the distance, and in an instant we were upon them.

"We move as fast as the wind, Aleron. Stealth is our cloak, for under its cover you'll survive for millennia. Without it, you'll surely perish. We're stronger, faster, and smarter than mortals; however, our numbers are few and the mortals are many, thus we fear their intentions lest they ever discover us and our true natures. We don't live among them. We do, however, interact with them, as they're our finest and most pleasurable delicacy. You see, my love, we survive by drinking blood. We thrive by drinking blood. We replenish ourselves by consuming it. Therefore, we become better predators as our prey remains constant."

*Delicacy implies that we can survive on the blood of other beings*, I thought.

"Yes, we can, but to deprive yourself of human blood is to be but alive. As I said before, I'm here to teach you to live. To live is to do exactly what I'm going to show you."

The candles were burning outside a theater. The marquee promised a performance of *Ozymandias, Pharaoh of the Exodus*. I knew him as Ramses II. But we were not there to see the play. We dared not attempt the front doors, for they would surely open into a great room full of people. Instead, Mynea led us to a rear door situated in the center of a dark and lifeless alleyway. The smell of unattended mildew and filth filled my nostrils, the unmistakable scent of decaying flesh nearby buried under some trash. This alleyway was only penetrated by street vermin and homeless mortals, on occasion.

I turned my attention to the door. The rust on the hinges and the debris scattered about the base told its true history. Mynea opened the door with ease, tearing apart the rusted hinges, doorframe, and the three steel locks that kept it secure from normal entry. The sound was muffled by the sheer speed. Without uttering a word, she told me to be silent. The side door had once been an exit from the back of the staging area. I could hear the performers entertaining the crowd. There were several oohs and aahs, interrupted occasionally by applause. I began to listen to the performers, for I'm well versed in Egyptian history, especially Ramses I, II, and III.

Mynea looked just past the curtains, surveying the crowd. She then eased her head back into the darkness and smiled at me. "I've chosen, and she'll make a worthy meal."

"What do you look for?" I asked, excited that she was hunting. "How do you come to choose? Are there any rules?" I asked.

"I was taught to hunt the wicked. The murderers, cheats, and viola-tors of society; however, I no longer subscribe to that lesson. I choose my meals indiscriminately, as God would choose who would live or die. I don't care what one has done in life, nor do I concern myself with whom they may have wronged. I simply let my will and their unfortu-nate fate guide me to them. There's no method. They're all my prey. Good and perceived evil alike. The young, old, strong, weak—they all will die soon enough."

The thought of draining the life from a child disgusted me. "This is not what God would sanction! How could you kill an innocent child?"

"Doesn't God allow the perfect child to be trampled by a horse? Do you not know of doctors and priests falling victim to petty crime? Do you not hear of the church condemning non-believers to death through some horrific means? Don't think or reason as if you're human. You didn't question the innocence or lifestyle of the young woman whose morbid fate you so clumsily and mercifully decided."

She was right. I was confused as to what I was to do. All my life I'd been a servant of God and my fellow man. Now it seemed I was supposed to be the self-appointed executioner of any poor soul I condemned to death. *I'm not sure I can do this! What is the price? What have I done? What have I allowed Mynea to do?*

"Nothing, my dear," she replied. "You haven't allowed me to do anything. You had no choice in the matter. I chose your fate for you and for that I'm your master. You'll learn from me. You'll watch me as I show you how to live with your new immortal life."

Again she was right, I had no choice. Even if I had, I still wanted her. She was my master, my teacher, my mother, my love. She was mine.

"Sorry, my love," I said to her. "Forgive me."

"I already have, Aleron. It's only natural that you question what I do, what you'll do. It's not necessary for any apologies. Kings don't apologize for anything. And you, my dear, strong Aleron, will be king!"

This time I took her in my arms. She looked and felt cold, though her eyes were inviting. I pressed her rigid body against mine and began to kiss her lips. Passionately and deeply we embraced each other. It was then that I realized that nothing would ever come between us. I would love her until life ceased to exist on Earth. She was indeed mine.

Mynea lifted her head and nose into the air, then inhaled. "It's time." She peered through the red velvet curtains again. I followed her lead. The crowd was captivated by the performance; not a single sound broke their concentration save the voices of the actors and actresses. Suddenly a woman arose and made her way toward the exit. Various people in the crowd began to chatter and look on in amazement at this woman's desire to leave during what seemed to be one of the most compelling parts of the play. Her decision seemed quite odd to me as well.

"Follow swiftly," Mynea whispered.

And so I did, and in an instant we were through the crowd, in the lobby, and then in the stairwell leading up to the balcony. No one in the crowd even saw so much as a blur as we scurried past their eyes, defying their senses. We stood in the shadows of the stairwell next to a door, waiting for it to open.

When it did, the lobby light shone through, outlining the woman who had left the performance. Mynea stepped into the light, while I stayed hidden in the shadows. The woman looked at Mynea with a familiar calmness.

"Hello, my dear," Mynea said to the woman.

She didn't respond. She just stood there in a daze. "Come closer."

The woman took a few more steps toward Mynea, farther into the stairwell. Mynea took the woman into her arms and embraced her as a mother would embrace a child she hadn't seen in ages. She then took the woman's neck into her mouth and punctured her skin just above the clavicle. The woman sighed out of both pleasure and pain. Her eyes shifted and found mine.

She looked at me as the life was being drawn from her body. I could see the reflection of my eyes in her dying gaze. Mynea continued to drink until the woman's body went limp. Mynea dropped her to the floor, turned toward me, and smiled, her mouth and teeth covered in dark, dripping blood. She took me into her arms again and began to kiss me. This kiss was unlike any other we had shared; the woman's life force was still ripe in her mouth and filled me with feelings of ecstasy.

She pressed her body against mine, and for the first time I felt warmth emanating from her. She felt softer than normal, though still too hard for human skin. I felt lost in her grasp. I began to see dynamic visions that weren't mine, memories and excerpts from a story unknown to me. I didn't let them distract me. I never wanted this embrace to end. But it did.

"You must learn to lure your prey. Avoid detection by allowing them to seek you while silently persuading them mentally. We're superior to them in every way. Know this and know it well, for once you forget who you are, it will be the end of you."

We left the stairwell as swiftly as we had arrived, returning to the shadows of the alleyway. We walked into the moonlight, and Mynea looked more radiant than ever.

"Aleron, our appearance changes slightly after each meal. I look and feel a little more human, though I'm more powerful than I was before I drank. This allows us to mingle among them for a short period of time without drawing too much attention to ourselves. Make no mistake, the mortals both see us and don't see us. Their ignorance also allows us to remain with them for centuries.

"Now the time has come for you to feed again."

"So we must take more than one a night to survive?"

"No. You must now because you're but a fledgling. I myself won't need another meal for months. However, I enjoy the hunt and thus will hunt again tomorrow and every day thereafter."

*Where do I begin? Whom should I choose? Should I choose a male or female? Is there a difference?* All of these questions could have been answered by Mynea, but she chose to act as though she could not read my thoughts. She wanted me to learn this basic step on my own, and so I did.

I took Mynea's hand, and we stepped out of the alleyway and began walking down the cobblestone road toward the distant roar of people conversing. The night air was refreshing in my lungs. I purposely led Mynea with a slower, more humanly pace in an effort to mimic the motions and movements I'd known all of my life. We passed several groups of people chatting about various insignificant topics until we came upon a local watering hole called the Peasant's Dungeon. I'd heard of this place, yet I couldn't recall from whom and where. The exterior was familiar to me, and I had a sense of the interior as well: broken wooden doors, the smell of leather, mold covering the seats. I could remember the barkeep and his daughter, who served the gentlemen more than just drinks. We approached the door, and a tall, burly man stood in our way.

"Strangers aren't welcome. Find another tap," he said.

Until now I made sure no one we passed saw my eyes or my face. I looked at him and grinned. *We'll enter and you will show us a clean seat,* I said to his thoughts. He did so. The place was exactly how I'd envisioned it, even though I was sure I had never been there. How could this be? I noticed the familiar scent of the woman Mynea had fed upon emanating from the barkeep. They were acquainted in some manner; I didn't know how.

"What you're remembering are not your memories, Aleron. They're the memories of the woman."

Of course, once we kissed, the blood had transferred from Mynea to me, and thus the memories from the woman in the theater had passed on to me. How fascinating! This was indeed how I found this place. I didn't realize until then that I was coming here with a definite purpose.

There were several small groups of people scattered about. The groups were made up mostly of men, though a few contained one or two women, who were there for entertainment purposes only. I began to observe. I could easily take any one of the lot. Was there a method or logic to this skill? Did I kill as Mynea described, like God, indiscriminately and without remorse? Or was there some grand scheme that was not to be realized until the last soul was separated from his body? As I looked around the room, I realized that all chatter had ceased and that everyone was watching us. I could sense the heavy breathing coming from some of the men as they undoubtedly noticed the way Mynea was dressed. The lust in their thoughts and intentions made her smile. She, of course, had noticed long before I had.

*I'm going to get that bitch and make her my personal slave,* one man thought. He seemed to command respect from the other lesser men in his group, for they immediately moved out of his way when he stood and approached us near the entrance of the bar. He stood between us and stared at me, thinking Mynea belonged to me.

*Stay calm, my love,* she whispered to my mind. Men, it seemed, didn't need to be lured using any unnatural persuasion, for they're creatures of habit and, alas, predictable.

Before the man opened his mouth, I could smell his rotting teeth swimming in a sea of ale. A drunken fool he was. "Hello, my lady," he murmured. "I'm Rathmon, and I would like to employ your services."

"Of course, my dear Rathmon," Mynea replied. "Many men have wanted me, and no matter how much they have offered, they must first seek the approval of my keep."

"Your keep?" he bellowed.

"Yes, my handsome brute. He stands behind you." The man turned around and looked me up and down, finally locking his eyes on mine. "How much?" he inquired.

"Let us walk and discuss this business in private quarters, shall we?"

I goaded. Relying on the woman's blood memories, I led the man out of the bar, down a corridor, and into a room. I could almost taste his anticipation for pleasure, for this room was the very room in which he had employed or stolen the services of many. I opened the door and he entered the room behind me. Mynea followed us in and closed the door without touching it. *Fascinating*, I thought, after witnessing yet another power that our kind possessed.

"Now that you have me here, how much for the woman?"

"Make me a fair offer, my good man, and don't insult the one you desire." He turned around and considered Mynea from head to toe once more. She made this glance unforgettable by allowing one of her breasts to be slightly exposed by a flutter of her silk gown.

"I'll give you three pieces of gold for the pleasure of knowing her," he said, completely bewitched by the allure of her exposed nipple.

"Surely you can do better than that, for she's young and unspoiled."

"Five pieces!" he retorted as saliva flew from the sewage of his mouth.

"That's more like it, my good man." The man approached Mynea with a bestial lust.

"Gold before the girl's intimate touch," I said.

"I'll pay you once I'm done with your wench. Now leave us lest I have you once I finish with her!"

She allowed him to grab both of her arms, and in an instant, and to my surprise, fueled by possessiveness and spite, my hand penetrated his back with ferocious fury, and I ripped out his heart! He turned around in shock and stared at his heart, still beating in my bloody grasp. The sight of the blood was too much for me to resist. Had this occurred but a day earlier, I would have surely quivered as I fought back the urge to expel my lunch and breakfast.

I marveled at it! His body collapsed to the floor, eyes wide open as he witnessed me drinking his life's nectar directly from the source. Mynea said nothing. She watched in amazement. Indeed, I didn't realize my new strength.

I began to hear hurried and clumsy footsteps coming closer. I was astonished by my ability to isolate the sounds of the footsteps entirely, allowing me to determine there were three men and a woman. Obsessed with bloodlust, my once-human desire for life was utterly devoured by a new compulsion for death. For a moment, I began to imagine myself killing them all and draining them to the point of oblivion. Yes! This was what I wanted. I must have more!

*We must go now, Aleron,* Mynea said to my thoughts. *You weren't quiet in your attack, and others will come if he doesn't return.*

"Then let them come and face his fate!" I retorted aloud. I felt invincible, a feeling that would prove to be an illusion.

"No, my love, remember, they're many, and though we're strong, we're few. To jeopardize yourself is to expose us all. That must never happen if we're to continue living." Mynea grabbed my blood-soaked hand. "Now make haste, for I can sense curiosity from his comrades."

Just as the door flew open, we were off into the night.

† † † †

We returned to the castle swiftly. We entered the great room, and Mynea took my hand into hers and kissed it. Her kisses became tiny licks and suckles. I looked down and noticed some of the brute's blood still smeared between my fingers. Even though I wanted to imagine that Mynea was kissing my hand from her sheer attraction and desire for me, I knew it was her lust for the freshly squeezed ambrosia that called out to her. I kissed her lips, for I, too, needed her succulent taste once more. We embraced each other as only unnatural beings could, an inseparable and impenetrable embrace that defied even air's request for passage. She looked at me with a mother's concern coupled with a lover's desire.

I tore off Mynea's gown, exposing her completely naked body to my touch. She answered by thrusting me across the room while holding my clothing, using the momentum to rip the clothing right off me. I landed on my feet, and she was instantly on me like a lioness pouncing on her prey. I wasn't nearly as strong as she, so to take command was impossible. She knew this. She held me down, pressing the fur rug tightly between my body and the stone floor. She mounted me with such fury that I felt pain and pleasure, the likes of which I had never felt before and can scarcely describe in words you'd be able to understand. Just know that our intimacy was heaven's bliss, though we were hell's instruments. We were one. Afterward, we remained utterly still in each other's arms, staring into oblivion, absolutely numb. Mynea broke the silence. "It's time, my love, for you to rest."

"I want to lie here with you until the sun rises, my queen."

"This you cannot do. Listen carefully to what I'm about to tell you. Don't forget these words, for if you challenge them, your immortality will be forgotten. You'll die if you expose yourself to the light of the morning sun. You're a neophyte, utterly unaware of what lies beyond the nest. And though you feel strong, as you rest you'll become even stronger. Rest will also allow your immortal mind to arrange your ill-gotten memories of those who were slain. This is only achieved through a deep vampiric sleep."

As she spoke, my body began to feel strange. "You see, Aleron. The sun is awakening, and your body senses its arrival. Your limbs will stiffen, and your mind will no longer be as sharp as it was this past evening. You will be weak and vulnerable. Over the centuries, the sun's effects will begin to subside."

I felt a deep sleep befalling me. "Will you be here when I awake?" I asked.

"Of course," she said. "Of course."

I drifted into complete darkness. Helpless, like an infant, I lay in complete dependence on my mother, Mynea.

# CHAPTER 4

glimmer of life returned to me, and my mind gradually grew sharper as I began slipping back into consciousness. The hunger from the previous dawn returned. I wasn't quite awake yet, but in my half-sleep I could feel my body preparing for reanimation. I began to hear my own heartbeat as it progressed from a faint sound to a pronounced symphonic bass, to acoustic, and then contrabass, until the solo tuba erupted with such fury and determination that ignoring it would be impossible.

As I listened, I noticed something strange about the rhythm of my pulsating heart. I could hear a faint, slow, steady beat, constantly filling in where silence should reside. I used the skill I had learned the previous night and isolated the sound. It was indeed a living pulse, but the constant drum wasn't mine. I realized that I wasn't alone. My eyes sprung open to find her.

Mynea stood several feet from me, staring out into the distance. She was completely naked in the dimness of the dying sunlight, defeated by the rising of the moon. The shadow she cast was intriguing. My eyes widened in awe as the silhouette came to life preceding the movement of her body. She turned around and looked directly into my eyes.

"You slept well, my love." She held out her arms, signaling me to come. I stood and began to walk toward her. With the paling light of the moon now surrounding her frame and with a nurturing calmness, she took me into her arms. Unlike our first embrace, she was, to my surprise, humanly warm. The chill of my touch instantly stole warmth from hers. She began to kiss my neck and chin. I could smell the meal she must have had before I awoke. The aroma instantly rekindled my insatiable hunger. At that very moment I could no longer think of anything else. Her kisses became a memory. Everything I'd become was forgotten. Life itself was an afterthought. I could only think of blood. My eyes opened wider than ever to see Mynea tilting her neck and inviting me to bite her!

"The hunger will consume you entirely if you don't feed soon after you awake, my love. Drink." Without so much as a forethought, I opened my mouth, and I gently punctured Mynea's neck with my teeth.

The feeling of her warm blood flowing from her body into my mouth was indescribable. I can only liken it to trying to describe an orgasm to someone who has never had one before. It was simply something one must experience for himself. It was the cure for all that was aching within me, the answer for any lingering question my body had. The absolute meaning and purpose of my very existence was all satisfied by the blood meal she gave me. If love is, then I was certain, blood is.

As I continued to drink, incoherent memories of a female rushed into my mind, walking swiftly, alone at dusk. She kept looking back, feeling a presence drawing nearer, never knowing what true fate awaited her when she stopped abruptly in front of an angel. My angel. My Mynea.

I continued to see strange visions foretelling the life of this poor woman in the first person until the images seemed to dissipate and the blood memoirs suddenly changed. The woman was no longer the protagonist in these new visions. A feeling of despair came over me. It was sudden, absolutely without warning. I felt hopeless. It was similar to the feeling one might have alone and in complete darkness, hands outstretched, hoping to grasp onto something but grasping only air. It was a feeling I didn't like.

Then a vivid picture came into focus. I saw a castle nestled deep within a vast mountainous region. As my curiosity increased, I sucked harder. I tried to focus in an attempt to understand these visions, but my efforts were futile. A dark and deep moat encircled the castle, denying safe passage to any, welcoming only the invited. The castle had a menacing quality. For the first time, the blood memories offered yet a new dimension in interpretation: sound.

"Mynea!" the voice said. In that very instant I saw black, colorless eyes. I couldn't distinguish a pupil or an iris. Both were an abyss surrounded by ancient flesh. These eyes were menacingly huge, larger than those of any humans I had seen. Thick and dark eyebrows hovered over unusually long eyelashes. Eyes that foretold a knowledge far beyond my understanding. They seemed to be looking at Mynea. As quickly as it had come, the vision faded.

*More!* I thought as I continued to draw blood from my queen. *More!* Suddenly, I felt Mynea's powerful grip clasping the back of my hair, pulling me away from her neck.

"That's enough, my dear Aleron. In time, my love," she said while releasing me to my feet. "You don't have to rush. Our bloodlust will last an eternity."

I had completely forgotten about the insignificant life of the woman Mynea had condemned. I was intrigued by something far more mysterious. I hadn't been able to see the face, but the eyes were burned into my memory. Mynea slowly turned away from me and focused over the horizon once more.

"You have questions, Aleron. As I said before, I will answer them. Just know that these things that bewilder you have no meaning to you as a fledgling vampire." Her voice was stern and undeniably chilling. Her shadow remained still, though her body moved. She turned toward me, and I knew then that my queen was indeed my queen, and I one of her subjects. She would only reveal to me what she thought was necessary. I truly believed the visions I saw would be explained in the future—or so I wanted to believe. I was certain that those eyes would haunt me from that moment on. The revelation would eventually be told to me, but not by the lips of my queen.

The brat in me wanted answers immediately, and she knew this. She knew my curiosity would diminish if I drank her blood long enough. The mere thought of her blood returned me to a state of calmness. I became a baby at the bosom of his mother, positively safe. Mynea must have sensed this, for she again took me into her arms. I embraced her cooling body. I must have drained some of the mortal warmth she stole from the woman in the visions. The thought of stealing from mortals made me smile. We are thieves, are we not? We steal the hopes and dreams of each and every victim we condemn to a fate that was once left for their God to decide. We steal the passions of those who love and replace this absolute emotion with absolute despair. We steal the joy of a mother and the security of a father, and for what? In the name of our survival, we are thieves!

The mortal radiance began to subside, and the only evidence of the woman in the remaining vision were minute droplets of blood smudged along the right side of Mynea's lips. I must have it! I kissed the very spot, and Mynea smiled as if she had purposely left them there for me. Either way, I was thoroughly satisfied.

She placed her head on my bare chest, and I took the more aggressive role. I rubbed my nostrils on top of her hair. How sweet she smelled! How deliciously sweet! A bath of flowers must have preceded my awakening. Lilacs, orchids, samba, and my favorite of them all, the blue iris. It was said that the blue iris only grew in the southernmost mountainous region of eastern Europe. Nearly impossible to find and even more difficult to acquire, this exotic flower was to be respected and never forgotten. To harness its fragrance was no easy task. One had to use a mortar and pestle to crush its petals into a fine powder. Heating the powder under a small flame, such as the flame of a candle, turned the powder into a paste. Women applied this precious gum to their fingertips and massaged it onto certain areas of their bodies, anywhere the fragrance would be enjoyed. I loved its intoxicating aroma.

I looked at Mynea, into the eyes of a lioness. How long had she watched me before making me hers? I had fallen completely in love with her upon seeing her. I don't know if she used her gifts to lure me into the women's quarters of the Promethium. However, it mattered not. I was physically drawn to her at first sight. Try to imagine God's most perfect angel—perfect face and perfect body, exquisite eyes that seemed eternally forgiving. Her poise suggested a timeless grace, complemented by a curly mane of shiny brown silk, and the coup de grace, a soft glow that created a sublime silhouette. That was the beauty that was Mynea. Her preternatural lure wasn't needed.

I could see from looking directly into her eyes that she also loved me. But I had no idea why. Surely there existed at least one male immortal whose looks far surpassed those of mortal men. There had to be a male vampire who knew of Mynea and loved her. Surely we were not the only two in existence. And if we were, where had she come from? What was her origin? Was she once human? Did someone or something change her? More and more questions arose. I needed to know the answers. This thirst for knowledge was fueled simply by the intimidation and intrigue of those eyes. Did I feel haunted? Yes. Was I scared? Somewhat. Ultimately, I was consumed by curiosity.

## CHAPTER 5

t that moment I heard tiny footsteps in the distance. A familiar scent filled the air, and I knew that Eliza was near. The enormous door began to move. Surely Eliza didn't possess the strength required to shift the great stone door in the slightest, yet it continued to open. I began to make sense of the vulnerability Mynea spoke of before our vampire sleep and wondered if we were completely helpless. Could we be killed if someone were to discover us during slumber?

The door was now completely ajar. "Come in, dear," Mynea said.

Eliza entered. Glancing up only for a moment, her eyes instantly retreated at the sight of our naked bodies standing near the far wall—rather, I should say, the sight of my naked body. She was holding clothing, which she laid across the chair. And then, without saying a word, she was gone.

Mynea dressed me. She was meticulous with every button on my black trousers. There was nothing extraordinary about the clothing we now wore. We resembled ordinary mortals, wearing what the common people wore during those times. The clothes suggested our destination was of no significant importance.

"Aleron, we're going back to the city. You'll learn to hunt as I do this night. You have no doubt discovered you're stronger than any mortal you've ever encountered or who will ever exist. Your hand tore through that man's flesh before your mind commanded. Though you're indeed powerful, your greatest endowment won't be revealed until much later. You must push your body to its very limits. Mental and physical boundaries must be forgotten. That's the only way to embrace your true nature."

"I'm a killer," I said with a disgusted undertone. "Slayer of men. A reflex that I can't control!" The thought of Rathmon's smoldering foul breath insulting my queen triggered in me a desire to end his life. It was a fury I'd never felt before. "I'm a monster!"

"Yes. We are killers, Aleron," she replied. "We're even considered monsters to some. However, we cannot deny our nature. Whom we choose to kill and why we choose to end their existence is our choice. How we kill is our choice."

"What about what we kill, my love?"

"You can feed on the blood of any animal you wish, but understand this. You'll temporarily take on some of the attributes of your host. In our efforts to remain in society, feeding on man allows us to hide our true nature right in front of their eyes."

*Take on the attributes of the host?* I thought. "In time," she replied in her soft yet authoritative voice. "Come with me, Aleron."

She took my hand, and as swiftly as a single flutter of a hummingbird's wings, we were off.

I so loved our impenetrable embraces, moving silently and swiftly across the black water, the wind in our faces, the moonlight reflecting on our beastly eyes.

At that moment, a vision beset my mind. Those eyes! Menacing. Large. Black. Though they were looking at Mynea, they seemed to be staring at me. Piercing my soul, or whatever was left of it. Tormenting me. I felt an unsettling chill. Mynea was now aware of the change in me.

She looked down upon me from the corner of her eye. Then she looked ahead. I felt more cautious than frightened.

Our journey took longer than the previous night. We were traveling in an entirely new and unfamiliar direction. I began to see flickering lights in the distance as we moved away from the water to travel above land, too stealthily and fast for any human to detect. Trees were but a blur. The creatures of the night sang a fading song. My anxiousness temporarily replaced the stalking eyes with anticipation of this night's offerings.

Leaves rustled during our passing, the night air filled my lungs, cool and crisp, soothing me, relaxing me. And in an instant, we stopped. Eyes focused, I realized we were not quite within the city walls, yet not far from them. We were purposely nestled in the middle of nowhere. She spoke to my thoughts with hers. *My love, I've brought you here for a reason.* Audibly I replied, "What reason is that?"

"For you to learn more about yourself. For you to test your limits and gauge your strengths and learn to respect your weaknesses. This lesson you should never forget, but I must see if your vampire instincts will carry you through the excruciating pain of timelessness. Immortality is a blessing and a curse."

"Curse?" I asked. "One can only dream of what it means to be immortal. What it means to live outside of time. Infinite life without the fear of sickness, famine, or death. Truly a curse," I finished with a smirk.

"What do you know about immortality?" she asked. "How can one who has been immortal for so little time understand what it truly means to live forever? You're an infant who embodies a god's power! Strength, you know nothing of. Speed, you can scarcely grasp the concept of. Abilities that could bring you victory or, if misunderstood, defeat." She spoke with authority. She was again my queen. "The night is young, and your lesson shall begin with a meal that I will prepare," she said, and then she was gone.

I was left standing in the middle of nowhere. I could no longer sense Mynea's presence. What lesson did she want to teach me? I didn't know what I was supposed to do, so I began to walk in the manner I was most familiar with, as a mortal man.

I was enamored with everything that embodied Mynea. My infatuation for her was greater than any feeling or emotion I'd ever felt. I couldn't decipher at the time if I loved deeper as a vampire or if I was simply under her powerful spell. All I knew for sure was that I cherished her a thousand times more than a husband cherishes his faithful and nurturing wife. I adored her a hundred times more than a baby adores its mother. It was love incarnate. Immortal love, perhaps. Nonetheless, love it certainly was.

I continued to take note of my surroundings, and I followed a soft melody to a nearby pond. The ground was damp and gave with every step, leaving a progressively deeper impression as I came closer to the inviting body of water. I bent down for a drink when I saw—me.

I had changed. I was surprised and startled by the reflection in the water. It was me, but I was something far more than my former self. Up until this point I had never referred to myself as beautiful. Sure I was handsome and desirable to some women and probably even to some men. But the vampire staring back at me was beautiful.

Picasso would have considered my cast a work of art. Though I was a young mortal not long ago with faint facial lines that told a finite tale, my face seemed to have eluded the shackles of time. Everything about me had changed. Even the feel of the water, now flooding my ankles, felt different. Anyone can clearly observe the hundreds of tiny waves created by a single minute disturbance in its calmness, but I could *feel* them. Hundreds, maybe thousands, of infinitesimal waves crashed against my leg, all invisible to the mortal eye and completely undetectable to the mortal touch. It was in that very moment, while observing my own reflection, that I felt extraordinary.

I clasped my hands together, bent down, and submerged them in the water, capturing an amount more likely to tease than quench my thirst. How refreshing. It felt revitalizing, cool, and crisp, traveling swiftly down my throat, a delightful and tantalizing contrast to my blood thirst.

As I knelt for a second helping, I caught a familiar scent. I bolted erect, turned, and found Mynea standing behind me. She held a young girl in her arms.

"I've made you strong, Aleron, and I assure you, that was no easy feat. You must now learn your strengths and respect your weaknesses." I could see that the girl was still alive, but she looked bewitched, undoubtedly lost in Mynea's allure.

"I've brought you a meal, my young Aleron, but this will become much more."

"What do you mean?" I asked. She gently put the girl on the ground, then caressed my face with her hand as I closed my eyes and pressed to intensify her touch. When I opened my eyes to capture the moment, Mynea was gone!

I looked down at the girl now lying on the ground. Thoughts of Mynea dissolved as soon as the girl's blood called out to me. I knelt on one knee and took her head into my hand. I placed my hand just beneath the base of her skull, causing her neck to appear elongated. The sight was intoxicating! The desire to drain her of all life drove me into a frenzy. I plunged my teeth into her neck, and the blood began to pour into my mouth. It was more powerful than a hundred mortal orgasms.

Her vivid memories began to convey her last moments: getting up from a table surrounded by men and women and walking intently toward my beloved, whom I could see through the girl's eyes. Mynea took her into her arms and retraced her path around the crowded table and room, seemingly floating just beyond the crowd's reach as they witnessed her unnatural movements. The men were furious, and the women screamed as Mynea carried the girl into the night. Indeed, my blood meal was appreciated, but it came with a purpose. Sinister purpose.

My senses heightened as the scent of unknown mortals filled the air. I could hear their hasty footsteps coming from the west. From the rhythm and space between steps I determined that there were two of them. The timbre and heaviness of their breathing suggested that they were males. Quickly I continued to consume the meal I started, careful not to completely finish her until the two men arrived. I knew allowing them to see me would spell death to them. The steps drew closer and then came to a swift halt.

"Let her go!" the shorter of the two shouted. *I'm gonna gut your ass as soon as you step away from her*, he thought.

I stood to my feet, holding the girl by her hair with my back to both men. I unceremoniously tossed her aside, and she landed with a lifeless thud. The taller man realized that she was dead.

I slowly turned around and set my sights on my prey. Towering over the men, I remained stoic, my face impossible to read. I then smirked and challenged the men aloud, "Cut me."

The shorter of the two leapt forward, drew his knife, and flung wildly in a failed attempt to slash me. I moved slightly to the left between them, and the shorter one connected with air and fell to the ground. I turned and smiled at the other man over my shoulder.

He drew two large knives and yelled, "Die!" He swung his arms, desperately trying to make contact. His look of determination reminded me of the face a child would make during a tantrum. It was comical. Pitiful, actually.

After allowing him to get frustratingly close with several swings, I moved ten feet backward without moving my feet. Neither man knew what to make of my peculiar movements. I could sense their anger building. The taller one was developing a plan within his feeble mind. The shorter one only wanted me dead by his own hand, right then!

He ran toward me and thrust the knife toward my throat. I leapt twenty feet into the air, and as his brain tried to comprehend what his eyes had just witnessed, I plunged down on him, my feet landing squarely on his shoulders. His legs crushed under the force, and I could hear the bones in his back and shoulders shattering. He screamed in agony.

The taller man quickly reconsidered his plan for revenge, instead choosing to flee. I sprang from the shorter man's shoulders toward his partner, grabbed him by his collared shirt, and lifted him off his feet. He was stronger and larger than the average man and not accustomed to being weaker than his opponents, which explained his bewildered look. I brought him closer. I wanted him to see the immortal me, to see what I saw in the reflection of the pond. I wanted to burn my face into his dying memory.

Even though his thoughts were sporadic and grossly incoherent, one thought was clear: *Not human.* He repeated this thought over and over. Not human, indeed.

I smiled once more, this time displaying my vampire teeth. "No," I said. "Not human anymore!" With this statement I plunged my canines into his throat, purposely crushing his neck with my bite. I almost found myself chewing as I sucked his blood. My limbs started to grow numb, and I could feel weakness creeping in. The feeling reminded me of my first blood meal. My bite had been too ferocious, and I had severed his veins! I knew the blood was tainted, but in my gluttony, I couldn't stop myself. The blood was too intoxicating to stop, and I wanted to continue at all costs.

*Even at the cost of death, Aleron?* I heard Mynea's voice in my head. I was drowning in this erotic pleasure, antagonized by the logic of my mother. Suddenly, I felt a sharp pain in my lower back. It was impossible to awake from the drunken stupor induced by the bad blood. I felt hot breath on my neck and hair and another sharp pain just above the last.

A man yelled, "Die, you monster! Die!" in my left ear, rendering it moist. This irritated me immensely. I wondered how I had not picked up the stench from his rotting teeth. My mind wasn't yet able to focus, but I could feel him on my back. He was much heavier than the two already slain by my hand.

The taller man's heartbeat faded to silence, and I released him. I felt my blood spilling from the wounds inflicted by the third man. He stabbed me a third time on my right shoulder. "You're gonna pay for what you've done!" he screamed.

I had to focus. The man put his arm around my neck and plunged his knife into the back of my head. Despite the excruciating pain, I took advantage of his mistake.

I felt myself growing feeble from rapid blood loss. I opened my mouth and bit into his hairy arm, and he screamed out. I began to suck, and before I knew it, I was standing. With him still on my back and his arm still in my mouth, I lunged backward with fierce momentum and crashed into a mighty oak. I could feel the warm mess of the crushed man. I spat out his despicable arm and stepped forward. Though I didn't turn around, I could hear the man's bloody flesh dripping down the tree. I could feel his body peeling off my back.

I was furious. He had actually hurt me. The arrogance of it! A query presented itself, his arrogance or mine? Mine, I reluctantly concluded.

Still somewhat lethargic from the tainted blood and not enough good blood from the third man, I searched for Mynea. I had heard her thoughts when I was drinking the foul blood, so she must be in the vicinity. My vision wasn't sharp. In fact, none of my senses were keen after the last snack. I could scarcely hear the creatures of the night. Each sound was muffled and without distinction. I looked down at my pale hands. My steps were no longer sure or graceful as I walked slowly back to the pond. Once I felt the water begin filling my shoes, I dropped to my knees and leaned forward onto my hands to keep myself from falling in.

Perhaps pure and simple water could be my cure. Leaning forward, I caught a glimpse of myself again, and again, I hardly recognized my face. My mouth was stretched. Weathered lines of age now resided in my face. My eyes appeared dark and sunken. My hair was an unkempt mess. I had a look and feeling of sorrow. I resembled a corpse! "Not Aleron," I whispered. This couldn't be me. It was some simple, rudimentary imitation of a Picasso.

I drank the water. Though refreshing, it had no profound effect on my weakened state. I began to feel the chill in the night air. I didn't sense the presence of anyone. Or, I couldn't. I looked around and saw the carnage I had left. I looked back into the pond, taking note of my reflection again. I didn't see radiance. I didn't witness divinity. I didn't embody immortality. I didn't resemble the king my queen spoke of. I saw vulnerability. I saw frailty. I saw mortality. I saw death.

I realized that Mynea was trying to teach me about immortality. I had been under the misconception that I couldn't die. As a fledgling, I misunderstood immortality to mean to live forever; I've since learned to the contrary. Vampires can be vulnerable to death. If I remained careless about my eternal life, I would certainly die. There are rules that must be obeyed if I'm to remain alive. This lesson, Mynea had instructed, should never be forgotten. And it never has.

I smelled more men approaching, and I could hear their chatter and their calls to those who preceded them. I couldn't tell how many there were at the time, for it was difficult to focus and isolate the sounds and nuances. I tried to read their thoughts, but my effort was futile. As weak as I felt, I knew there was no way I could defeat them all. I realized I had few options. I had neither the time nor the strength to escape. I slid quietly into the water, trying desperately not to cause a disturbance. I swam toward the opposite bank.

When the men came upon my massacre, they erupted into angry shouts. Their cries faded the deeper and farther away I swam. My strength was fading, and my muscles ached with every stroke. The water was cool against my skin, yet it seemed to be an almost impenetrable barrier holding fast as I desperately tried to swim. My mind was overwhelmed with thoughts of mortality. I could feel my lungs pleading for air. The surface seemed out of reach. I felt panic and desperation in my lungs. My movements began to lose purpose. I tried not to inhale, knowing that when I did, all would be lost. My immortal life would be no more. With open arms, the angel of death was ready to accept my offering. *Condemnation to hell*, I thought. *I'm going to die!*

Reality was now lost. Logic and reason were but a memory. I was suspended between life and death. The underwater scene seemed surreal, and the surface above danced with the distorted reflections of the moon. Darkness fell over me. Motionless I sank, my eyes still open. In the moments before losing consciousness, I could think only of her.

# CHAPTER 6

 awoke in Mynea's powerful grasp. She pressed her right wrist against my lips. Instinctively I bit into it, and the blood flowed from her body into mine, her heart pumping vigorously to serve an additional body. My sensibility began to return, and I could focus my mind. I began to suck more and more vigorously. Visions began to play before my mind's eye, many reminding me of the last time Mynea had fed me from her own bosom. Suddenly she wrenched her arm away from my overzealous mouth and stood. The look in her eyes was one of disappointment and fury. "You fool! You would trade life immortal for one blood meal?"

Though she posed the admonishment as a question, I dared not answer. I just stared at her. I had no answer. I had heard her clearly warn me, yet I continued in a fiendish rage.

"Knowing what you are is just as important as knowing how to live as you are, Aleron!" Her voice, while remaining stern, had love and forgiveness in it, perhaps even pity.

"Those men could have killed you! You could have drowned in the black water. Had I truly left your side, you would have perished. And even more devastating, they could have caught you! Catching you would spell doom for the rest of us. You can't allow your petty pride and vanity to endanger your life, let alone all of our lives. You must understand your limitations and your weaknesses if you're to know who you truly are and realize your true potential."

I remembered that look. I first received it from my mortal mother, Camilia, when she was lecturing my sister and me about God's word and how we were charged with spreading His word. We were to devote our entire lives to this notion. "Everything else pales in comparison to the glory God would bestow upon thee," she would say. Though my sister listened attentively to every syllable, I was more interested in what all teenage males were interested in—teenage females. My mother knew me all too well. Nevertheless, she tried desperately to get through to her son. After several failed attempts at gaining my attention and acknowledgment of our duty, she gave me a look similar to the one now delivered from my immortal mother, one of disappointment. Mynea's silent expression unearthed memories from when I was a defiant child. I thought of my mortal family. Until that moment, they had been lost to me.

The look of disappointment in her eyes faded. "Aleron, be mindful not to interfere with the lives of those who knew you as a mere mortal. It's forbidden to return to loved ones and acquaintances after transformation. We're taught this for good reason. The road to rekindling past relationships with our mortal families and friends leads to intense pain and suffering—the likes of which I desire you never to experience."

I wanted to ask why, but before I could, she answered, "Your mortal feelings will return and linger about for an eternity. You will live forever, and your mortals will certainly die. Loneliness, then sorrow would follow. And loneliness, my prince, is the very reason some of our kind go mad. It's an incredible blessing to live for an eternity; however, it's a curse if misunderstood."

She stopped as if interrupted or just alerted to some interloper, "Aleron, come with me. Dawn is near, and we need to get back to the castle."

I stood and took her hand. As we began our journey back to the castle, I realized we weren't far from where I had slipped into the water. We took to the treetops, enabling me to see the ground below, where limbs and body parts were scattered about. I counted eleven heads, including the crushed skull hanging from a detached spine near the base of the oak. Four were dispatched by my hand. Mynea must have slaughtered the rest before she pulled me from the water. This would explain the many incoherent thoughts and visions filling my head while she fed me.

We returned to the castle and again to her bedchamber. "Your body will feel numb soon and you'll be unable to move. The scars that tell the story of your encounter will be but a memory when you awake. You'll be as beautiful and radiant as you were at the start of this night. Rest now, my child. Embrace your slumber with open arms."

I still couldn't speak. I simply did exactly what she told me. I lay on an animal fur next to a roaring fire, welcoming the warmth. I tried to keep my eyes on her as she disrobed, but my sight became blurry. I felt like a paralytic. Alas, I could only bear witness to the flickering light of the flame growing dimmer and dimmer, until it was no more. I heard nothing. I felt nothing. I wasn't drowning this time, simply resting.

As always, when I awoke, Mynea was already awake. She was again standing at the same great window intently studying the night's full moon. Her thoughts, I imagined, were of a distant place, one unfamiliar to me. Suddenly she turned around as I stood. "Come to me, Aleron."

She didn't need to ask. I walked toward her, desiring a much-needed embrace, to feel her immense power. She loved me. I knew that once I touched her, she would never let any harm befall me. And I, her. The thought of any harm to my queen would drive me to madness. If love is, then blood is.

Mynea and I carried on in this fashion until a routine developed. The nights became weeks, and weeks became years. We dutifully left the castle in search of victims. My bloodlust began to match hers. My strength even began to rival hers. I knew this to be true because, though Mynea loved to be held, it aroused her more to exert her will on me, to show me what true power she beheld. This was proving to be more and more difficult as the years progressed. As my vampire abilities began to manifest themselves under her constant tutelage, I became faster than my mother. I could leap higher and farther.

In my eagerness to please her, I drove myself hard to learn the lessons she gave. The results exceeded both our expectations. Though gravity still held a firm grip on my mother, it started to lose its grip on me. More and more often I led our airborne travels, holding Mynea in my arms. She would look upon me as though she were a proud mother observing an obedient son. Hunting became second only to breathing. I had a true vampire's lust for it. The choice. The lure. The capture. The dance. And, of course, the blood. It was all so enchanting.

Upon our return, we alighted as one, and always directly to the bed-chamber we would go. Expressions of our love would completely eclipse the amour shared by Romeo and Juliet. We followed blissful lovemaking with hours of conversation, Mynea answering as many questions as I could ask. I madly wanted to know about the ancient abyssal eyes I experienced through her thoughts, but I restrained myself from asking, though not knowing filled me with discontent. Nevertheless, intercourse with her would always comfort me.

Our lovemaking often began with Mynea pressing my head to her neck and allowing me to drink. While I drank, she would explore my body and further stimulate my desires until I reached complete and total rapture. Finally, we would drift into the type of sleep that only a vampire could ever know—slumber that numbed and nourished our entire bodies while drawing together vivid pictures and encounters that linked all of our kind. Dreams more akin to latent memories, never to be forgotten once transmitted during our sleep. We would awake strong and fully refreshed.

The rules that governed the life of a vampire were taught to me. Mynea would speak of them mostly while we were hunting. Many, I admit, were self-explanatory and simple, but there were some that baffled me.

"Aleron, I know you'll eventually long for your mortal family." She was right. I couldn't deny that I periodically thought of my mother and sister. Many a time I would see acquaintances while hunting near Alexandria; however, I would purposely avoid places my mother and sister frequented.

"You once had a life as a mortal. You must forget that life and never attempt to return to it. It's gone, forever. You'll simply become a loving memory to your mortal family and all others who knew you. You must never try to see them or let them discover you as you are now."

I understood this from the previous lectures, but the understanding didn't eliminate the desire to see them again. However, I was still determined to obey her commands.

Life at that time was complete bliss, except when Mynea withdrew and became distant. When this happened, I would sometimes ask her to tell me what was bothering her, for it was still virtually impossible to penetrate her thoughts, and she would simply reply, "Nothing of your concern, my love." Hearing the words "my love" escape her lips was often all it took for my unease to subside.

The second defining event following my transformation into a vampire happened one night when Mynea and I were preparing for a hunt. I had noticed earlier in the evening that there was something different about Mynea. Then my suspicion was confirmed when I saw it in her eyes as she touched my face.

"My dear, Aleron. My love. My prince. My king. My lord. I won't join you this night. I must tend to other affairs. You shall hunt without me." If it weren't for my keen senses, I wouldn't have noticed the slight quiver in her voice as she spoke. Mynea's expressions to many were undetectable, but not to me.

Before I could ask to accompany her, she slowly and subtly shook her head, solemnly signifying the request would be denied. I remained silent as I kissed her lips, then I took to the night sky.

I couldn't understand why she chose not to hunt with me, nor what affairs she spoke of. However, I wasn't terribly concerned, either. I wanted to hunt alone, for I knew wherever I went, she would surely be close. She would no longer be there for protection, only for companionship. She was my bride. Everything was for her. I would often sneak out and bring her flowers, which she would discover upon opening her eyes. I learned how to mask my feelings around her so she wouldn't suspect what I was doing. I began to fall asleep after she would, always in my arms. I would pass my hands softly and attentively through her hair, then I would kiss her lips, her cheeks, her nose, and her forehead as she slept. This would be my ritual until I, too, fell asleep.

Mynea meant everything to me, and as I reached southern Cairo, I couldn't stop thinking of her. Now there was a feeling in the pit of my stomach that nearly equaled that of the anticipated blood meal. I was longing for her. That longing did not go away as the evening progressed.

The night was wet with a steady rain, perfect ambiance for enjoying the victim I'd been tracking for several weeks now. Eli was wanted for every crime one could think of: theft, kidnapping, rape, even murder. He began his evil deeds in Sharkia, in Lower Egypt. Understand that Lower Egypt was north of Upper Egypt. The name came from the upstream flow of the Nile River, which separated the two regions.

Eli was a middle-aged man who had a commanding stature. His size demanded respect from others. His voice was deep and raspy. He had a habit of chewing on twigs or the shriveled butts of used cigars. He was in the habit of spitting awful-looking globs out of the side of his mouth. One may wonder what attracted me to this vile specimen. It wasn't his disgusting disposition, nor his habit of wearing the clothing of his victims. Eli personified what my kind truly represented. He took whatever he wanted without regard to law or the well-being of his fellow man. He stole possessions of the lowly as well as the aristocrat. Watching him do his deeds provided entertainment for me on countless nights. I would often feed in places where I knew he would be, just to observe his wretched ways. It was a true delight.

The townspeople thought he was responsible for the many disappearances, and they feared him. I continued hunting in his territory, and as a result, he was blamed for things he didn't do, things he couldn't do, such as murders in the dozens.

During this time I often wondered how long Mynea had watched me. I wanted to know why she chose to give birth to me instead of feeding upon me. Why did she choose to love me and not to bury me or leave my carcass to the rodents? I guess I was more than Eli, much more than he would ever be.

I guess one could say that I was responsible for all of his murders the day I decided to kill him and didn't. Sure, I could have dispatched him whenever I wanted and perhaps prevented bloodshed by his hand; but who was I to prevent bloodshed? Eli represented much more than an interesting meal. I wanted to follow him. I wanted to study him. I wanted to know him.

I admired his cunningness and uncompromising skill at disposing of his victims. I was amused by his arrogance. I witnessed many of his chilling encounters with those unfortunate enough to cross his path. The theft of an old lady's possessions after he knocked her unconscious with a swift punch of his hairy fist. The rape and sodomizing of a young man and his wife, the death of the woman, and the man left to be tormented by his memories for the rest of his life. Of course, I couldn't let him go on living under such anguish. I, after Eli vanished, took whatever life he had left. I considered it a mercy killing.

I witnessed dear Eli slitting the throat of a local merchant for his money. He later went to the man's home, having acquired his keys and address from his belongings, and visited with his family. He forced the man's wife to cook for him, pleasure him as if he were the patron of the house, and then killed her and their daughter. He overlooked a young boy who was hiding, so I took it upon myself to relieve the child of the miserable life he would endure as an orphan. Of course, I don't kill children, for children are inherently innocent, and this case was no exception. I simply peeked into the child's mind and took him to a relative's home, where I left him with enough gold to be cared for until adulthood.

Eli was neither neat nor discrete in disposing of his victims' corpses. Though he knew he was wanted, he still did not clean up his messes. Perhaps he knew one day he would be caught. This notion was correct. He just didn't know he was going to be caught by me, the slayer of men. Eli didn't know that darkness had chosen him that day in late September.

After tracking him for several weeks, I was able to predict his whereabouts from night to night. It took only a bit of logical deduction on my part. Once I was within a few cubits of him, his signature heartbeat would direct me to him. I knew this night his conquest would take him to Damiat, near the mouth of the Nile, so to Damiat I went.

The journey to Damiat took far less time than it would have decades prior. I was now able to propel myself several kilometers at will, without the aid of the wind. The laws of physics were now bending to my demand. I was no longer bound by the rules of gravity. My ability to fly intrigued Mynea. She told me no other vampire whom she had known could take flight as I could. The others could move swiftly, as well as make enormous leaps, but not actually fly. This gift manifested within me and was mine and mine alone.

As soon as I arrived in Damiat, I began listening for his steady heartbeat. Once I isolated it, I began my pursuit. Within minutes I had him. But he wasn't alone. I could read his mind and learned that with him was a woman of tender age, a girl. I took to the sky and perched myself on a rooftop seven stories above, peering down on Eli and the girl. It was a dark alley and, except for them, completely deserted. Eli coerced the girl into following him with something he stole from his last conquest, a silver necklace. He motioned for the girl to turn around so he could affix it to her neck and, as she complied, he grabbed her! The girl's screams were muffled by his filthy, wet, hairy paw of a hand covering her mouth. Her feet struggled to gain ground but only futilely splashed in the puddles that accumulated from the steady rain. He lifted her off her feet, and her legs churned the empty air. But, alas, her feet found nothing to connect to. Hopelessness filled her heart.

I surveyed the other corners and finally the main road. No one was around. She would indeed be his next trophy. Soon her body would be discovered by a passerby and reported. Her memory would be added to the fear already spreading through the region, her family grief-stricken, her future stolen by this fiend.

I turned my attention back to Eli and the girl. He had completely subdued her. She lay flat on her back, and he held her head to the ground. He tore off her shirt with his other hand, exposing her underdeveloped breasts. It was disgusting to watch him fondle and grope her to his liking and to her dismay. Realizing he was simply too strong for her, she finally gave up her struggle. Her eyes went blank as her tears mixed in with the raindrops falling upon her face. She looked up and whispered a prayer, and in that moment, she saw me.

*Please help me! Please! Please! Help me!* Her thoughts screamed out to me. Usually I would not be so sentimental, but she reminded me of someone important in my mortal life, my sister. I obliged her.

I leapt down from the rooftop and landed purposefully louder than usual. This startled Eli. After noticeably flinching at the announcement of my presence, he turned his attention away from the girl and onto me. He leaned back down within an inch of her face and snarled, "I'll be back to finish once I show our guest out."

Eli looked directly at me and ran a paw over his face. Just before he began to speak, I did something I hadn't done in years, since that night at the pond. I spoke to my dinner.

"Hello, Eli," I said in the manner of an old, long-lost friend. His well-rehearsed battle face that no doubt struck fear to the hearts of his opponents was instantly replaced by a look of bewilderment.

"Who are you and how do you know my name?" he stammered.

"It's of no consequence, but if you must know, I am Aleron. But for tonight, for you, I shall be called Death."

"Is that so?" he replied. "Well, we'll see about that."

I turned my gaze to the girl. "You're free to go now, young one."

Unsteadily she scrambled to her feet and ran away. Her steps quickened the farther she got from Eli, until she was in full stride out of the dark alley and into the night.

Eli, watching her flee, reclaimed his battle face. His eyes focused. His nostrils flared. His mouth dropped open, exposing rotten and missing teeth. He pulled out his knife, no doubt the very one he used on the old woman weeks prior.

"I guess tonight Aleron is on the menu," he gravely spat out, shifting the knife from hand to hand.

Hearing him say my name was queer and unfamiliar to me. For decades I'd only heard my name spoken by my beautiful Mynea, who made it sound like music, the sweetest symphony. Eli demonstrated how my name sounded when spoken by anyone else.

I swiftly closed the gap between us and grabbed his neck. I scaled the building with him in tow, and in his astonishment, he dropped the knife. I heard the tiny splash it made as it landed in one of the puddles. I landed firmly on the rooftop with him still in my grasp. I squeezed his neck, careful not to crush it, while I forced him to the edge of the building. With each step closer to the edge, he gasped for air. I held him over the building. He struggled to look down from the corners of his eyes. Completely satisfied, I closed my eyes, lifted my face, and allowed the rain to tease my senses. I opened them to see the moon. Yes, it was more than enough light for him to see me. If there was ever a meal that I wanted to see my true nature, it was Eli. Death had arranged a special messenger for him. He'd be reunited with his victims in a manner that only a vampire could deliver.

Eli affixed his eyes upon me. I grinned and revealed my vampire teeth. He opened his mouth and spattered, "You're not human! Are you the devil?" Saliva flew from his lips and onto my face as he strained to speak. Coughing profusely and hardly able to formulate more words, he muttered, "Are you here to take me to hell?"

I slightly loosened my grip. "Eli, I'm surprised at you. For months you've played Death's reaper to the innocent. Seventeen lives, to be more precise. And though they begged you to spare them or their loved ones, you answered with either your knife, or your penis and then the knife. So for you, yes. I am your reaper! I am your devil! I will deliver you to whatever afterlife awaits you."

Once dangling, he did not struggle out of fear that the slightest movement would send him plummeting to his certain death. "What are you going to do to me?" he gasped.

A strange yet inviting feeling took over me. I had the sudden urge to put the laws of gravity to the test. And so I did. I stepped off the roof into the open air. I allowed Eli to look down. He realized there was nothing holding me, and total despair filled his face. I brought my nose within an inch of his, as he had done with the girl. I smiled again and took him straight up into the night air, twirling him to further exacerbate his unease. I bit into his neck as we soared, draining almost all of his blood. I didn't want to kill him just yet. He stared at me as we flew.

"I've drained you nearly to the point of death, Eli," I softly told him.

"But I won't kill you. I'm merely an instrument." Then I dropped him. Too weak to scream out, Eli expelled a pitiful sigh as he started his descent. I could see his fear; it was a look he must have seen at least seventeen times before in the faces of the unfortunate innocent. I could hear his once steady heartbeat race, just as the pulse of his victims had soared. His grizzly deeds played over and over in my mind as my vampire eyes followed him down.

Before he hit the ground, Eli struck the corner of the building. I heard his vertebrae shatter in several places. I could also hear his heart beating so profoundly that I knew it would burst from the shock of death racing upon him. A bane on society, Eli preyed upon the public, and it was only fitting that his end should be public as well. Eli landed in the middle of the square, a heaping, bloody mess for all to see. Screams and gasps filled the air below. It was fitting.

I alighted with stealth, much differently from when I announced my presence to Eli. I wanted to see the justice I dispensed personally. I wanted to scan the thoughts of the people who witnessed the aftermath of this gruesome death. I needed to see.

Landing just beyond the crowd, I raised the collar of my coat to create a bit of a shadow on the profile of my face. Though fresh blood was coursing through me, my skin appeared quite unnatural in the full moon. I drew in and buttoned my overcoat to hide Eli's only contribution to this world, his blood. I wiped his offering from my mouth and stepped toward the onlookers now gathering en masse around the body. Avoiding detection, I looked upon him. Poor Eli. His wish had been granted: eternal, blissful death.

I was about to depart unnoticed, as I'd arrived, when I heard a familiar voice say, "Thank you." It was the girl, and she was, again, staring directly at me. She had seen me take to the air. She had seen how easily I had disposed of Eli. She knew I wasn't human. She knew! By the code, she was condemned to death. Mercy again played its part. I couldn't bring myself to kill her after saving her, for she reminded me so much of my little sister. Her innocence. Her naivety. She walked toward me, and I started walking in the opposite direction. Her pace quickened. I stopped and waited. Her footsteps came to a halt a few feet from me.

"Thank you," she said again, this time softer, yet more direct. I turned around and raised my hand to give her something, the silver necklace that Eli had used to lure her into the alley. As she opened her hand and marveled at the bounty, I slipped away into the darkness, never to be seen by her again.

I arrived back to the safety of the castle just before daybreak. I found Mynea lying on the bearskin that we usually slept on together. She was barely awake. The coming of the sun had taken its toll on her, too. Or so I thought. We didn't talk this time. We simply embraced, kissed, and drifted.

# CHAPTER 7

*'m lost in your arms, Aleron. I chose you above all oth-
ers. I've watched you for decades and you never cease
to amaze me. With me, you have known pleasure the
likes of which humans cannot imagine. I've taught you
all of my knowledge and wisdom while making you
stronger than any of my other children as well as all others of our kind.
You'll stand alone atop an empire that I'll create for you. You will be
king. You've given me the one thing he never will: your heart, my love.
He forgot passion long, long ago. His icy core never thaws. I'll show you
what he's shown me and more. When you awake, you'll long for what is
rightfully yours by birth—me. The void in me will be no more. For now,
go and master your immortal gifts. For this lesson I'm no longer needed.*

"My lady," Eliza expressed softly. "It's time. You must start your
journey. All has been prepared for you in the hills of Moeciu, as well as
in the innermost chamber of the Carpathians. I wish you well, my lady."

"I know, my dear, sweet, and loyal Eliza. Thank you. Provide for

Aleron as you have provided for me. There's no need to fear him. When he awakens, he'll have a hunger unmatched by anything you've ever witnessed. And even though he knows you are of me, it may be difficult for him to control his hunger. You mustn't let fear dissuade you from the task at hand. He'll call out to me and be unanswered. You must go to him and soothe him. You'll serve him as you serve me. I can't tell you where my destination is, for he'll read your thoughts and follow, only to find his death."

"And what stops him from killing me, my lady?"

"He won't, my dear."

"And if he refuses to listen to me and travels as far as the Carpathians in search of you?"

"Then he'll be on the doorsteps of a monster, the likes of which he's never encountered nor possesses the strength to conquer. He's seen the castle within my blood, for he's grown strong, and it's more difficult to hide my memoirs from him. If he allows his longing for me to set him on that path, he'll kill us both, leaving you vulnerable to those of our kind who are unclean and follow no laws of the immortals. So you see, my dear, your survival depends on his."

"How long until your return?"

"I won't be gone long. I know you're troubled with thoughts of your own mortality. You've come to understand my immortal blood has made your heart strong and granted you unusually long life for a mortal. I will return before Father Time claims possession of you."

"Thank you, my lady. All will be done exactly as you wish."

"Goodbye, Eliza. Until my return, farewell."

† † † †

While drifting in and out of consciousness, I experienced dreams so vivid I could feel, smell, hear, and taste the realism they mimicked, places I'd never been. An unfamiliar castle, immense in size and more dark and mysterious than the one I'd resided in for so long. This fortress stood overlooking a vast and rugged mountainous region. At its base was a moat that was just wide and uninviting enough to deter even the most curious of creatures. My awareness seemed to flow through the solid stone walls like smoke through a screen door. This drifting was unobscured and without the slightest effort on my part. I was being drawn in. Many candles lit an otherwise dark and damp place. Rodents roamed freely in and out of the many cracks and holes along the base of the walls. Paintings of nobles covered much of the dark stone walls, similar in style to the ones I saw in Mynea's castle. The air was moist with the smell of mildew and the unmistakable stench of wet dog.

Suddenly I could hear someone speaking in an unfamiliar tongue, the dialect so old as to have been beyond mortal recall. Increasingly, the voice became louder, as if I were getting closer to its origin. I continued to penetrate a number of walls until I saw beings that resembled people standing in a room, their faces blurred, their movements unnatural for mortals. There was a lone man standing as inanimate as a statue before them, draped in black and red robes from collar to foot, hands outstretched, palms up, as one would imagine a priest's would be when offering forgiveness. I drew closer. It seems I was being drawn in to him. His features remained blurred, save his eyes, which were the same eyes I saw when Mynea shared her blood with mine, the same eyes that have haunted me day after day. Yet again, they were focused on me—so I thought.

An unexpected appearance by my lovely princess being summoned by him! I reached out for her. I cried out with a loud voice, yet she didn't respond. Closer and closer she drew toward him, farther from me.

I felt my senses retreating from the dream as if I were being sucked backward. I retraced the path on which I came, backward through the chambers, through the walls, and into the air. The castle began to shrink into the distance. The vast moat reduced to a splash, the creatures of the night resembled scurrying ants. The moon became a speck. His eyes remained until the last detail of the vision was extinguished. And as his evaporated, mine opened.

When I awoke, I immediately sensed that something was different. For the first time in decades, Mynea's naked body wasn't sharing the warmth of our bed. I got out of bed and looked around the room. I scanned the surrounding areas with my mind and vampiric senses. I sensed nothing. I silently called out to her and searched for her thoughts. Again, there was nothing.

Suddenly I felt an excruciating pain, pain I've only felt twice in my immortal lifetime, this time being the first.

It was a feeling of unimaginable loss and utter loneliness, complete and total despair. I was a child who's lost his parent, a man who has lost his wife and best friend of sixty years to some debilitating disease for which he can offer no salvation or cure. He can only witness her passing. And even these emotions described herein are human. The anguish I encountered then was a thousand times more debilitating. An uncontrollable deep shudder overtook me as I dropped to my knees like a stone.

I heard a wail that could wake the dead and was surprised when I realized the wailing came from me. I held myself, wrapping both arms around my body as if clinging for dear life, my hands gripping my limbs, my nails tearing at the flesh beneath them. I was crying, though no tears fell, only dry sobbing.

Eliza entered the room and saw me kneeling. I didn't have to turn and look at her eyes, for her thoughts told all. She felt sorry for my anguish. She understood my affliction, yet she wasn't surprised. She knew. She knew before I did. If she knew, then she had known!

The cloudiness caused by Mynea's disappearance and my distress evaporated. I released myself. The wounds resulting from my nails ripping my skin healed instantly, leaving only dried blood in their place. I slowly stood and turned toward my servant.

"Eliza," I said with a calm and authoritative voice. "Where is she?"

Eliza's face immediately displayed anxiety. "My Lord Aleron, Mynea has left me with instruction to care for you as I cared for her," her voice quivered with each word spoken.

"Answer me!" I demanded with a countenance that was unforgiving.

Tears began to well in her eyes and tiny translucent drops slid down her cheeks. "She's gone, my lord. Her whereabouts are unknown to me." With her head down, looking at the floor, she continued, "She knew that if I knew that you would read my mind, and—"

I lifted her by her arms. Her feet dangled helplessly, searching for the ground below.

"I won't ask again, Eliza. Know that I'm not Mynea; I still don't quite know my own strength. However, I would much rather test my limits of unspeakable cruelty on another."

I held her close to my face, close enough for my stinging breath to leave moisture in her ear. I spoke softer and slower. "Make no mistake, my dear, I still have an enormous hunger burning within. Your blood would be no different from that of a vagabond at the Peasant's dungeon!" Though the rage in me was building, I wouldn't harm Eliza.

"My lord, what I tell you is true. If you don't believe me, then take my blood into you and satisfy your curiosity. But I beg of you, please don't take my life, for I must do what my mistress has ordered."

I already knew she was telling the truth. However, an offer of blood was still too irresistible. "I will oblige your request, and I hope, for your sake, that the blood memoirs are cohesive and depict what you've told me," I said while maintaining my stern glare. I allowed her feet to slap soundly onto the stone floor as I released my grasp. Her knees buckled slightly. She continued to stare at the floor as she meekly raised her wrist in offering.

I drank, and true to her testimony, I saw no visions of where my queen had gone or when she would return. Nevertheless, Eliza's blood sent me into a frenzy. A battle ensued within me. Why should I let her live when her life meant nothing to me? I intensified my hold on her. She gasped. Her encounters with Mynea began to flash in my mind. I watched her memories as vividly as a motion picture. I could see and hear their intimate conversations, confirming that she spoke the truth.

Periodically, Mynea spoke candidly to Eliza about the life of a vampire, in which she detailed the agony of the immortal heart. I witnessed visions of Mynea in a weakened state being comforted by her faithful servant; Eliza raising her wrist in offering to Mynea; Mynea's acceptance and rejuvenation from the sacrifice. In the reflection of Mynea's eyes, I could see the expression of envy and lust on Eliza's face. How badly she wanted immortality. How she longed for an intimate kiss from our queen. And as the blood continued to flow into me, I saw it—Mynea giving Eliza blood. Vampire blood! I now witnessed Mynea squeezing minute drops of her immortal blood into the waiting mouth of Eliza. I saw this action occur repeatedly over decades. Still, Eliza remained human. The blood had made her life unnaturally long while it slowed the sands of time. More than a mistress and servant, the two were symbiotic, thriving off each other. Before I knew it, Eliza's heartbeat began to slow. Her eyes were wide open as mine regained focus. Then I heard the sweetest voice, "Care for him, as you care for me."

I noted my queen's voice via her memories. Every fiber of my body wanted to drain Eliza of her soul completely and soundly, driven by the thought of being able to hold on to her visions of my queen. But I stopped. Her eyes weren't as wide as before, but they remained open. She had an exhausted expression on her face. Her complexion had lost most of its luster.

She continued to stare right into my eyes as I gently laid her on the white bear fur. Her expression had changed. Previous feelings of comfort had been replaced by fear and intrigue. Realizing the possibility of her own mortality had strained her usual calm state. Indeed, Eliza spoke forthrightly. Even in the face of uncertainty, she had told me the truth. She feared what she didn't understand. My intentions remained a mystery to her—and to me as well. I guess the combination made me ever more intriguing and terrifying to her. My thirst satisfied and now assured that Eliza hadn't withheld anything, I knew there wasn't anything else to gain this night from her.

I picked up Eliza and carried her to her quarters. While in my arms, her head swayed to and fro to the rhythm of my footsteps, teetering on the brink of death. How terrible I began to feel! The harm I brought to such a beautiful creature, who catered to our every desire, grieved me. Eliza never questioned a command given by her lord or lady. She had truly won the favor of Mynea. *What a monster I was. How could I do such a thing?* I thought.

Though I didn't look at her, I knew Eliza was staring at me as we traveled up the stairs to the third level. Her head must have felt twice as heavy dangling on her swan-like neck. I adjusted my grasp to support her head. Her thoughts began to speak to me. *I can see why my lady loves you so. I've always been fond of you, Aleron. My lady talks of you to no end, and you've haunted my dreams for decades and, I pray, for decades to come.*

I proceeded to her room. As I approached the closed door, I envisioned it opening, and before I reached out, it opened inward, more forcefully than I had intended. The momentum of the door caused a glass of fresh apple nectar to crash to the floor. The sound of shattering glass ricocheted off the stone walls. It took me only a few steps to reach the bed. This chamber didn't display the luxury found in the many other rooms throughout the castle. There were cotton curtains in place of silk. The only thing that hung on the wall was a mirror, which was situated above a small wooden desk on which stood an old lamp. The room felt drab and simple. Embers burned in a circle of loose stones in the center of the room. Eliza gracefully fell from my arms onto the wooden bed. I was surprised to see that the sleeping pad was made of down furs and feathers, definitely better accommodations than I'd seen within the quarters of any slave girl. But Eliza was more than just a slave.

Eyes sunken and nearly as pale as the dead, she strained to speak. "Please don't leave me like this, my lord. I won't last through the night. Please. You have the power to spare me."

She was right. I noticed the lines in her face were more pronounced than ever before. The excess skin under her eyes sagged. Her hair seemed thinner. Her bones seemed feeble. She had aged and continued to age right before my eyes! It seemed I had sucked the youth right out of her body. To save her, I knew what must be done.

I sat beside Eliza and took her head into my arms. It flopped lifelessly against my chest. I punctured my wrist and allowed the crimson wine to drip into her mouth. With every bit that landed on her tongue, she swallowed and took me into her. I could feel vigor returning to her bones. I didn't know how much to give. However, she, it seemed, knew how much to take, and suddenly she stopped. This was unlike my kind, feeding on one and bringing him within an inch of his life, more often beyond. With the steady flow and the abrupt turning of her head, some of my blood dripped down her face and neck. Within seconds, my self-inflicted wound was gone. Her eyes were now closed. I could feel passion and renewed life electrify her entire body. Her body warmed, a direct contrast to my much colder soul. I loosened my hold.

After I had decided to sit with her for a while, I picked up an interesting-looking book on the table next to her bed to help pass the time. The book looked as if it were of a different time, of a different place. I was intrigued. I picked it up, and suddenly a flash memory of those haunting eyes invaded my mind and then disappeared just as quickly. I turned to Eliza to see if she saw what I'd seen. Her thoughts didn't reveal such a vision. I lifted the book closer for observation.

It was heavier than its physical dimensions suggested, much heavier. There was no inscription on the front or back. I turned the book to its side; there was no writing on the spine. I ran my fingers along the binding and realized it had been stitched with fine, dark hair. The hair had not originated from the head of a mortal. Tiny imperfections as human hair grows didn't accompany this binding. The smell of it was familiar, and that's when I realized it was vampire hair—from the crown of my queen!

I opened it and explored the first page with my eyes and hands. The pages of this book were made of thin, dried, tanned skin. The ink reminded me of the masi used in India, made from burnt bones. The book had an unusual scent. If old had a smell, then this book would epitomize it. It was written in a language and alphabet I hadn't encountered throughout all of my nights as a historian. I perused it with my vampire eyes and began to recognize a word that was used frequently throughout. Indeed there was one such word, rather a name. I silently said the word, and the eyes that had plagued me for so long, gazed upon me yet again. I had summoned Vlad.

# CHAPTER 8

 desperately tried to understand the rest of the writing. When I turned the page, I recognized Mynea's handwriting, also in the unfamiliar language. I turned to the next page, where I noticed that tiny blood vessels littered the leaves. What poor soul or souls contributed to this tome? Page after page I searched for something, anything I could readily understand. Only the name Vlad was recognizable, nothing more.

Eliza had found the strength to sit up on the bed, and she was looking at me.

"Is this your book?"

"No, my lord. It belongs to my lady."

"Can you read it?"

"No, I cannot."

"Then why is it here next to your bed?"

"It was the only book in my lady's library I couldn't read, my lord. I've been trying to determine what language it's written in."

"What have you found?"

"It's not any language of this region. That's all I'm able to determine, my lord." She shook her head slowly. "I've seen my lady write in this journal many times. She's had it since she enslaved me. I never dared to inquire about it, and when I thought of it, she would command me to do various things. I've cared for my lady for decades, and at least twice every seven days I would see her writing in it."

"If it's Mynea's journal, then why is it in your room beside your bed?"

"My lady left hastily. She must have forgotten it. For every other time she left the castle for more than one night, she would take it with her. This time she didn't."

"Why is it in your room?" I repeated.

"I was intrigued by it. For years I've been reading the books within my lady's library; however, the opportunity to read the one I was most interested in never presented itself, until now. Since the first time I saw it, I wondered what was within its pages. On one occasion my lady caught me with it and punished me for trying to read it." She finished her sentence with her head down and eyes closed. The memory was apparently particularly painful for her to bear.

Just as she began to describe it, a vision entered her mind, which depicted Mynea lashing her within the very same room in which I was born. She was left lying in the fetal position, while her blood found its way into the tiny imperfections that riddled the stone floor. Punished indeed.

"The discipline only baited me more. I was given permission to continue reading the other books, but I wasn't to read this one. Like a child, I couldn't resist. When I realized she had left it, my disobedience overtook me. For this, I'm truly ashamed." She spoke softly, as tears filled her eyes.

I couldn't help but feel answers to long-unasked questions would be revealed within the pages of this strange book, especially where Mynea had gone and when she would return. More pain entered my heart as I silently called out to Mynea yet again. Again, I heard nothing.

Eliza placed her hand on my face in an effort to soothe me. I found myself wanting her warm touch. I instinctively pressed my face against her palm and closed my eyes. I could only think of Mynea's touch when I heard her words from Eliza's mouth.

"Your thoughts are heavy, my lord. May I suggest you go out and feed?" The last part Eliza spoke very softly.

Mynea's words were spoken by this beautiful yet mortal creature. Even after my ruse earlier, threatening her life, Eliza was still genuinely concerned for me. She always had been. However, the pain in my stomach and the loss I felt nullified the desire to hunt. I didn't want to move. I didn't want to do anything. For the first time in decades, the blood thirst subsided. "Not tonight, Eliza."

With Mynea's journal in hand, I turned to exit Eliza's bedchamber. She motioned to say something but chose to let the moment be mine and remained silent. I strode into the hall. I had frequented this hall hundreds, maybe even thousands of times, yet this time it seemed much longer and narrower, almost constricting. My heart pounded, and the knot in my stomach grew. Though I hoped for Mynea's swift return, deep down I expected otherwise. I was devastated.

I steeled my legs and proceeded down the stairs to Mynea's private room. It was one of the few rooms I'd never been in. I stared at the enormous stone door. I could've entered, but I didn't. I wanted the room left exactly as she had left it, undisturbed. I guess I was still hoping she would return.

I placed my hand on the door, thinking that maybe by touching it I would somehow feel her. This room was as sacred to her as she was to me. But, alas, there was no sense of Mynea.

I continued down to the lowest part of the castle, where I often went to think, to occasionally relive memories, and to try to forget those whom I loved as a mortal. However, that night wouldn't be filled with thoughts of my former life. That night was consumed with torment and despair, full of loneliness and heartache.

I entered the dungeon, my chamber, the place where I awoke that fateful night long ago. This cell was my link to the world of light, the world I left and have tried to forget. No one disturbed me in this room. It was my salvation. Though vampires often enjoy the company of other vampires, we're generally solitary creatures. I understood this many years later with the help of another, one who shall stay in the shadows for now.

I lay on the cold, wet stone floor. I wanted to sleep. I wanted to dream. I wanted to see her. I needed to feel her. I hugged myself as I had earlier that night with one difference, I held the book close to my heart. And though the moon was still awake, I drifted off.

During my slumber, I remembered Mynea. When I would wake up, I would place the journal on my chest, lie with my hands behind my head, and stare into the darkness. My blood thirst remained a distant second to my longing for Mynea. Though I felt weak, I had little desire to hunt. Several months passed, the longest I had ever gone without blood. Every once in a while Eliza would call out to me. The frequency of her calls increased as the days passed, though her voice began to wane. I could sense that she was weakening as the blood I gave her lost its strength. She didn't call for another feeding. She called out to me for the same reason I was in the deepest and darkest part of the castle—loneliness.

Her own bloodlust was secondary, as was my own. I summoned Eliza silently to come to me and drink. She did so. She drank only enough to replenish her strength and maintain her youth, though she sucked a little more fervently than before. Eliza's feedings were the only times when Mynea's journal wasn't touching my heart. But I always kept it in my grasp.

Eliza would return to her quarters even though her thoughts revealed her desire to lie with me. I wouldn't permit that to happen, for I wanted to wait until my queen returned so I would be unspoiled to her touch, even if it meant restraining myself from Eliza's radiant beauty.

I passed the months paging through the diary, staring at its pages, burning the tiny symbols of the unknown language into my memory. I inhaled the odor of its pages and binding, the sweet scent of Mynea's hair. Though I couldn't understand the words, the book nevertheless provided me with solace.

Eleven months later the blood hunger returned, rivaling the first time I felt its call. It wouldn't be ignored again. Slowly, I stood. My muscles were feeble. I wearily walked up the stairs to the main level. My legs shook with every step. I used the wall for support. Eliza must have heard my moaning, for she appeared at the top of the stairs.

"My lord," she stammered, shocked to see me in such a weakened state. The concern in her voice was genuine. And though I heard every word, the sound of her heartbeat muffled everything else.

I looked up at her. The thirst had returned with a vengeance. I could feel my flesh wanting her, needing her blood. Eliza must have misunderstood the desire in my eyes, for she proceeded to walk toward me—or perhaps, she understood. She took me into her arms and aided me up the stairs. It took tremendous strength and every ounce of my concentration not to sink my teeth into her. How excruciating it was to hold back! I wanted to devour her! Just as the thirst began to overtake all reasoning, she raised her wrist to my mouth and said, "Drink, my love. Drink." I couldn't believe my ears. Nevertheless, I drank.

The blood flooded me with immediate satisfaction, each drop fueling the fire of my desire, every swallow a testament to the very fabric of life that holds us all. I grew stronger by the second. Eliza's memories swam around in my head. I faintly heard her speak, "Please, Aleron, stop."

I did. She withdrew her arm and collapsed into my body. I carried her to Mynea's bedchamber and gently laid her on the fur. The sight of her lying there eerily reminded me of the night after Mynea left, months ago. But this time, I didn't drain her to the brink of death. She kissed me on my lips, but I didn't return the kiss. The dominant part of me wanted to, the part that needed more blood.

In the moments before I spoke, I realized a change had occurred within my caretaker. For the first time since I'd known her, Eliza called me by my first name.

"I will return, Eliza. For the night is calling out to me, and I must answer."

"Please return swiftly, my lord. I will be waiting."

Eliza had a familiar look in her eyes, one that I hadn't seen for years and had never witnessed from this host. It was passion once displayed by Mynea. I welcomed the stare.

At once, I left the castle and flew into the night.

# CHAPTER 9

 moved swiftly through the trees and brush until a vile odor caught my attention. I followed the foul smell through the shadows until I saw a human slumped over at the base of a rotting tree. He was panting for air while blood flowed freely from his abdomen. I could hear his heart fainting as his chest rose and fell to an abnormal rhythm. I dared to relieve him of his misery.

I knelt and picked up the wounded man by his shoulders, as one would inspect a shirt. He let out a gurgle-filled gasp. Blood bubbles escaped his mouth and nose, filling the last few breaths he possessed. His eyes, once rolling in the back of their sockets, now struggled to focus on me. I propped him against the tree and raised the hand he held over the wound in his stomach. It was drizzled with blood. He began to slump over as I licked the dripping red nectar from the fingertips to the wrist of his hand. How sweet and easy this meal was. I straightened him and examined his face. His thoughts revealed his name to be Canaan.

He looked over my shoulder, and suddenly I heard the rustle of leaves. In my lust I had failed to notice the sounds of footsteps. The steps grew louder and more frequent, and I realized that a man was running in our direction. I peered into Canaan's eyes and could see the reflection of the man wielding a large knife closing in on us. In an instant I turned around and caught the man by his throat. Desperately trying to free himself, he plunged his knife into my torso, which was completely exposed since I had not worn a shirt beneath my black jacket. He pulled the blade out and attempted to stab me again, but I tightened my grip around his neck, causing him to drop his weapon and frantically try to free himself.

"Let me go!" he wheezed, and so I did. He fell to the ground and scrambled to get to his feet. However, he was too terrified to gather himself. Still on the ground, he shuffled backward on his buttocks. Keeping my eyes on him, I lifted Canaan up from the base of the tree and dangled him before the man. I flashed my elongated canines, which gleamed in the moonlight. I bit into Canaan's artery, crushing his clavicle as the blood began to flow into my mouth. The man on the ground stared, frozen in terror. The meal was short, for Canaan had already lost too much blood and, within a few deep gulps, he was dead.

While I fed, the other man found the strength and focus to reach for his knife. During his effort, he noticed the wound on my torso had completely healed and only a smear of blood remained. In a clumsy frenzy he found his footing and ran off into the night, screaming.

I raised my head and nose toward the sky and deeply breathed in the fresh night air until my lungs were cool. My hunger wasn't yet satisfied. Then I affixed my eyes on the fleeing man. Up into the trees I went.

Fascinated by the speed of this human, I decided to follow him. Keeping my distance, I glided across the treetops, never letting him escape my sight. He ran toward the city gates. If he had made it, he would've surely caused a stir, and of course I couldn't let that happen. I drew closer. His adrenaline propelled him more frantically the closer to the gigantic wooden gates he got. Gasping for air, he threw himself into the entrance and attempted to cry out for help. But before he was able to gather air into his lungs to give voice, I had him.

In a flash he was gone to anyone who may have been watching. The only evidence of my presence was the wisps of smoke floating up from the torches that my swift movement had extinguished. Only moonlit shadows remained. Darkness fell over the front gates of Alexandria's marketplace.

To Pharos Island we went. During our flight, I held him by both wrists within the grip of one of my powerful hands. Had I squeezed a hair more, his bones would have been reduced to fragments and dust. He strove to free himself every moment of the way, kicking his legs and screaming frantically, hoping to somehow shake his body free, wishing I would take pity on his pitiful soul. I approached the district of Gumrock, near the eastern shores of the Mediterranean. As a mortal, Old Alexandria was one of my favorite places, and Gumrock was desolate that time of night. There would be no disturbances.

The ancient tombs of Anfushi were our destination, south of the palace of Ras el-Tin in central Gumrock. We approached the stone stairway that led to a square courtyard below. A stream ran down the center of the courtyard. Miniature trees lined a stone walkway, which gave way to tombs.

My captive had passed out, most likely from the speed of our travels. I had forgotten the fragility of man. I dropped him seven feet onto the cold stone floor between the tombs, and his body landed with a hard thump. The fall didn't wake him.

It was no coincidence that I chose this destination. The ancient society of Caracalla was notorious for locating and capturing the most elusive of criminals, blasphemers, rapists, and murderers of twelfth-century northern Egypt. The Caracalla didn't believe in the laws governed by man, only the laws set forth by God and those implied in the Bible. This belief led them on a vigilant quest that often ended in a grotesque obscene ritual perpetrated to release the "evil spirit" that had consumed the minds and hearts of many.

A dark, reddish hue covered the marble and alabaster walls and Greek- and Egyptian-influenced statues. The color was believed to be the result of blood splattered during numerous beastly slayings. The Caracalla wanted people to fear the laws set forth by God, which I found a fascinating paradox. It seemed the Caracalla didn't truly understand who the ruler of this world was; however, they served him well.

The blood recollection from Canaan revealed a truly disgusting past for my dear Ammon. I saw visions of Ammon beating and raping Canaan's daughter, Cena, a young girl no more than fifteen years of age. Ammon entered Canaan's home as night fell and let himself into the young girl's quarters. The floors of the home were made of marble. Two oil paintings by Peter Paul Rubens hung across from each other in the hallway: "Fall of the Rebel Angels" and "Le coup de lance 1618." Canaan was obviously of influence.

Ammon crudely managed to knock "Fall of the Rebel Angels" off the wall as he forced himself onto the girl. Hearing her screaming, Canaan burst through the door, only to see his daughter on her back and the behemoth on top of her, his filthy trousers pulled down to midthigh. The silk red bow Cena usually wore at the waist of her dress lay untied and torn on the floor. Her dress was pushed upward and undergarments ripped, exposing her young flesh for Ammon and the cold hard marble floor.

Enraged, Canaan grabbed Ammon's muddied black shoes and pulled him off his daughter. Cena feverishly sat up and pushed herself back into the corner of the room where she continued to scream and cry out, her arms wrapped tightly around her legs. Her lips were bloodied and misshapen from the assault.

Canaan lost his grip on Ammon's legs and fell backward onto his rear. Ammon quickly pulled his pants up and leapt to his feet, one hand still holding his trousers. With his other hand he reached into his pocket and pulled out a knife. Canaan swiftly recovered from his tumble and lunged at Ammon, landing several punches. Though outmatched by Canaan's size and speed, Ammon managed to plunge the knife into his stomach several times before receiving Canaan's massively incapacitating blows to his head and throat. Ammon narrowly broke free of the barrage. The ringing in his inner ear disoriented him, but he instinctively fled toward the outer reaches of the city, followed by the heavy, hasty footsteps and ranting of the wounded father.

Ammon pushed his way past several men, women, and children, knocking them around like rag dolls. It made no difference to him whom he injured. The escape was all that mattered.

The knife wounds took their toll, and the blood loss weakened Canaan to a point where he could no longer pursue Ammon. He fell to his knees beneath the tree where I had found him. Then I saw a familiar face in his memories. It seems another predator, albeit of an immortal nature, was also lurking about.

Ammon obviously wanted to take full advantage of his new opportunity to exact death from another. His mistake was the assumption that I was human. Realizing his knife had no effect on me, he made another miscalculation: He hoped I was forgiving. His hope would be eradicated momentarily. I wanted him to be awake to witness the conclusion of his fate.

I left the most recent blood splatter on the walls and ceiling of Anfushi. The Caracalla would've been excited and satisfied by my offering of justice. They would also have come to realize their methods for punishment and disposal paled in comparison to what I had in store for my dear Ammon!

# CHAPTER 10

tanding in the opening of the catacombs, I sensed movement coming from between the tombs. Ammon was awakening and whimpering, no doubt at finding himself in the unfamiliar surroundings. I imagined him turning in horror to recognize the tombs, with their menacing dark shadows and stench of decay. His hands searched for steadiness, only to find thousands of tiny bone shards, roaches, scorpions, and other creatures that would make any human's skin crawl. I listened as his breathing became the panting of despair. And then his eyes found me, standing under the arched stone doorway, silhouetted against the moonlight. Although I wasn't looking directly at him, I could hear his thoughts.

"Please don't kill me," Ammon stammered, the words barely audible through his blubbering. I slowly turned to see him, to see the helplessness, to see what he saw in the eyes of the fifteen-year-old whose innocence he had stolen.

"Thieves, are we not?" I said. Not to him, but aloud to myself. He began to crawl slowly toward me. *How brave*, I thought. This one was indeed impressive. He clearly witnessed my delight in completing the job he didn't finish, and he no doubt realized his fate would be similar, yet he continued in my direction.

"I'll repent my sins!" He continued to plead his case, and though I was amused, it was futile. Ammon must've thought me to be the hand of God, to have a forgiving spirit for one as vile and cruel as he.

"Tell me, Ammon," I replied with a tinge of agitation, "why should I spare your life? Was it not you who stalked Cena? Was it some other man who made his way into her quarters and forced himself on her?" I stared directly into his eyes. "Was it a random vagabond who stabbed her father after he witnessed the atrocity you brought into their lives?" I looked away and began to walk toward him. "Did Canaan not engage you and force you into the trees where you returned to not only finish what you started but to include me as a bonus?" I stopped and stood directly in front of him.

Towering over Ammon, I pierced his soul with my eyes. The fear in him began to boil as the feeling of total anguish crept into the deepest corners of his eyelids. His pupils fully dilated, searching for any resident ambient light. I could feel the tension building in his soul. Again he crawled toward me, though he was ultimately sabotaged by his injured wrist, which I had carelessly crushed during our journey from Alexandria's front gates. His clothing was full of dirt from dragging himself in my direction. He didn't seem to notice the roaches and scorpions crawling on him. I believe Ammon realized he was in the presence of something far more terrifying than the bugs that now riddled his shirtsleeves and trousers.

He began to plead again. "Oh, God, please have mercy." Was he speaking to me, or was he speaking to God? I didn't know. In the sense that only God can decide the fate of humans, then to Ammon, I was a god by implication, for his fate was my choice, and my decision had already been made.

I couldn't wait any longer. I could feel his heart beating. I could smell the blood coursing throughout his veins and arteries, that succulent dark-red delicacy that served as a witness to all of his misdeeds. The very thought of showing him mercy infuriated me!

He rose to his knees and began repenting in a combination of Slavic and English dialects. He then planted one foot for a lunge toward me, which of course I knew about as soon as he planned it. Quickly he leapt forward while punching wildly at my head. I simply moved slightly to the side, causing him to miss me and lose his balance. And with his momentum, his footing caused him to stumble, and he fell backward against the stone wall. He struggled to see me in the darkness. Again he dashed toward me, this time gritting his teeth in an effort to draw upon some forgotten strength.

Expeditiously, I ripped open the top of one of the coffins, sending it across the air until it crashed into the wall and then fell into a heap of stones. I raised my knee and with much force pushed the topless stone coffin into his path, knocking his legs out from under him. He landed awkwardly in the sarcophagus and began waving his hands frantically, trying to hoist himself out. The remains of the dead that he now desecrated belched a cloud of dust that invaded his lungs, compelling him to cough uncontrollably. He choked as he cried out, "Let me go! You're no better than me! I saw what you did to Canaan, and you're no better than me!"

Like an animal I sprang and landed on the coffin edges. I looked down on Ammon, and then I lifted him up by both of his arms. Holding one wrist in one hand and the remains of the other in my other hand, I stretched them apart, pulling him nearer to me. I wanted him to see me up close. I pulled him a few feet to a spot under the skylight, which granted entrance to the magnificent moon.

"I am no rapist!" I snarled, face-to-face with Ammon.

He screamed ever more loudly, "My arms! My arms!" I wanted him to see my perversely perfect features. I wanted him to look upon my predator eyes. I wanted him to be utterly terrified in my presence! I wanted to be his harbinger. I wanted to be his god. I wanted to be his devil! He looked at me as if I had come out of the sea with ten horns and seven heads. Indeed he looked upon me as Satan. I wanted him to see in me what Cena had seen in him as he raped her. I wanted his heart to burst with fright. I wanted him to feel how Cena must have felt when he covered her angelic mouth with his filthy, clammy paws. I wanted him to taste the stench of hopelessness while looking into certain doom. I wanted him to see . . . Aleron!

He squinted to study me more closely and thought the word *unnatural*. I grinned enough to display my most beastly attribute, my fangs. At first glance, vampire canines seem just a bit larger than those of an ordinary human's. However, when inspected closely, as closely as I held Ammon, one soon realizes the animalistic proportion of the canines to the rest of the teeth. One would deduce that they are long for a purpose. It is the most frightening realization preceding death for those who become the victim of a vampire.

Suddenly, he was silent. His body became rigid in my grasp. His eyes opened wide, lips fell slightly ajar; I could feel his pulse racing. He was completely within my trance. My hypnotic stare terrified him to the point of near paralysis, yet he was too captivated to look away. He wore an expression of utter terror.

The wait had come to an end. I sank my teeth into his neck the way I imagined a Siberian tiger would bite into the neck of the antelope, crushing the throat completely to suffocate its meal. Crushing, yes. Suffocating, perhaps. I didn't care. I only cared about the blood that flowed rapidly into my mouth. How delightful it was. His expressions conveyed his pain, for his throat was no longer capable of producing sound, only a choking hack.

*Is it murder when you kill a murderer?* I asked myself. Nonetheless, I continued my torment. I tore his right arm from the socket, and with minimal effort, I removed it from his torso completely. I continued holding him in the air with one arm and bit into the severed arm's artery. The blood was so warm. I could think of nothing else for the moment. I sucked. He struggled. I sucked.

Once I had drained the arm, leaving nothing but withered muscle and bone, I discarded it inside the open sarcophagus, which I stood atop of. I turned my attention back to my dear Ammon, who danced between the world of the conscious and unconscious. "Scream for me," I whispered. "Scream for Cena!"

I licked the blood that had dripped onto his shirt and the rivulets under the fabric. Once there was nothing more to savor, I drank from the wound where I had ripped the arm off. His eyes rolled up. I mustn't let him die too soon.

I turned Ammon upside down. I wanted him to see the corpse that lay beneath us, the mouth of the skull freckled with drops of Ammon's blood. How fitting. I lifted him slightly and sank my fangs into the lower part of one of his thighs. My teeth ripped through his fleshy thigh, and I pulled at the bone until I tore off the leg. Ammon opened his mouth wide, and I imagined that, if he could, he might ask our dead host, "Is being dead as painful as death?"

In the time of my adolescence, healers would use the mandragora plant for amputations. The mandragora would cause the wounded to drift into a comatose state, thus feeling little pain, if any at all. Not for Ammon. How excruciating it must have been to have an arm and leg ripped off, leaving only a blood-dripping torso on one side and paralysis on the other. I drained this detached limb in the same manner as the previous one. He began to lose consciousness.

"Oh no, Ammon! You must remain coherent for the finale!" I said to him and turned him back so that he was facing me. His eyes rolled back into place; the look of terror was replaced by despair and hopelessness. "The dead have no answers for you, Ammon. However, I do."

Even though Ammon had one arm in the sarcophagus and a leg stuck in another dark corner, his heart was still beating, so I wasn't done. Though I knew he wanted desperately to die, I plunged my hand into his torso, tearing through the skin and cracking open his ribcage in my quest to secure his feverishly beating heart. The beat slowed, and I drank from his neck before his heart stopped beating entirely. I completely drained the blood from his body. Good and bad, I had to consume it all. His body began to wither. I withdrew from suckling and opened my mouth as wide as I could. Then I completely severed Ammon's head with a flesh-tearing bite! It hit the edge of the coffin with a thud, finally settling on the ground. Right away, hundreds of insects swarmed over it.

Though Ammon's body was now limp, the heart still pulsed. I saved this delicacy for last. I licked the blood streaming down my arm before I bit into the heart. I couldn't let any of Ammon's blood escape my hunger. There could be nothing left of his treachery—nothing! I reveled in the living dessert.

Ammon's eyes were frozen open, staring up at me as something like a millipede bore into his ear. Ammon was gone, but I wasn't quite done. I unceremoniously tossed the rest of his body into the coffin. Then, with one final blow, I lifted my foot and crushed the partially flesh-stripped, severed head. Ammon's right eye popped out and rolled along the ground. I picked it up and looked at it. I brought it close to my face. Even in death, Ammon could see me. I tossed it over my shoulder and turned toward the entrance. Upon my exit, I could hear the scorpions' thanks for the last bit of the feast I provided. It was truly music to my ears.

# CHAPTER 11

left Anfushi invigorated by my latest encounter. I felt alive. For the first time in months, I felt purpose! I was, once again, Aleron—the Aleron my queen gave birth to, immortal Aleron, powerful Aleron. Though the thoughts of Mynea never left my mind, my desire to hunt was revitalized. This night my longing for her company was finally eradicated by my inherent bloodlust. Even though vampires are not restricted by time in the way mortals are, time still heals wounds of the heart.

Almost intoxicated, I traveled more slowly to safety before the impeding sunrise. About a hundred miles from the castle, I strode the backstreets of Old Alexandria. In those wee hours, they were empty. Suddenly, an unease came over me, deflating my high. I sensed an unnatural presence. I looked around. Though I could see no one, I could hear the faint steadiness of a heartbeat. It was bizarre, long, and slow—too slow for a mortal. Steady. I became on high alert.

"Show yourself! I know you're there!" I yelled in the deserted alley that smelled of rotten garbage and urine.

*Watching me*, I thought. *Watching me without fear!* The heartbeat didn't quicken. It was the slow drum of a cautious yet curious being. The rhythm was calming to me. I continued to look around, and with my vampire speed I covered the entire area, every crevice where someone or something could hide. Then I took to the rooftops.

"I know you're here," I repeated in a voice softer and more inviting than before. "Reveal yourself to me, and I will spare you death."

To my surprise, I heard a quiet giggle. And then all at once the heartbeat was gone. The only thing left was an unfamiliar scent. I took it into my lungs and into my memory, never to forget it. Even unto this night, I never have.

I began moving faster than I normally would. I wasn't nervous, only cautious. The presence was unknown and obviously gifted, for my search ended unfruitfully. Naturally I was curious and guarded. Moreover, the approaching sunrise caused me to propel myself harder; thus I covered the hundred miles in mere minutes.

Once in the castle, I climbed to the third level and strode into the long corridor that led to Eliza's quarters. I knew she was asleep, but I simply wanted to see her. I quietly opened her door, glancing upon her much like a loving father would his sleeping daughter. She was safe, unharmed. I closed it softly and proceeded down the stairs to the lower level. Being surrounded by the familiar sounds and smells of the castle settled my uneasiness temporarily.

I entered my dungeon and lay on the cold stone floor. My hands found and gripped the only window my queen had left to peer through, a window that possessed foggy panes that didn't allow me to see what lay beyond. I tried to read the journal, but again, it was indecipherable. I stared up at the ceiling and thought about the latter part of the evening.

How long had it watched me? The laugh suggested it wasn't afraid and knew I was something more than ordinary at the very least. Soon I began to feel the effects of dawn as my eyes began to close. I couldn't deny the lingering thought in my mind. Had Mynea returned to me? Darkness fell over me.

# CHAPTER 12

concentrated on my prowess and on sharpening my skills and became more deft with each kill. My speed increased to near teleportation. I took flight with less effort and more effectiveness. I punished my body as I explored my limits in an effort to distract me from the pain of missing Mynea.

Dutifully I provided the necessary sustenance to sustain Eliza's frozen countenance whenever it began to thaw. However, after several moons and feverish hunting and sharing, a strange feeling began to creep into my soul.

Desire called upon me. Not the desire one would assume, but a longing to be free of this castle. I felt captive by a force stronger than anything I'd ever encountered. I felt as though a weight had been placed on my chest, relentlessly pressing on my heart, suffocating me. I needed to be free from pain, free from love, free from sadness, free from Mynea—free from this place.

I scanned the castle and found Eliza settled at the dining table in our grand and luxurious kitchen. She was radiantly beautiful, appearing unspoiled by time. Silently I observed her. Flawless skin covered her naturally high cheekbones. My eyes digested every inch of the right side of her elegant silhouette, finally resting slightly above her delectable collarbone, on her carotid artery, which prominently thumped to the soothing rhythm of her beating heart.

She was drinking lilac tea when I entered. I must have startled her, for she nearly toppled over when she realized I was standing right beside her.

"Good evening, my dear." My hands stroked the top of her head, through her hair, and down the back of her neck. With both hands around her throat I gently, yet forcefully, lifted her to a standing position. I nudged the chair to the side as I spun her around so that I was now behind her, our bodies pressed against one another. A small gasp escaped her lips as she leaned slightly to the side, inviting me to draw upon her sweet nectar. I kissed her neck with only a slight urge to take her life.

"Aleron," she was again mesmerized by my presence and soothing touch. "I dreamed of you again last night, as I have every night for many months." She turned to face me. "You'll never leave me, will you?" Her question was sincere yet full of sorrow. Her deep rich chestnut eyes searched my face for a sign. Big and round, they searched, pleaded. I saw my own face in their reflection; however, a sign she did not receive.

"Don't trouble your mind with such thoughts. You've been at my side for decades. You're more essential to my existence than any number of victims I choose to dine on."

She closed her eyes and smiled while pushing her face against my hand, as a cat searching for its master's affection might. I caressed her warm skin with my cooling touch. I could always feel her skin tighten in the areas where my cold hands touched her balmy flesh.

"There's something I must do, however. It will involve you."

"What would you have me do, my lord?"

"Know that I do not wish to remain here another day. It's agony to dwell in what reminds me of her. I'm leaving and will send for you in due time.

"Where will you go, my lord? When will you send for me?"

"I shall go into the island of Philae, just along the Nile in upper Egypt. When I've settled, I'll send a vessel and messenger along the Nile. She'll come to you, and you shall trust her. Leave everything except the gold and jewels when I send for you. I'll have all you'll require in our new home. As for this place, when you leave I'll no longer concern myself with it. Don't worry, for I'll send for you before Father Time calls your name once more."

"Of course, my lord."

I punctured my wrist and exposed the dark gift within. Gently I raised my arm to Eliza's waiting mouth. She began to suck. I couldn't help the feeling of ecstasy that immediately followed sharing my blood with her. I was indeed aroused by her eagerness and tenderness as she drained me of what immortal life I would allow her. Something in me wanted her to continue, though I didn't know at the time what would happen to her if I allowed her to do so, or what would happen to me. Then she stopped.

She was indeed strong willed, more so than I. I would have had her drain me completely dry. In that moment I found a feeling that nearly rivaled my love for Mynea, my desire to feed, and my desire to live. It was a new craving to share the life force that had come and gone with every life I stole. The blood gift. What could this new feeling mean?

I opened my eyes and Eliza was staring at me. She looked more radiant than she had ever looked before! More beautiful. Though my heart didn't seek another, if it had done so, that other would be she. In the blink of an eye, my erotic daze was replaced by spine-tingling focus. I straightened my posture and took a deep breath.

"I'll be swift, my dear." I left to return to my immortal cradle. I knew that if I'd stayed in Eliza's presence, woe would have befallen my heart. Though she was exquisitely enchanting, she still reminded me of the one my heart longed for. Through her devotion, she commanded loyalty and trust from me. I couldn't leave her to die, for a swift death awaited her if I chose to stay away too long. Her strength would leave her. She would lose the ability to walk and speak. Her heart would begin to crawl. Her skin would lose all elasticity, and her bones would begin to rapidly deteriorate before, ultimately, turning into dust. The immortal blood had made her vulnerable to our will, for, she, too, knew of her mortality. She was a slave to life. Aren't we all?

I made up my mind at that moment that I would keep my word and return for Eliza. I didn't lie to her about returning when I was talking to her; however, I would have said anything to leave. She knew it. I could sense her uneasiness when I began to depart, and her thoughts cried out to me as I left the castle: *Please, my lord, Aleron. Don't abandon me. Please don't leave me to rot.*

I went down into the lowest room of the castle, the dungeon, which provided me with the salvation I needed so desperately, and took with me the last relic forgotten or bequeathed by my queen, the journal. And then I was off.

After crossing the water, I turned and looked back at the castle, which was now illuminated by the glow of the moon. I was captivated by its splendor and sheer size. For decades it had been my home. I had grown quite fond of its menacing exterior and luxurious interior. I remembered my first night in the dungeon. Vivid memories and random exotic rendezvous with Mynea began to fill my head. I took a moment and remembered her touch, her sweet and soothing voice. Her scent. She completely embodied everything I'd come to love and desire. The feeling of losing her would never weaken. I didn't know at that time which scared me most, her leaving or not knowing where she had gone.

A vampire's lust for blood is insatiable, so if a woeful heart can overshadow the appetite for life, one could conclude the intensity of my love and despair. It was enough to tear apart the very fabric of my immortal existence. I temporarily lost my desire to live. Without Mynea, nights had grown longer, and the urge to bathe myself in sunlight increased. Life eternal without my love would be unbearable. Night after night I had been torn between searching for her and waiting for her to return. Somehow I had convinced myself that one evening I would awake, and she would be lying naked next to me. This single thought kept me from leaving the castle for months.

I turned away from the castle and looked at the city below. The thousands of flickering lights served as a fitting ambiance for my liberation from that woeful feeling. Of course, my preferred method of travel was flying. That night, however, I decided to simply walk. I closed my eyes and allowed my animalistic senses to guide me to my eventual destination, the ancient island of Philae. And by closing my eyes, I would dispel the darkness created by the shadow of the enormous castle, which mocked the moon. As the distance lengthened between me and the castle, its shadow faded, a shadow that kept my heart in complete darkness.

As I made my way closer to the city of Alexandria, the various sounds of the insects, rats, and other small creatures scurrying about were replaced with the chatter of people and sounds of string instruments. The rough and littered cobblestone streets forced mortals to step carefully. I, however, was able to move through the streets quite easily, and as I did, the millions of imperfections from stone to stone beneath my feet created a silent yet rhythmic tale of their own.

It was easy to walk among humans, for I wasn't my deathly pale self, given the blood of my last victims coursing through my body. I must remember to thank all of them when I see them again.

I walked slowly around the districts until I came upon one that smelled familiar. I opened my eyes and realized I was standing in the district of al-Montaza, the land that was once my home.

Though I had often avoided al-Montaza for obvious reasons, I felt a sense of relief, a sense of belonging—or perhaps a sense of longing, yearning to be with those who loved me and whom I'd loved. I coveted companionship. Not just any companionship. I hungered for amity with those who knew me. And that desire had led me back to the living. A craving was born in me to forget the nightmare under the guise of a dream. To forget the demon under the guise of an angel. To escape my immortal self and return to the bosom of Alexandria. To forget her. To forget Mynea.

I knew and remembered very well the rule Mynea spoke of regarding reaching out to my mortal family. I simply didn't care. I burned to see my mother and father, whom I hadn't seen in decades. I wanted to see Shani, my sister, whom I'd missed tremendously.

† † † †

It was late when I arrived at my father's home. Grass had grown over my mother's once well-kept garden. The lawn was overgrown, as were the shrubs and bushes surrounding the house. Ivy grew untamed over the outside walls of the house. Several ant mounds had erupted around the yard. As for the house itself, it was dark, with the exception of soft candlelight coming from my father's study. I used my mind to scan the thoughts of all who were present. Indeed, my mortal parents still occupied this home. I listened while my father read to himself. The book was of no significance. What was important was what happened next.

He stopped suddenly, stood, and looked out the window. Of course, I didn't allow him to see me, but he knew someone was watching. My father was always protective of my mother and sister. He hardly slept when I was a child, always on edge and ready for anything that posed a threat to his family. Once his query was satisfied, he would return to doing whatever he was engaged in. This time, he remained at the window unusually long.

I could hear the steady breathing of my mother in the next room. She was fast asleep. I listened for a second steady breath but found none. I couldn't sense my sister. Shani wasn't in my father's home this night.

Aknon stepped away from the window and returned to his chair. He continued reading. I didn't want him to see me just yet. However, I desperately needed to see my mother. I entered without making a sound through an open upstairs window. Swiftly I proceeded to their bedroom, where I found the door slightly ajar. I walked in and closed it all the way without making the slightest noise. I stood still and read my father's thoughts again. He was undisturbed.

I looked at my mortal mother sleeping. She had changed. She was older and looked sickly. I began to feel sorrow. The room was tidy, small, and quaint—as I remembered it. I could smell the mix of dirty and clean garments behind the closed closet door. The faint stench of mildew saturated the air, too faint for mortals to detect. The walls, no longer bare, now had a figured covering on them. The colors were faded. The edges of the walls revealed where the plaster began to peel away from the wall. Dust lay beneath.

I walked over to her bedside and looked upon her. I gasped silently. I expected to see my mother sleeping peacefully. I had expected to see a slightly aged yet still beautiful Camilia lying before me in my mother's bed. But what I saw was what was left of my mortal mother after some disease had stolen her youth. She had dark rings around her sunken eyes. Her lips were cracked and pale. I could hear her unsteady and unsure heart beating. My eyes were lying to me, and only by touching her could I escape their deceit.

I extended my cold right hand, touched her forehead, and she flinched uncomfortably under it. The eyes rolled beneath the lids, but she did not open them. Her eyebrows twitched slightly, conveying her discomfort. She inhaled deeply through her parched lips, making a sucking sound. The outline of her body beneath the thin canary cotton cover went from small to smaller. Her entire body tensed as she withdrew into herself. If I had kept my frigid touch upon her head, she would have awakened. I didn't want this to happen, so I lifted my hand, and as I did, she exhaled, releasing the stress I had brought.

Suddenly I heard the door swing open and crash into the wall. Quickly I melted into the shadows of the room just beyond the sight of Aknon, where I remained perfectly still. I witnessed my father surveying the room with his gun. I had lost connection with his thoughts, distracted by the sight of my mother's deteriorating condition. He must have felt a presence in the room and blindly charged in. Though he couldn't see me, he remained steadfast. Aknon, the protector. His eyes probed, his pupils dilated, drawing on the faint light. His head turned in unison with the barrel of the shotgun. He strained his ears for the slightest sound. They would hear nothing unnatural. They didn't sense me. Notwithstanding the temporary annoyance of my father's buckshot, I couldn't let him see me this way.

He lowered his guard as he turned his attention to my mother, who was still asleep in the bed. He walked over to her bedside, almost standing in the very spot where I had stood. He lit the lamp next to her on the small wooden chest.

Forty-two years had taken its toll on my father. Though his heartbeat was still strong, his outward appearance told a different tale. His once jet-black hair was now a silvery-blue mane that nearly reached his shoulders. His skin had lost its color, and his bone structure was much more pronounced than before. Hair escaped the confines of his nostrils and ears, and his facial hair was a mess, suggesting a man who had more important matters to confront. My father's nails were uneven and long, though clean. These changes may seem understandable and accurately representative of the elapsed years; however, my family had always been noted for looking far younger than their true age. My father looked as though he was in his late nineties or more, not the ripened age of eighty-six.

He leaned over and placed his hairy ear to my mother's chest to hear her heartbeat. My mother's arm began to move. Though her eyes never opened, she rubbed his head gently and lovingly while it rested on her breast. She smiled.

I could hear my father's heart quicken. A tear ran down the side of his face onto my mother's gown. He was indeed saddened by her declining health. He knew the end was near. And that knowledge was tearing him apart. I, too, felt tremendous sorrow and decided to leave as quietly and swiftly as I'd come. Seeing my parents in such despair made me want to comfort them. That I simply couldn't do at the time, so I left, knowing I would return.

I stood frozen across the street from the place I once called home. I wanted to go back in and reveal myself; however, I couldn't. I simply stared at it. Just before I turned to walk away, I saw him in the window again. He was looking around, but his thoughts didn't reveal him seeing me. Ever watchful, ever protective, honorable Aknon.

I began walking in the direction of a place I had rented shortly before my transformation. An eerie feeling came over me and grew with each step I took. Slipping immediately out of sight and into darkness, I surveyed the area. My senses heightened as my eyes pierced the moonless night. It was here. The very same scent I had committed to memory was upon me once more. Yet, again, I could see no one. I heard no one. And then it was gone.

I knew at that very moment that someone or something was following me, stalking me. Perhaps I would be the prey of some unknown and powerful adversary. The thought made me smile, as Ammon was recalled to me. I thought not. I didn't sense any actual danger. Whatever was following me posed no threat, I concluded.

I returned to the streets, for the hunger in me had returned, and it was time to feed. The air was dry and smelled of rain. Musk and wafts of perfume came and went, carried by the unsure wind. The temperature was only warm, but the people were steamy and hot, burning from the desires of life and the wants of the flesh. I was surprised by the number of people out at this hour, especially the young ones, whom I seldom saw. Though I quickened my pace, a few caught sight of the ghost of the night. I entered the Sharak district in Eastern Alexandria. This was the city's second most populated district after al-Montaza. Therefore, the district was predictably rife with bandits and lowlifes. It wouldn't cause too much of a stir if a few of them went missing.

I entered Saad Zaghoul Square, which was known for its many open-air markets where the townspeople shopped for jewels, clothing, medicine, and food. Gambling, prostitution, and crime were also prevalent in the area. This commerce made it a haven for thieves and murderers, an evil a la carte, so to speak. I scanned the minds of many people and was soon able to locate my prey. The preparation and partaking of this particular meal was neither a major concern nor a matter of importance. All I cared about was that he would bring new life to my undying existence. A new life to be cherished. As if we vampires lived for the kill and were sustained through those we killed. We saw their lives from their perspective in the blood memoirs and thus lived vicariously through each of them. This contributed life to our lives and thus lengthened our existence, or at least made it more bearable to live indefinitely. When this cycle was broken by our kind, we ceased to exist. We became victims of our own immortality.

After feeding, my flesh was warm, my complexion less ghostly. It was time to return to al-Montaza. Aknon would be less likely to be able to see who I'd become. I needed only to stay out of direct light to deceive my severest judge: my father, who knew me better than I knew myself; my father, who had trained me to be the man I became and an absolute force in the vampire I'd become. Aknon, whose stare could penetrate my soul as a mortal and make it waver even in its immortal form. I do have a soul, for all living flesh are souls. I'm not a specter that travels like energy from the dead. I am life itself.

In less time than it takes to enjoy a sip of tea, I was, once again, standing in front of my father's home. I could sense my father was still awake and diligently alert The book he was now reading was *The Sorrows of Young Werther*, ironically about a tormented man who's fixated on an inaccessible woman. Oh, how my mother's health tormented Aknon. It aged him and was driving him to the very edge of sanity. He felt powerless, and that was the root of his agony. Johann Wolfgang von Goethe spoke to Aknon through the words of this novel, and my father listened.

I let myself in unnoticed through the same upstairs window. For as long as I could remember, this window was kept unlocked, for it was too far from the ground below for a thief to enter. Well, perhaps an ordinary thief.

I entered my mother's room. I walked over to her bed where she still slept and knelt until my weight rested on one knee. Memories of my mortal mother were instantly cued, various visions spanning my childhood and adolescence, times nearly forgotten. We were so happy then. She was so vibrant. This wasn't the woman I remembered lying before me in my mother's bed, wearing Camilia's gowns. She also wore Camilia's scent. But if this were Camilia, she'd been reduced to a mere shadow of herself, a shell of old feeble flesh. I had to see her eyes. Only her eyes would reveal my birth mother to me. If only I could see those soft, beautifully accented brown eyes. The thought of Eliza's eyes came to mind.

I already knew my father was approaching the room, but I simply didn't care. At that moment I heard the sound of Aknon's Spencer and Roper twelve-gauge shotgun cock, and then my father was standing directly behind me with his shotgun pointed at the back of my skull. I wasn't worried in the slightest, not only because I was immortal, but also because my father knew that there was no guarantee if he fired a shot that my mother wouldn't be wounded. Besides, it would have been messy. Thus, the shotgun's role was one of intimidation. Had Aknon been standing behind another human, the person would have been utterly paralyzed. Fortunately for both of us, it was his supernatural offspring who stood before him.

In an effort to somewhat ease the situation, I raised my hands into the air. "Stand up slowly," he said in a hushed yet sturdy voice.

I did, carefully and silently. From behind, my father couldn't see my face. I wore my oversized collar turned up to obscure most of my features, and the room offered little light.

In a slow and calculated voice, he said, "Turn around slowly and go out of the room into the hall." I did exactly what he requested. In a slow, deliberate dance, Aknon followed me, step for step. My father, with his uncompromising manner, kept the business end of the shotgun planted to the base of my skull. Together, we completed a circle, and once our places were traded, he nudged me forward. We stealthily inched out of the room. He quietly and, without taking his eyes off his intended target, closed the door behind him. We walked slowly down the hallway and stopped with just enough distance between us and their bedroom door. Aknon began to speak with the gun still nestled on the collar of my shirt.

"Why have you come here? What do you want?"

I said nothing.

"What do you want?" he repeated slightly louder this time, while pushing the barrel even more firmly against my head.

"I wanted to know," I said just loud enough for him to hear.

"Know what? Who are you, and why have you entered my house?" Though my father wanted to know why I was there, his thoughts affirmed his greater desire to know how I got in without his noticing. This burned him tremendously.

"I didn't mean to startle you, Aknon." This was the first time I had ever said my father's name when speaking to him. It felt strange, but it also seemed appropriate since I was now something other than the son he had known.

"Turn around slowly," he said, thinking, *How does he know my name?* I could sense his nerves quickening, the finger on the trigger unsure, his heart racing.

I turned slowly until I was facing the shotgun and Aknon. Though the light provided by the flickering bulb was still insufficient in the hallway, his eyes widened, and he began to lower the shotgun.

"My God! Aleron?" he questioned in almost a whisper. Many things came to mind in that moment; however, I only managed to reply directly to his question, "Yes."

His instinct was to hug me, but the dominant alpha male in him couldn't allow such a gesture just yet. He simply stood there looking at me for what seemed to be an eternity. My abnormal features were cloaked by the lack of light. No matter how I tried, the voice emanating from my mouth was inconsistent with what he remembered. Though he hadn't seen me in decades, he knew I was somehow different from the Aleron he knew, for a parent knows his child. Aknon remembered me from the very last time he saw me those many years ago, and I'm sure he couldn't have imagined me as I'm now. How could he?

His eyes left my face, and a once-staunch stare retreated into confusion. He completely lowered his shotgun and walked into his study, passing a colorless portrait hanging on the wall that depicted a young father and mother with two gleeful children. I followed slowly.

The flicker of the candlelight on his desk disguised the movements of my shadow, which had often appeared to have a will of its own. He turned around to face me.

My father's stature was shorter than mine. This, coupled with the natural deterioration of his bone structure from age, created a surreal visual of a son towering over his father. There was no intimidation in my father's eyes or heart, only curiosity, which turned into anger.

"Where have you been?" he blurted out! Traces of spatter escaped his mouth while saying this. "We all thought some terrible fate had befallen you. We all thought you were dead, or worse!"

*Interesting,* I thought. *Worse than death?* I guess one could suggest that my encounter with Mynea and eventual transformation could be considered worse than death. One could.

"Not so far from the truth, father," I replied, desperately trying to mimic the voice of mortal Aleron, his son.

"Why did you leave?"

"I had no choice in that matter. It's complicated."

He looked perplexed. "Why return now? What do you want?" Aknon demanded.

"I didn't wish to remain away for so long, but understand, it wasn't my choice, and I want nothing," I heard myself reply. It was a difficult question, for even I didn't know what I wanted.

My father lowered his head and, in an insecure voice said, "Your mother, she's not well." He raised his head again. "And I know it was you in her bedroom earlier."

"What's her ailment?" Before I could finish getting the question out, his thoughts told me: a broken heart.

"We searched tirelessly for you. I neglected my customers. I closed my business and employed many men to search for you. I spent our entire wealth looking for you. Your mother and sister went door to door, all throughout this district and the neighboring districts. Nothing. Not a word. Not a trace. I went to your employer. He had already begun a search party of his own. We talked to the many men who spoke of their conversations with you at the Promethium Gala. None could remember where you went or what time you departed. What we found out next led us to the worst possible conclusion. There were traces of blood in the woman's quarters. Upon learning this information and not finding any trace of you, your mother and I feared you were dead."

He looked directly into my eyes, which were still disguised by the candlelight. "Your sister fell into a deep depression. You don't know how much you meant to her. Neither did we, until that day. For the next few months your sister became more and more withdrawn from everything. She would get in frequent arguments with your mother and me, fueled by a rage and depression we've never encountered, the likes of which would be second to the depression that befell your mother after Shani left Egypt, for the Americas. Your sister didn't consider how losing both children would affect her mother. Nevertheless, your sister's mind was quite sound when she made her decision and left for her new beginning."

*The Americas*, I said to myself.

"Your mother became ill soon after. It began with constant fatigue, followed by constant irritability. She would go days and sometimes weeks without eating more than a slice of bread or leaving her bedroom. The doctors were all perplexed, and understandably so, for they couldn't cure a broken heart."

My father walked over to me and wiped what felt like a tear from my cheek. Suddenly, his gaze shifted from one of sympathy to one of amazement and intrigue. I learned why when he retracted his hand, and his finger was dressed in a diluted red liquid. He rubbed his thumb against his red-soaked index finger, trying to feel the consistency of the liquid. He stepped back and removed the candle from its holder on the wall. He wanted to see me. I could have vanished in the blink of an eye, but I decided not to. I remained in the same position, for my thoughts were with my mother and nothing else mattered. How could I have let my selfish desire to be with Mynea allow me to neglect those who loved me the most? A monster, I was. My father was looking upon the monster I had become.

*Dare I?* I thought. *Dare I disregard the very essence of what Mynea taught me about staying among the shadows? Never allowing any mortal to look upon us without devouring them shortly thereafter? Dare I peel back the veil of secrecy that has kept our kind safe for as long as we have been? Would I be the first to reveal himself in this demonized angelic splendor?* As I grappled with these questions and thoughts, I came to the conclusion that I didn't care!

He held the burning candle up near my face. His eyes widened. I already knew what he saw—the wavering eyes of his son, larger than what he remembered and a thousand times more menacing and captivating. I didn't move. He raised his other hand and touched my face.

"My God" he whispered in awe. "So cold. Hard like stone! What has happened to you?"

The statement 'My God' coming from my father was a paradox. He was never one to quote or refer to any religious teachings or scripture. He openly loathed the fact that my mother and sister had spent countless days spreading the word of God. This must have had profound meaning coming from Aknon. His utterance couldn't be taken lightly. He was genuinely moved by what he saw, and he sought divine understanding. Who was I to deny him this? He withdrew his hand.

"Aleron, what happened to you?" he repeated.

I chose my words wisely. "I'm more than the son you knew." My tone was humble yet powerful. As my father, he demanded my respect, as a human, my restraint.

"Are you the son I knew?" he whispered, almost more to himself than to me.

With only a thought, I caused two candles to catch flame and illuminate the room. Then I appeared in the opposite corner of the room. Completely surprised and caught off guard by my sudden movements, he nearly leapt out of his skin as he turned toward me. I allowed Aknon to see his immortal son. He looked at me slowly and carefully, eyes full of confusion and compassion. He continued to stare.

Astonishment only briefly displaced his fear. Fear was an emotion not readily accessible to Aknon. For all of my mortal years I had never known my father to fear anything or anyone. My father, the eternal protector of his house and all who reside within it, the pillar of our family, was as strong as the cornerstone to the great pyramid of Giza. But this man was in fear of what stood before him, the chilling countenance and unflinching stature of his son standing in his home. He knew I was unnaturally cold. He knew I wasn't the son who disappeared that night when I was taken by infatuation and force. Had it been more infatuation, or more force?

Aknon continued staring at me. With mouth agape, his eyes followed my new endowments from head to toe, from my long black coat to my black shoes, which carried the various reminiscences of towns I'd had the pleasure of visiting that night and every night before. My hair had grown to a mane, a side effect of vampirism. My clothing, though dark, was noticeably caked with dried blood that I hadn't bothered to clean off before my return, and this startled Aknon.

"What happened to you, my son?" his tone that of a forgotten father's love for his son. "How did you get like this?" His face slowly transformed into disgust. "You're not my son! You're a specter! A demon!" His pulse hurried as sweat began to drip from his hair down the side of his face.

Before I could answer, we heard a faint murmur from the bedroom. My father turned slightly toward the room while I remained as unflinching as stone. He turned his attention back to me.

"She can't see you like this. I won't allow it!"

"What makes you think you can stop me, Aknon? What makes you so sure you can exert the strength necessary to keep me from doing my will? Why do you think I came here?"

"Have more respect for my wishes in my house!" he retorted sharply and with rejuvenated confidence. "The sight of you like this will terrify your mother. She won't be able to sustain an encounter such as the one you desire. You know this to be true!"

He was right. Seeing me would spell her death. Seeing me could arrest an already faint and weakened heart. My mother deserved my respect and my understanding. But did I deserve her forgiveness? Before I could respond to Aknon's demands, I felt what he truly must also have felt, complete sorrow and sadness. For he knew my mother would be gone soon, and he wanted her undisturbed. He wanted her to breathe as long as her lungs would allow, without laying her sunken eyes upon her vampire son. Surely she would drift off to her eternal rest immediately after the initial shock of my return and my inhuman appearance. She would indeed die.

"Aknon," my father's name struggled to find its way from the other room through my mother's dry, cracked lips.

"Stay in this room and don't leave! I'll check on her and will return." He walked past me into the hallway. As he passed, he knew his commands no longer held authority with me. I wasn't going to stay. I was going to leave the moment he entered my mother's room, and so it came to pass.

# CHAPTER 13

pon leaving the home of my mortal life I wandered the streets of al-Montaza. I couldn't stop thinking about my mortal mother, her sickened state, and about Aknon's disapproval of my presence. I thought about the thoughts he held closest to his soul, of my transformation, or becoming a demon, as he put it. A demon. Ironic, considering the notion of God's true purpose for mankind on Earth, to live within the physical boundaries for all eternity—until the true demon persuaded the first mother to be disobedient. Treachery was the charge and death the sentence. Life for man changed at that moment. Life meant death. From that moment of original sin, man was born to die. Man would spend his entire existence preparing for death. But as for vampires, life meant forever. Aknon believed me to be a demon, though as a vampire I was closer to the true nature and purpose of man than all of mankind. Why then were we the damned?

As I pondered the thoughts I had stolen from my father, I came to realize that it was an enigma. We killed to live. We seized the blood, thus forsaking the life, the soul, the gift from God to live. This was why we were demons. This was why we were the damned. We stole from God. Thieves. Aknon was indeed right. We were demons!

Dawn began to approach, and I sensed the onset of the paralyzing metamorphosis. I sought salvation in a tomb at a familiar place. There was a graveyard between Cairo and Alexandria that housed more than the dead. Many migrants traveled the route, passing through it in search of a more prosperous way of life. The journey was long and sometimes impossible to accomplish. Those who couldn't continue took shelter within the confines of the graveyard. Thus its name became the City of the Dead, for the city never slept even though most of its inhabitants were dead. Those who resided in the City of the Dead were poor and tended to keep to themselves, often not speaking to another inhabitant for several days or weeks. It was the perfect temporary resting ground for me, a demon.

As I approached, I caught the unmistakable scent of death. It permeated the air, and even those who were alive wore its funk. The graveyard was as vast as it was old and neglected. Its statues had always fascinated me, born from timeless marble, stained with dirt and decay. They resembled angels and people, perhaps depictions of the more permanent residents they celebrated. The portraits of the dead were larger than life yet perfectly proportionate. The garments they wore, though perfectly still, were in a constant flow of motion. The faces were always melancholy. Their eyes, open without an iris or a pupil, stared into nothing, frozen in a timeless state of sadness.

The angels suggested something else entirely. They stood gigantic and towering, commanding allegiance to all whose eyes captured them. Their wings were never outstretched; they rested—enormous, spanning the entire length of the body, adorning the face of hope, justice, and love. They did not wear garments, which, of course, made perfect sense, for clothing was manmade and originated from earth, while the angel was made from the very hands of God and thus was inherently perfect. And one doesn't hide perfection.

Of course, the City of the Dead had its fair share of crucifixes. I believe there were more crosses of varying shapes and sizes than the dead who found eternal rest there. There were traces of flowers that dressed some of the graves; however, their splendor had been forgotten long before my arrival.

Many centuries ago, this burial ground was for the wealthy. Therefore, no expense was spared in the preparation for the final resting place. The tombs were as big as small homes. How fitting it was: garments of silk, a house of marble, a guardian angel or deity, complete with one or more crucifixes, symbolic of a pathway to what lay on the other side. A fitting place for me—a demon.

I would come to find rejuvenating slumber beneath the earth, adjacent to the permanent residents. I thought the disturbance would go unnoticed if I borrowed a sarcophagus for one day.

I arrived and was completely out of sight before anyone could notice—any mortal, that is. There was indeed another near me who was well aware of my presence in the City of the Dead. I felt it. I found myself racing against the coming sun as I eagerly searched for a suitable place, away from everyone and everything, including my follower, whom I had begun to fear, for it was innate to fear the unknown.

I chose a tomb where life had left long ago—a tomb whose size and weight would be more than enough to deter any mortals from disturbance. I moved the stone covering from the mouth of the tomb and entered. It became increasingly difficult to maneuver and position as the hour grew early and the night's strength in me began to subside. Immortality has its ironies. Though we were depicted as free of time's boundaries, we were bound by the very celestial bodies that determine daily and nightly progression, and so we were confined and regulated by a much smaller timeline than that of a mortal life, ironically immortal.

Slumber found me faster that day than any other day I could remember. The thought of the stalker reminded me of the vulnerability I felt the time Mynea saved me from the lake after I slaughtered those men.

A vampire was stalking me, and it wasn't Mynea. It had the same grace and same pace but a different scent. If this vampire was pursuing me and the effects of the sun didn't cause it to abandon the hunt, then this vampire was older and perhaps stronger, I concluded. I felt the vampire getting closer to me. I began to hear the moving of the dirt beneath the stone entrance. My body stiffened as I desperately tried to keep my eyes open. It was futile. I was at the vampire's mercy.

"Sleep," the vampire said with a soothing voice. I heard her as if I were awake and listening to her; however, I was already asleep. At that time, I didn't know how to will myself conscious. It was a skill I would perfect a few years later.

The damp ground beneath me gave as I lay beneath the cemetery. Visions of mortals and immortals alike flooded my mind, with places and sounds only familiar to me during my vampire sleep. Night after night, week after week, year after year, I dreamed about a distant castle, whose ancient inhabitants were unaware of my curiosity and presence and where the central figure towered over all he commanded. His voice I shall never forget. Yes, these dreams, though unwelcome, returned again and again.

Day after day they revealed more and more. This time was to be no exception. However, the dream du jour wasn't of a rich, dark, menacing castle along a mountainous region. The dream wasn't of places Mynea frequented or of people and places our shared and unshared victims remembered upon their death. No. This dream was of someone I hadn't dreamed of in decades. It was a dream of my mortal blood sibling, my long lost Shani.

We were young and carefree, running through the house playing hide-and-seek. There were three rooms, a kitchen, a common area, and five closets at our disposal. The floors were hardwood, so one had to tiptoe to disguise the direction of their chosen hiding place. I welcomed these memories, for it reminded me of a home full of life, full of love—a home that contained several portraits characterizing my sister and me, along with our parents, paintings of sunsets as well as abstractions. Our furniture was always handmade by my father and sewn by my mother. Yes, I welcomed these memories.

Shani was counting, and I was hiding. As a young boy, I could always find a hiding place secret to others. Our home had many nooks a child could hide in, but I found the best. This proved most frustrating to the patience and expectations of a young girl. She spent many minutes searching for me, which can seem an eternity to a child. I found a small spot within the attic of the house where the light couldn't reach. As I waited quietly, I could hear her stumbling footsteps below searching for her seemingly vanished brother. I held back laughter as she went to and fro beneath the attic door. Exasperated, she began to call out to me and then began to cry. I purposefully made a noise just loud enough for Shani to hear and return to the spot beneath the attic. Sensing I was near, she began to climb the unsteady stairs to the attic. I readied myself to scare her. And as I saw the top of her head peek through the pitch-black opening, I sprang from the shadows, and I yelled out to frighten her.

Her eyes widened immensely as she screamed, and something I didn't consider occurred next. She fell backward and landed awkwardly on her arm. With another scream, a thousand times more dire than the first, she called out to mother. I knew she was hurt. I rushed out of the attic and down the stairs. She was holding her shoulder, and her arm looked slightly out of place. I knew in that moment, when her innocent and tormented eyes met mine, that I would never cause such despair in my sister ever again. I would always protect her. I would always look after her.

My mother must have read the expression on my face, for she didn't scold me. She picked Shani up and took her into the kitchen. I followed, and Shani stared back at me over my mother's shoulder. I felt the same sadness while dreaming about it as I had experiencing it. My mother sent me to get some rags and a sponge. I retrieved the items as fast as I could. She cleaned the blood from my sister's arm and wrapped it with the rags to steady it. She then left the kitchen to get my father. Shani looked sad, but not for herself. She saw the hurt in my eyes and felt sad for me. Shani, even then and as always, was completely selfless. Tears had begun to well in my eyes as I turned to the counter that held the water pitcher and poured her a cup of water. She took a big swallow as I held the cup to her tiny lips, then she looked at me.

"Thank you," she said. However, in my dream, it wasn't Shani's voice. It was the sweet and innocent voice of the young victim of the murdering fiend Eli, the voice of the girl I saved right before I took Eli away from the land of the living. Eli's victim's voice coming from my sister left an eerie feeling in me. The dream sequence faded as darkness triumphed.

Often my dreams would be saturated by countless thoughts and visions of Mynea. Between and throughout the disjointed sequences, she would appear and disappear. Sometimes she would speak and sometimes remain a silent observer. Sometimes I would dream of a woman who had Mynea's voice and scent but different physical features altogether. This particular day, I heard a female voice that wasn't Mynea but the voice of the one who told me to sleep. I saw Mynea's visage, but it was another immortal's voice instructing me to take her hand.

She took me to a place deep beneath the city walls and out of reach to most. There were candles and torches instantly lit, transforming the utter darkness into dancing shadows. This place didn't resemble the castle I had called home for decades. There were no paintings on the stone walls, rather, the walls were covered in old dirt and moss. There were no furs along the floors and hallways; instead, cobblestone adorned the wet floors. No doors distinguished individual spaces. Running water trickled down the wall, creating a slight vertical pathway. There were no sheets of silk aligning the walls, simply natural cracks that had occurred throughout the ancient history of its existence.

This abode was in ruins. Mynea's possessor took me to the primordial city of Ephesus, a city I had studied as a mortal. I recognized the Greek goddess Nike standing next to the goddess Diana, etched into marble. We were within the confines of the antiquated Library of Celsus, built in the tenth century before the Christ. Indeed, I was intrigued by this location. The rich Christian and Roman history of Ephesus had always enthralled me. Perhaps I chose this setting subconsciously for a reason.

Mynea began to speak in my dreams with the voice of the other vampire. The melody of the sound was soothing, but there was an ancient manner in her diction. There was a semblance shared by one other I was aware of, the immortal master of all he surveyed, the one with the eyes that pierced through me to arrest my soul while mocking my immortal existence. I would never forget his eyes, or the voice and tone that accompanied them.

During this vivid and surreal encounter, Mynea stretched out her right arm and summoned me to come to her side. I was lifted from the ground without the use of my own immortal gifts and brought to rest next to her. She was unusually radiant, even for Mynea. Everything was exactly the same, save her eyes. Her eyes were smaller than I remembered and a slightly different color. With outstretched arms she drew me into her. I remembered this embrace. I needed her touch. I desperately wanted her lips, and then my want became my reality. Her lips found mine. This vampire was a princess by every measure of royalty; however, Mynea she wasn't.

Her touch was as real as any other touch. I could actually feel her while I was dreaming. I could feel my skin feeling hers. I felt my lips kissing hers. She began to speak. "I'll tell you what you wish to know. I'll give you the freedom you seek, Aleron. I won't hold anything back from you. You'll learn everything about yourself from me. You'll learn about us, the vampire origin. You'll learn about the one whose eyes follow you in your dreams. Mynea was wise to keep you hidden from us. She knew of the master's limitations. Clever for her to have chosen such a location to give birth. Her blasphemous betrayal of the master will spell her doom."

I felt her lips touch my neck. I felt her fangs puncture my artery. I could feel her sucking my blood. I thought, *How could this feeling be just a dream?* I could feel the flow of my blood drawn by her throughout my entire body. How could this be a dream?

She only sucked for a short period of time, and in that moment of time I was reminded of ecstasy. I was reminded of a time when I was in love with a vampire.

The dream began to fade. Mynea's face became insubstantial. I began to rise above the ruins of Ephesus, rising out of Turkey and falling back into the City of the Dead. I felt the reanimation of my limbs. My mind rapidly grew sharp. I began to hear rustling and my eyes sprang open. I looked around as I leapt to my feet. There was no sign of any intruder. Everything was as it was when I closed my eyes. I rationalized that the various sounds from my dream had originated from the inhabitants of the graveyard. Nothing more. Though I could still feel her touch, no scent was present that reminded me of a possible encounter with another vampire. It was simply too surreal to be real. I deduced it was simply a dream.

I removed the large stone blocking the entrance and looked up at the young night sky. The anticipation of the night's offerings invigorated me. Before this night's victim, I wanted to drink water, for I desired the coolness against my throat and the satisfying quench that only pure water could achieve. Even though I hadn't walked as a human in decades, I walked in a perfect interpretation as only a vampire could imitate. There was a central point within the City of the Dead where pails of water for drinking were kept. I approached.

There were four pails of water, one of which no one was near. I walked to that one and grabbed the ladle inside. I dipped the ladle in and withdrew it. I drank from it while noticing my reflection cast by the dark water. As I finished the first drink and almost submerged the ladle again, I noticed dried blood on my neck. I examined my dark and vague reflection in the water. I could see the traces of two puncture wounds healing in the very spot where Mynea's likeness had drawn blood from me. I raised my hand to my neck and felt the wounds. I wiped the dried blood and looked at the smear now on my fingers. I tasted the blood. It was mine!

<h1 style="text-align:center">CHAPTER 14</h1>

he vampire was with me while I slept, following me from town to town. She even followed me to al-Montaza. She knew where my father's house was. The unknown danger caused me to take to the air. I didn't care who may have seen me soar into the darkening night sky. Swiftly, I advanced toward my father's home. I had to be sure my parents were safe.

Once in the area, I searched every neighboring street and alleyway, even the rooftops of the homes in the vicinity. Once inside and before appearing behind my father, I searched every inch of the house to make sure we were the only inhabitants present. And we were. I used my mind to scan the area. I also raised my nose to the air to pick up any familiar essence that may have told of her presence. I sensed nothing, only my mother resting and my father looking out the window in his study.

Aknon was not surprised by my return. He also knew I was there at that very moment. I could sense it in his thoughts. "Show yourself," he whispered beneath his breath. "I know you're out there. Whatever you are now, you're still my son, and I know of you."

Aknon turned around abruptly to find me standing behind him. A little startled, he almost lost his footing. He braced himself against the table. "Aknon, I'm here for the last time. I'll obey your wishes and leave your house, but before I do, tell me what you know of Shani's whereabouts. Tell me where she has gone and with whom."

"She mustn't see you like this. She mustn't look upon you as you are now. She'll notice as I did that you haven't aged. She'll know you've changed into a demon. She knows what the Bible says about demons, and she'll shun you. She'll absolutely shun you," he replied while shaking his head.

He was right, but I needed to see her nonetheless. He didn't have to tell me through words. I knew if I posed the question, his mind would answer it, and it did. She had gone to New York. That was all I needed to know.

"I disagree with you, Father, but I won't press you any longer. I'll find her through other means. I do have one last request. I'd like your permission to see mother before I leave your house for good."

"If I said no, would you listen? Could I even stop you?"

"No," I replied.

"Then your question was out of respect."

"Yes."

Reluctantly he replied, "Come on, while she's still asleep."

Aknon went past me toward my mother's room. I followed. Before he opened the door, a strange feeling came over me. I felt a presence similar to the one I had felt just hours before. I rushed past my father and pushed the door open. The force knocked it off the bottom hinge. Instantly there arose a disturbance in the curtain covering a once-closed window. My mother was awakened by the sound of the door crashing against the wall. I moved too fast for my mother to see me as I followed the presence through the opened window and onto the roof of the house.

*Don't worry, Father. I won't return,* was the mind message I passed on to Aknon's thoughts, as he struggled to comprehend what had happened. I knew I'd brought death to my parents' doorstep. I had invited a demon into his home and into my mother's chambers. With the blood meal she stole from me, she knew all! I couldn't let her get away! I had to find her.

I isolated the slightest sound of the treetops rustling in the windless night. I dashed through the air with fury in that direction. When I could hear calm breathing, I knew I was drawing near. I could hear footsteps quickening to vampire speed. I drew closer still, with sudden twists and turns through remote areas of the district. The vampire continued to elude my sight, but I could hear and smell her. I gathered all of my strength and flew faster.

I saw a black gown and black hair traveling incredibly fast just beneath the treeline and scarcely touching the ground. She moved like a cat. What happened next almost stopped me in my tracks. She turned around and looked directly at me and smiled! Then she vanished.

I slowed my progress and landed in an open area between the trees. I looked in every direction but saw nothing except darkness and the half moon. Neither sound nor thoughts that came from her lingered.

A sinister thought entered my mind. Maybe this wasn't a chase but a lure. Maybe she knew the limitations of my speed and the lack of strength I suffered by not having fed before our encounter. Perhaps she allowed me to see her just long enough for me to descend on this very spot.

I looked around once more, and, by chance or a design unknown to me, I saw something on the ground. It glistened in the night light, and I walked over to it and picked it up. It was a ring. I recognized it, and it contained her scent. It belonged to my mortal keeper, Eliza, whom I left waiting in Cairo. The female vampire lured me here to show me this! She wanted me to know how much she knew. I knew I must return to Eliza, for I didn't know if tragedy had befallen her.

Suddenly I heard a voice. The vampire had returned without detection. "Eliza is safe, Aleron. She's being looked after."

Before I could turn around, I felt her hand caressing my neck and back. I turned around instantly, and she was again gone. Then, right before my eyes, she reappeared, this time several feet from me, cloaked by the shadows of the great trees surrounding us.

I took a step in the opposite direction, then faster than the blink of a vampire's eye, I had her! She struggled with such strength and power, yet my grasp was too much for even this powerful immortal.

"Futile, isn't it?" I questioned in her ear. "To struggle will only bring you closer to me. Now tell me what I desire to know!" I lifted her into the air, and we flew.

"I know who you are, Aleron. I know who made you. I know your secrets. And I know what you desire most."

I stopped in midflight and began to descend rapidly to the ground. We landed with such a massive force that the trees surrounding us shook. She was temporarily stunned.

"She made you powerful. Mynea must have wept down to her very marrow when she decided to leave such a mate."

I tried to read her mind but only saw our encounter from her perspective, nothing more.

"You're too young to read my mind, Aleron. Your strength is undeniable, but your mental skill as an immortal tells of your true age."

"Who are you?"

"I'm Pandora, and no doubt you have concluded I'm a vampire."

"Where do you come from?"

"I come from a land you have visited in your dreams, far to the west of Egypt, deep within the Carpathians. As for whom I come from, that would be the very same origin of your beloved dark mother. We are of the same bloodline. However, I'm much older than she."

I began to feel an uneasiness. Why would Mynea keep the existence of others away from me? Especially those who knew of her? Pandora stood perfectly still, and I began to pace back and forth before her.

"You haven't had a meal, Aleron. Here, drink from me and know what I tell you to be true. Drink from me and know that lies have not assaulted your ears."

With her hand, she caressed the back of my head, inviting me to drink from her alluring outstretched neck. The artery began to call out to me as her steady heartbeat increased. I drew closer, opened my mouth, and gave her the vampire kiss once reserved for Mynea.

Out of love, lust, or hunger, I began to draw from her the life force, the blood nectar that was much more potent from a vampire. The blood of humans was indeed an undeniable lust, but the blood of an immortal was a thousand times more saporous. This was simply a meal I couldn't resist. It was a reflex. It was the equivalent of the need to take that first deep breath after holding one's breath underwater. It was more than a desire. It was more than a want. It was a necessity.

Pandora's blood flowed willingly into my mouth. The feeling was greater than any feeling I had ever felt in my mortal or immortal years. My blood ignited! I could literally taste her strength. I could feel the power she beheld. I felt my own strength increasing with every passing second. I don't remember ever swallowing. Pandora's blood simply traveled from her body to mine. I could feel her pulse within me. I could sense her persona all around me, sensual and powerful. More powerful than Mynea, I concluded. For, with Mynea, I was at least able to withdraw from her flesh at will, but with Pandora, my will yielded. There were no bounds nor climax to my lust. This must simply last forever. I would have drained her dry if that were possible. Had it not been for the need to feel this feeling again, I would have tried, but I needed this again and again. I needed this immortal kiss.

By nature, vampires are solitary creatures, but we desperately need and yearn for the companionship of another immortal, if only to exchange a blood kiss and death omen alike. I needed Pandora!

My entire body was elevated by Pandora's blood. I could see her memories as clear depictions in a motion picture. I saw glimpses of a mother watching her young daughter's reflection in a mirror as she combed through the daughter's dark flowing hair. They were of wealth, no doubt. I saw brothers enjoying the adolescent company of their younger and only sister. Suddenly I saw her father and mother scolding her with raised voices regarding some man seen the previous evening lurking about outside the window leading into the daughter's bedroom. Then, I saw the familiar castle, the castle I saw in my dreams, the ancient stone walls I witnessed in Mynea's memoirs, and then, I heard him—the very voice I'd come to know and almost fear.

His voice was immensely in command, speaking a forgotten language with impeccable diction. His enormous eyes were larger than life, disproportionate to the skull they rested in, darker than an abyss. They were dismal to look at, yet intriguingly mesmerizing. Pandora was telling the truth thus far. She knew of my immortal mother, and she knew of the places and visions I'd seen in countless dreams, running themes seemingly inherent to vampires. It was a common psychic connection drawing us closer to one another, while simultaneously driving us further apart. I wanted more, so much more. It was unbearable to think of anything else. I needed Pandora.

As I continued suckling with an immortal's lustful frenzy, I heard the voice of my vampire mother. "Beware, my prince." I imagined the voice, born from the guilty pleasure and infidelity I was engaging in.

Suddenly I felt Pandora's powerful hand on the back of my head. I fully expected her to tear me away from the puncture in her neck, for I had far exceeded the time allowed for sucking the blood from Mynea; however, to my surprise, she pressed my head in full submission to my will, accepting my desire, feeding my need to continue. She had so much to offer. How I wanted to take it all. She knew.

We went on in this fashion for an eternity. I began to feel her pull away from me. My lips and tongue struggled to continue, but she had already separated us. I opened my eyes and saw that she was staring at me. "She must have cried for months when she left you."

My head was swimming with fulfillment. I was strong yet weak. I felt a new strength boiling within, yet I only wanted to rest. So many visions, some blurred and less distinct than others. Most of the memories were disjointed and impossible to follow. Though I could feel the rejuvenation in my body, my mind only sought understanding, discernment that only she could give. I looked at Pandora. She was looking into the distance.

"There, young one. You're now as you were and more. I've much to tell you as you have many questions, for I can sense you're rattled by the incoherent visions and memories you saw in my blood." Pandora's voice was soft and full of endowment, reassuring, kind, and accepting. She had been following me with purpose.

She turned to me. I could now marvel at her beauty. She was a creature whose allure rivaled Mynea's. Her height and general stature were almost identical to my immortal mother and lover. Her breasts were slightly larger and thus more supple. The garment she wore was little more than a silk gown that clung to every sensual curve. It was almost transparent. She wore no shoes, for vampires rarely needed them and kept them more as a lingering habit. There were no blemishes on her skin, no discolorations to accent the creamy olive tone that covered her. Her hair was dark brown. Her eyebrows matched her hair in color but remained untamed. Her cheekbones complemented her tiny nose, bearing narrow nostrils that nestled perfectly under two bold eyes, suggesting the greenish blue colors of the Aegean Sea, and just as clear.

Looking directly into Pandora's eyes led me directly to her soul. She was more radiant than my queen. I knew my possession was no longer relevant. It no longer applied. "My queen left me," I said.

"She did, but with good reason, young Aleron."

I stood. "Why did she leave me? Where did she go?" My voice was elevated and bothered.

"Be still, Aleron. Allow my blood to circulate within you and give you calmness and focus unmatched by any previous meals, mortal or immortal alike."

She was right. Though I was standing, she could sense the anxiousness in my posture and tone. I rested on the back of my heels and took in the cool night's air. Sensing I was calm, Pandora began.

# CHAPTER 15

"My story begins long before your beloved immortal Mynea came to be. Your questions must be fully answered by going back to a place and time we're all familiar with, yet most of us misunderstand."

Sitting on the ground, facing me, she placed her hand on the nape of my neck and caressed the lower back of my head. Her eyes spoke as softly to me as did her lips.

"Your dreams may seem incoherent and jumbled. However, they have purpose and profound meaning, the likes of which you can scarcely comprehend or imagine, given your relative youth in the realm of immortality. You'll come to know that our age is significant in our existence. Some of us are much stronger than others. We're all alike and different at the same time. Commonality, however, we do possess, outside of the dreams, outside of the hunger, outside of our will to live and die. This commonality is where I must begin. This common existence has a single origin, a beginning that spawned many immortals, all of which are alike. With one exception—you."

Pandora's eyes changed from sea green to a reflective pearl off-white. She was looking through me. I was about to ask what she meant by the exception, but she continued to speak.

"Mynea told you what you are and how you should survive. These lessons are essential. However, she failed to tell you *who* you are. Knowledge of self starts long before your birth. It starts beyond the birth of your parents. It starts at the very beginning of your lineage. It starts with the first of you. It starts with the first of us all."

The thoughts of Mynea's journal flashed in my head.

"Vlad is where we began, Aleron." Pandora stole the words from my lips as she released my head and stood over me. She began to pace in a slow, calculated manner, maintaining a familiar royal grace. "Vlad is where our bloodline began. You have seen this name in Mynea's journal. Of course her journal is written in an ancient language you know nothing of. It's a language forgotten by mortal tongue, it's a language revealed and taught to us by our father, as all things we've come to know. Vlad's eyes eventually find all of his children; you have seen them before. Yet there are limitations to his reach, which is why Mynea chose Egypt to cradle you."

Who was this Vlad who had been in my dreams? In Mynea's blood memories? In Pandora's memories?

"Your thoughts and questions are expected, young prince. That's why it's important for you to listen and learn all that you can from me. Know that I'm not Mynea and that I won't deceive you. Know that I'm here to teach you. Protect you. Love you. All this you'll come to accept in time."

She looked into the distance and continued. I remained seated on the ground, eagerly listening. "I don't know much more than what I'm about to share with you regarding our immortal father. He doesn't speak much of his mortal days or how he came to be, though legend has revealed a few things to me. So I must start with my first encounter with our king."

She paused for a moment as if distracted. The illumination of her eyes was momentarily concealed by their lids. I could see her chest rise and fall, and after a sigh she continued.

"The year was 1463 when I awoke in my master's arms. I knew tales of him before that night. I'd fallen in love with the legend of the ruler, once a prince of Wallachia, who fought tirelessly and victoriously against the Turks. I loved the tales of the vicious and unforgiving knight fighting for all Christendom, the poems of the slain prince who defied death to rise again from the grave. I fell deeply for the legend of Vlad, and for once my dreams weren't at all dreams. They were thoughts induced by the very knight who infatuated me. Vlad, who visited my bedchamber every night for seven days, haunted my dreams. I was a young woman of tender age when he took me from my home. I begged him to take me. I prayed for him to take me. Every waking moment from the first night he came to me, I thought of nothing else. I belonged to him long before he became my master."

She licked her lips slowly, as if reliving the first intimate encounter. "In his arms that first night, I felt a love like none other. I desperately wanted to be with him. I wanted to be with him for all eternity. Of course, at the time I didn't truly know what I was asking for. I didn't know what Vlad really was. I had no knowledge of his immortality. I only felt his love. My love for him was unmatched by any, save his love for me. The legends and folklore about a fallen and slain conqueror were false, for the man lay with me, and we were one flesh every night. He couldn't have been more alive and the legends more wrong.

"I began to loathe the day, for it meant my heart would go unfulfilled. Without him, living in his castle was excruciating; to feel his unnaturally chilling touch night after night, only to be alone with his servants and housekeepers day after day. I began to live for dusk. Every evening at the same exact hour, Vlad would come to me. I simply couldn't exist without him. At the tender age of nineteen, I felt I'd lived a full lifetime each day that passed in his absence. Eventually I began walking around his immense castle against his wishes.

"His fortress was just north of Curtea de Arges in Romania. In those times it was called Poenari. The grand abode was menacing at first sight. An acropolis, it stood at the highest point of Bucharest, surrounded by extremely tall trees. The fortress of concrete, stone, and brick lay utterly impregnable to outsiders. Legend told of an abandoned citadel, its walls thick and tall. It is the very one I speak of, and I assure you, it was no more desolate than this city of Alexandria is a ghost town. Its steps were steep and unforgiving to the foot. Harsh! The mouth of the edifice was a monstrosity.

"Some of the weather-beaten statues made of marble surrounding the front door were of angels. Some were of demons. One stood out among all others. In the center, just above the door, hung a beastly and grotesque bust of a three-headed canine of some sort. This creature had originated in the bowels of Hades. It found its final resting place above a gigantic door, fit for the Nephilim, long before recorded time. Just above the bust hung a cross, the one signifying the demise of the Apostle Peter. It hung upside down, bottom to heaven, top to hell. I remember closing my eyes and smashing my face between Vlad's chest and arms as we approached for the first time by horse and carriage.

"The castle reminded me of a cathedral. Vibrant mosaics and paintings littered the walls. Frescos covered the apex of the round ceilings. Each picture was a portrait of a man resembling the man I loved. However, I thought them to be of relatives, for the clothing spoke of a different time.

"The hallways were wider than usual, as were the doors inside the castle. At every door stood a statue of a uniformed knight, wielding an iron sword. His manservants and maidens forbade me to continue my exploration though they were well aware of the affection their master lavished upon me and the consequences to them of making me unhappy. So they left me to my spoiled and immature vices, so a princess I truly became.

"Curiosity led me to explore rooms I hadn't dared enter until then. I discovered a seemingly endless library. Wall after wall lined with books. A desk in the corner made of dark solid wood. A chair partially hidden by the desk. A quill and ink blotter lying beside a small jar of red ink next to a stack of documents, which I explored with a curious and untrusting eye.

"The top document was a ledger containing various entries. The documents below the ledger were land deeds drafted by a peculiarly acute, unnaturally steady hand. Every letter was identical from word to word, sentence to sentence. The lettering resembled art more than script, all written by Vlad's hand, no doubt. Vlad was an established businessman as well as the ex-ruler of these lands. His influence and power were a force. I was intrigued by his aptitude. Even though it didn't at all seem possible, I began to miss him even more!

"I would have his maidens wash me just before sunset every day, after which I would lie without garment on his bed and await his arrival. It always startled me how he would seem to instantly appear in the blink of an eye, how his gaze would guide me to him with the slightest physical effort from me. Completely and utterly helpless I felt. He was my master.

"We went on in this manner for weeks until one early evening during Vlad's absence, my brothers came for me. They entered Vlad's castle with weapons of war, feverish anger, and contempt. Every manservant was slaughtered. Every maiden was killed without regard to the code of war. One by one, my three brothers and two cousins entered every room of the castle searching for Vlad. They took me and made me leave with them. I begged and pleaded for them to spare his life, but my cries fell on deaf ears. In their eyes was madness, all of them in a drunken stupor, with the exception of my oldest brother Mordekai, who was enraged by my disappearance coupled with the known duty of protection charged to the men.

"One door, at the very bottom of the castle, they had yet to open. The corridor leading to the door was dark, nearly devoid of all light. One of my cousins raised his torch in the darkness, and a sudden hush fell over all of the men. They stood there visibly shaken by what they saw. On the door was a smaller version of the bust from hell that was nestled at the apex of the front door. However, it was a thousand times more menacing at eye level and in close proximity to us, its mouth outstretched, bearing canines. Nevertheless, it didn't serve its purpose to deter the will and desire of my brothers and cousins, for out of their temporary bewilderment came several attempts to break the boundary that stood between them and the unknown. All of them began kicking the door furiously.

"The enormous door was finally defeated, and a stench seeped through the cracked wood. Everyone covered their mouths as the door swung open. Mordekai and the rest began coughing and gasping for fresh air. But their efforts were futile, for the air in this lower part of the castle was thick and rank with death. A cousin held out a flame to illuminate the room, which seemed to be a dungeon, a place of torture and captivity. Severed limbs, partial skulls, eyes, fingers, and every other despicably disgusting extremity originating from a human were strewn about, all in various states of decay. If there was a hell on earth, we had stumbled upon it!"

Pandora paused for a moment. The pacing ceased as she relived the frightful event. Her eyes glazed over, and she stared into the distance, her voice quivering, showing some semblance of her once-mortal life. She looked at me again and continued.

"I was too afraid to continue into the darkness but more afraid to stay behind as the flame and the footsteps progressed. Reluctantly I followed. We came upon a coffin. I was terrified of it! Mordekai and Jonathan began to pry open the lid with the hilts of their swords, and after a great struggle, the sealed coffin gave. My eyes closed tightly as my nose was assaulted by the odor. "God damn you!" Mordekai yelled. "Where are you, fiend?" his voice echoed within this dungeon.

"I slowly opened my eyes and cleared them of the tears blurring my vision. The room was empty, save for a familiar handkerchief that I had given to my beloved just the night before to wipe some dark red wine he had spilled while not in my presence, the reddish smudge still in plain view on the once pure white cloth. Suddenly one of my cousins, standing just to the right of me, was swept into the black abyss. My brothers rushed with their torches to where he had been standing, and nothing was there. He had simply vanished! Mordekai and Jonathan, along with my youngest brother and remaining cousin, called out to him, "Alexander! Alexander!" The call was loud and answered only by its echo, mocking all of us.

"Then another short and sharp cry came from Demetri, who was standing behind Jonathan in the shadow of the torch. We were not able to find him, either. The men, baffled, began to look at each other and around the room. There was nothing to be seen but plenty to be heard. Jonathan screamed Demetri's name with a yell that was equally horrific in magnitude as Demetri's cry had been when the darkness took him. Once the echo of the chamber released Jonathan's voice, we heard a strange noise—the sound of crunching or breaking. It sounded like the chewing of bone. My youngest brother, Lucian, ran toward the entrance, followed by Jonathan, who continued yelling for Lucian to stop. Then right before our eyes, Lucian was lifted into the air and into the shadows in the same manner as the others. We then heard something splatter. A gasp came from Jonathan. Mordekai raised his torch to find Jonathan turning around slowly to face us. He was covered in . . ."

Pandora paused again briefly, then continued.

"He was covered in blood. Lucian's blood drenched Jonathan, covering his hair, face, chest, and arms, his mouth agape with his younger brother's blood covering even his teeth. It was abhorrent. Mordekai swiftly grabbed my wrist and yelled, 'Run!' With this command, Jonathan turned and ran toward the door through which we had entered the room. We ran up the stairs, terrified of what followed. We couldn't see what stalked us, but we could hear its footsteps. We were being chased by some beast. I could feel its breath on my neck. Mordekai dropped the flame, and in its extinguishing light I saw the face of a demon. I beheld the grotesque visage for less than a second, but as horrible as the beast was, it felt strangely familiar. With a shimmer of the evening sunlight at the top of the corridor, it was gone; it was only when we escaped through the front door of the castle that we realized Jonathan was gone, too.

"I tried desperately to free myself from Mordekai's hold as I didn't want to leave without Jonathan. I pleaded with him, but he tightened his grip on me and led me to one of the carriages waiting just beyond the drawbridge covering the moat.

"In that moment I took note of the unusual sunset. I remember the sun looked more red than yellow. It looked like a blood sun. The early evening sky disclosed the falling sun and the rising moon simultaneously. Though I'd seen countless sunsets prior to this one, I couldn't remember their brilliance and luster as I did that evening.

"I also felt a presence watching us, following us outside the carriage. The horses must have felt it, too, for they were restless and disturbed.

The carriage wheels hurled with the speed of the two mares frantically escaping an evil that seemed relentless in its pursuit. We detoured through a passage known by the Ottomans that led to the southern tip of the vast mountainous regions surrounding the castle.

"When I came to the castle for the first time, it had been in the middle of the night. This was the first time I had actually looked upon the monstrous castle in the twilight. Any mortal would have easily been frightened by the mere sight of it. However, I could only think of the night when my prince would return to me and take me back to what I considered to be my new home, And though I feared the beast lurking beneath, my thoughts were completely mesmerized by my master. For his fortress was where I belonged.

"Finally we entered the Carpathians. The feeling of being watched never subsided. The carriage wheels continued furiously grinding against the cobblestone path beneath. I remember the thunderous smashing of the rocks beneath the hooves of the horses and my brother yelling for them to continue their feverish retreat, flailing the leather straps that kept him in command. He had lost all hope, save that of escaping with my life and his own.

"Mordekai and I arrived at my father's home in Budapest as the moon stood at its highest. He had a look of despair, his mouth permanently ajar in total disbelief of the day's events. His eyes told a tale of sorrow for our brothers and kinsmen who were lost to the darkness, lives taken by some ungodly creature on my behalf. A creature whose eyes resembled the eyes of my beloved prince. My prince, who only came to me at nightfall. My prince of darkness.

"Only after we were presumably safe inside, with all the doors locked, did Mordekai begin to cry. It was the first and last time I'd ever seen him cry in such manner, sobbing uncontrollably. His emotions overwhelmed him, and he was reduced to a mere child. What was strange to me was that I, too, had suffered great losses at the hands of a beast, but I only felt longing for my prince to come and get me. I hugged my brother around the neck as he sobbed. He was comforted by my gesture—and a gesture is all it ever was. My mind and soul were elsewhere. Had this tragedy befallen any other, they would surely be broken by the horror of it and terrified that they might be next. But I felt nothing of the sort. I could only think of him. I know now that Vlad was within my mind, controlling my thoughts.

"My brother held me tight, but I was compelled to slip away to the window. There was a mist surrounding the base of the window ledge. It seemed to speak to me and instill in me an eerily familiar feeling of protection and love. It was not just any love. It was the greatest love. My prince was near, and I surrendered to his call. The mist engulfed me, and I felt Vlad's arms. I could hear his heartbeat. Though surreal, it was impossible to turn away from it. I closed my eyes and heard my name. Pandora. 'Take me with you, my prince,' I called out. 'Take me with you.'

"I opened my eyes, and my prince was holding me flesh to flesh. I was in his arms once again. Somehow the man I loved every night for weeks had materialized within the mist. I didn't care that this defied logic. Whatever sorcery was present, I welcomed it. I only cared for that moment.

"Mordekai noticed our embrace just outside the window and gathered his strength and sword once more. Vlad was looking directly into my eyes when my brother lunged at him, stabbing Vlad in the shoulder. Vlad swung his hand with such power and fury that he knocked my brother against the stone wall. Mordekai slid helplessly to the ground. Bruised and broken, my brother's body went limp, and his eyes lost their glimmer. He died.

"Vlad's expression changed. His eyes never left me as he struck and killed my brother, and I watched his expression change from one of fury to one of sorrow. At first I thought Vlad's look of sorrow was due to this wound, but he seemed unfazed by the blade protruding from him. Still holding me, he bent his arm into an unnatural position and slowly began to remove the blade. It was then I fully realized the magnitude of my brother's dying blow. An excruciating pain befell me as Vlad continued to remove the blade. I knew that I, too, had been deeply wounded. I didn't have to look down at it. I only had to look in Vlad's eyes. They told the story of my mortality.

"The blade made a sharp clang as it hit the loose stones on the ground.

I let out a gasp. I could feel the blood flowing internally. Vlad knew I was bleeding inside. He slightly withdrew himself from me. The sight of my wound seemed to raise fire in his eyes. This fire, however, wasn't the look of anger. It was the look of lust.

"There was something about my wound that seemed irresistible to him. I coughed and a little blood escaped my mouth and found his cheek. He wiped it off and licked his fingers. I looked at his eyes, and they changed color right before me. What was once a deep blue became pearl, his pupils dilated. I knew then my prince was more than I thought. I knew that Vlad was not of this world. I knew that the legend was true of a beast that spread a blood plague throughout Eastern Europe, the demon that haunted Bucharest and Transylvania, a manner of a being that was more than human. My prince was supernatural.

"I grew weak and began to slump over. Vlad pulled me close to him, and we traveled fast as the wind. He led, but his back was to the direction we were traveling in. Seemingly within a few moments, we were back in Vlad's castle. There were no servants. There were no maids. There was only my prince and I.

"I felt myself slipping away. The darkness was calling out to me. My breath became weak, and my vision began to blur. I began to feel nothing of the wound. I began to feel nothing of this world. I began to feel nothing at all. My time was nearing its end. Vlad removed his shirt while still holding me with one hand. Even though I was doomed, I wanted to see how badly he was cut, but there was no wound, only streaks of dried blood. It was at that moment that I chose to speak.

"'Don't let me die, beloved. Life or death without you is the same.' I wanted to share whatever dark power my prince possessed. I couldn't exist in heaven nor hell without him. His face spelled only sadness as I began to fade into darkness. Then suddenly I felt the chill of him closer to me. He pressed my lips to his hairless chest and softly said, 'Drink.'

"I opened my mouth and tasted his blood! And that was my last night as a mortal."

# CHAPTER 16

"I awoke smelling of rose blossoms and clothed in the finest garments, in the arms of Vlad. I awoke, a vampire.

"Vlad taught me what it meant to be immortal and how to survive as a vampire just as Mynea taught you. Though I was an immortal, I remained humanly naïve. There was one thing I was sure of, however—the one feeling that grew with veracity, the warmth that allowed this body to endure for centuries to come—and that was my love for Vlad. It was similar in magnitude of the love you felt and still feel for Mynea.

"For years Vlad lavished riches upon me. We traveled from city to city, country to country, even traversed vast oceans to different continents, from the Carpathians to the southern tip of Africa and all of greater Europa. Vlad had dwellings in every country we visited. Some homes were more extravagant than the castle you see in your dreams. Some were little more than a room deep within the ground. All were luxuriously furnished."

Pandora paused, knelt, and placed her hands on my face, her eyes examining every inch of my countenance. She exhaled and continued.

"While in Vlad's care, nothing seemed more important to him, save the need to feed his hunger. He rarely allowed me to hunt with him after he taught me the basic rules. I often wondered who made up these rules, who passed them to my prince, and if another existed then or even before my master. He dispelled this thought before I had a chance to ask.

"'I'm the beginning, my love,' he said kindly and lovingly. 'There are no others of our kind. You and I alone reign, and I forbid you to condemn anyone to a life of death.'

"And reign we did. Vlad still commanded a boundless army through his many lieutenants. His army was composed of the soldiers of the Ottoman Empire, along with hundreds of Turkish traders. They used to fight for all Christendom. Then they fought for their displaced king, their immortal sovereign. They were so willing to lay down their lives for a man who, unbeknownst to them, could not be killed—one who would remain long after their great grandchildren were dead. They dismissed the rumors and legends of Vlad being captured when he was the ruler of Wallachia and beheaded for vicious war crimes on humanity. Unfortunately for the magistrates of that time, Vlad was already dead before they took his head.

"For all others who witnessed his death as a mortal met with gruesome untimely deaths of their own by an unknown beast. It was conjectured and later believed to be the doing of some type of wolf. I know it to be my beast," Pandora smirked.

"During the day, my prince continued growing his wealth by making strategic land deals."

*During the day*, I repeated to myself.

"Yes, Aleron, our lord slumbers by choice, not necessity as his children must; though he somewhat resembles the walking dead during the hours of daylight. None of us can escape the effects of the sun. It simply deters his hunger, and lack of fresh blood weakens him and leaves him less luminous. Even though he is weaker, his powers of persuasion are heightened by a force or will unknown to me. This is how he continued to amass a fortune that rivaled the ancient Egyptian pharaohs. He could easily persuade aristocrats to sign over their deeds of land. There were some humans who weren't affected by his mind control, but they soon became his meal. Then he would simply forge the necessary documents. The signatures, of course, were a perfect match.

"Vlad soon commanded the armies of Northern Europe and all of Eastern Europe. Bucharest became a sovereign destination where kings and royal families would gather to pledge their allegiance to his growing empire. Christ was no longer the motivation. Greed and wealth replaced God in the eyes of man. Vlad knew this and used man's lack of faith and understanding against him. His influence corrupted the Islamic as well as the Christian movement.

"Decades would pass, and Vlad would withdraw more and more into his quest for power and dominion. There would be weeks and sometimes months before I would see him. I was forced to hunt alone. Confined to loneliness within the Carpathians, my longing for him became an unbearable cross to carry. When Vlad finally came to me, I could tell his focus was elsewhere. He was distracted. I enjoyed the company of his body, but his mind drifted. His eyes no longer looked upon mine with love and lust. They were withdrawn. This I couldn't understand. Then, one night, an unfamiliar scent planted itself onto Vlad's cloak. It was the unmistakable scent of a mortal. A female.

"Vlad hunted and killed men in the most grotesque and animalistic manner, but he refused to dine on women. I often wondered why this discrimination existed within him, but I decided it would be wise not to inquire. As a result, I felt powerless and infused with anger."

Pandora's voice grew sharp, her eyes looking keenly into the distance as her heart began to echo louder within the tiny frame holding her lungs. Her pace grew more rapid. I stood, thinking my movement would somehow calm her. It didn't.

"My prince had taken a fancy to a mortal woman. I couldn't bring myself to ask, for the answer was known. Even before I could inquire, he would quickly sink his ferocious teeth into my bosom, and he would drink. All feelings of anger subsided. Again, I was lost in his spell. I couldn't feel my body once in his grasp. His hold on me far exceeded my own. My body was his. My immortality his. My thoughts, visions, senses all belonged to him. I was simply helpless.

"When I would awake, Vlad would be gone, and the anger would return. Who was this mortal? Where was she now? Was she filling the bed of one of his many castles? Peles? Sighisoara Citadel? Rasnov? Or his beloved Bran Castle? Was he visiting her as he visited me before my rebirth? Why was he drawn to her?

"I began to search my memories from our last blood kiss for a trace of her. I needed to see her. I needed to see him with her. I didn't want to. I needed to!

"There was nothing. From that moment, I knew my prince could mask his thoughts from me. He could choose what visions I would see when we shared blood. I myself have learned to use this ability to a lesser extent. Vlad would see all. And I would gain nothing from my journey through his thoughts—nothing more than the scent he left of her essence in the room we shared. I left the room at once, wanting no more of her within me.

"I dashed down the narrow corridor and knocked one of our mortal servants against the stone wall. The manservant gave a cry and slid to the ground below in agonizing pain. How fragile he was. He could be easily broken in two, his bones brittle like the branches of a dead and withering tree. I turned around to see him cowering in my presence. In his eyes resided fear, desperation, and death.

"As vampires, we're invulnerable to disease. We'll never fall victim to aging ailments, viruses, or any other sickness one could imagine. But we share a common frailness with our human prey. Our hearts are fragile—even more fragile than that of a mortal's. With the intense love we have for one another, we can also have great sorrow.

"And when the essence of a mortal woman filled the air in my home, my heart fell. It cowered in agonizing pain. Our hearts are fragile. Though immortal in nearly every sense of the meaning, love can, too, drive us to an emotional death—a place that's darker than even Vlad's beastly eyes. In this place I felt a ferocious hunger, which matched my first. It wasn't the hunger to feed, but the hunger to destroy. To kill!"

In the moonlight I could see her teeth, glowing in their splendor.

Pandora's mouth was open with her tongue slightly exposed, almost as if she meant to taste the air or savor the recounting of her memories.

"I persuaded one of Vlad's lieutenants to disclose his location. Of course, he knew nothing of the true nature of his commander, and as any man, he was within my power before he knew it. Constantinople would be my destination. I left swiftly on foot.

"I arrived in Byzantium, the capital, just after midnight. It didn't take long for me to read the minds of men to find my beloved Vlad. Many here had come to know him through his business dealings and land ownership. The townspeople envied him. The women were drawn to him, but there was one woman he was drawn to.

"Her name was Mynea Ardelean. She was of noble birth, her parents Count and Countess Ardelean of Constantinople, aristocrats and descendants of bloodlines that reached long before the birth of Christ. I knew of her family when I was a mortal woman. Wealth beyond wealth.

"Count Ardelean lived in the Rumeli fortresses north of the city. Built by the Ottomans, Rumeli was erected to give the Ottoman Empire complete control of the ships passing through the Bosphorus River. After the conquest, it was turned into a prison for war criminals, housing mainly the officers. Count Ardelean purchased it for the countess once it was damaged in a failed siege and rebuilt it with the modern luxuries of our time, marble columns and statues with the likeness of the Ardelean lineage. Though the location was well known by all, penetrating it would be an altogether different task. With its menacing appearance and natural moat borders complete with cannons atop thirteen towers, it was truly a difficult feat for a mortal army. However, it was simply a minor delay for an enraged vampiress!

"As a young vampire female, I developed the ability to seemingly disappear and reappear. This, however, is quite impossible. I simply move with such speed that even an immortal's eyes cannot follow. The dark gifts are different within all of us. I used my stealth and unnatural speed to enter the well-guarded fortress my prince obviously so freely frequented while my bed remained empty. My purpose wasn't to draw unnecessary attention to myself, though I felt a slight urge to drink.

"Once inside, it took no time for me to pick up Mynea's scent. She was in the higher levels of the enormous home. I passed many servants who knew nothing of my passing, save the wind they felt after I was well out of their eye and ear range. Though there were no windows to produce such a wind, the sentiment was to add it to the growing mystical sensation that became the very basis for supernatural rumors within this town. No doubt most were rumors about the comings and goings of my prince.

"As the scent became stronger and stronger, I quickened my already devilishly fast pace. The anticipation numbed everything else. I was a cheetah on the trail of its prey. I was going to look upon the mortal woman who had stolen Vlad's heart from me. I would anticipate our confrontation. What I would do with her, however, I didn't know.

"Finally, I was looking directly at the door to her bedchamber. There was a man standing there half asleep. His duty to guard the door was prompted by Mynea's father to guarantee her chastity. My frenzy took hold of me as I snatched the man from his half slumber into my blood-thirsty and vengeful grasp. Before he could utter a sound, I ripped out his throat with my mouth and drained him. I accomplished this without the slightest sound or detection.

"I opened the door swiftly and threw his body in. I closed it and turned to my nemesis. She lay fast asleep. I had to see Mynea. I had to see what drew him to her. What did she possess that I didn't?

"Her quarters were lush with floral arrangements, gorgeous and vibrant. Dutch amaryllis accented by anthuriums. Purple lilacs and lilies highlighted a bed of pinkish-red roses. The arrangements numbered eleven, all situated in magnificent vases, her furniture simple and impressive, a vitrine and cabinet housing a tortoiseshell jewelry box. I stepped over the white animal fur lying on the ground and quietly examined the jewelry box. As soon as I opened it, my heart fell. A necklace identical to the one my beloved had given me lay gleaming within the confines of the tiny box. The once soft candlelight burst into an inferno as my fury climbed. I turned my attention back to Mynea.

"Quickly I appeared before her. I looked at her lying there, blissfully unaware of the fate before her. She was angelically beautiful, sleeping peacefully and completely unaware of my presence. I took in every breath she took. I felt every move she made. I read every thought and examined every image within her dreams. Her eyes danced under her eyelids, consumed by visions, thoughts, and dreams of my prince, now hers. She was as I, when I was mortal.

"She was beautiful, as was I, her skin, an olive tone, as was mine, yet slightly darker. Height proportionate with weight, as was mine. We were twins. Mortal and immortal alike. I had to see her eyes.

"I laid my back on the headrest of her large epicurean bed. Gently I situated myself behind her, carefully raising her into my arms. Her head rested on my breast. I spoke to her mind, *Wake*, and her eyes opened. She wasn't startled, for her mind was being controlled by me long before I ever approached her. She looked directly into my vampire eyes, hers a golden brown with slight hints of orange that were imperceptible to the eyes of mortals but radiantly visible to me. She couldn't speak, for I wouldn't allow her to in my presence. I wanted to see what my prince saw.

"The rage began to build again. Uncontrollable fury filled my thoughts. My body began to shake all over. This mortal woman had found fancy in the eyes of Vlad. And while my hatred was at its paramount, I sank my teeth deep into her neck, and I sucked rapidly. Her death would be the only solution. Vlad would look upon her no more. He'd return to me. My heart would be whole once more.

"I continued to drink. Visions of Vlad from her memories filled my thoughts. I realized the extent of his love, his passion, and his desire for her. And at that moment, that passion again belonged to me. This drove away all remaining sanity. I wanted to drain every drop of blood from her. Memories of her childhood, her parents, her teachers, her family. They were all mine. I was becoming the mortal I once was. With her death, I would have my life again!

"Being completely captivated by this bloodlust numbed the feeling of a powerful hand throwing me across the room and into the stone wall. Mynea's body returned to her pillow with a soft thump. Her eyes nearly void of life remained open as her chin dropped to her chest.

"I felt pain for the first time in decades. The act was much too powerful for a mortal. My arms and legs were completely useless for the moment. I could feel my lungs and heart begin to bleed inside. My vision was clouded by the blood that dripped from my eyes. It took tremendous strength for me to lift my head and see my assailant, though I already knew that there was only one who possessed such power.

"I could smell the unmistakable scent of death incarnate. His breath was heavy, his mind sharp, and his fury beyond measure. He came into focus as he knelt over Mynea's withering body. He then whipped his head around, faster than my eyes could see, and pierced through my soul.

"I didn't feel sorry for what I'd done. I didn't feel fury for what was subsequently done to me. I felt devastated by the look of sorrow in the eyes of my master. It was the same look I had seen in his eyes on my last mortal night, when death was at my door. I knew then what he saw in Mynea that he didn't have in me.

"He saw me in Mynea. He saw me as that mortal girl I once was. He was drawn to her mortality. He was living through her life. I realized he had made me what I am only because he couldn't bear the thought of being without me. He lived by watching her life. He wanted to see her eat. He wanted to see her love. He wanted to taste her warm flesh without condemning her to a life of eternal damnation. He truly fell in love with our humanity, the tale of Beauty and the Beast told in this distorted form.

"My body began to heal rapidly. I could feel my bones realigning themselves. My internal bleeding came to a halt. The blood tears dried on my cheeks. Still dazed, I stood slowly to my feet. Vlad's eyes had grown red with grief. 'I have caused enough pain for this night,' I thought. I vanished as quickly as I could. I left him there with Mynea. I robbed him of his attachment to the world of the living. For that, his forgiveness would take an eternity. So I thought.

"I returned to the castle and retreated to my bedchamber. I was noticeably shaken, and the servants knew something was amiss, yet they dared not query.

"Night transformed into day, and the vampire paralysis took its hold on me. Slumber was inevitable, and my eyes found the darkness they had sought since the night began."

# CHAPTER 17

"efore I opened me eyes I realized I wasn't alone. When I opened them, I saw Vlad. He was sitting in a chair staring at the flame of a candle. Without turning to me he began to speak, slowly, as if chewing and tasting each syllable: 'I am regretful, my love.' His voice was filled with pain and affliction.

"I lay motionless in my bed, silent. And he began again. 'To hurt you is to hurt me. The betrayal you think you committed is not a betrayal at all. No doubt by now you have come to realize the meaning of it all and my desperation for mortal companionship.'

"He turned toward me and seemingly floated to my bedside, his open cloak flowing behind him. Remembering his gentle manner, he lay down with me and pulled my head to his chest.

"'My love for you grew out of desire and necessity,' he continued as I listened to his heartbeat. 'Immortality is a death. To be immortal means to die slowly every day and every night. You witness the passing of your family and loved ones. You cling to them desperately as you watch their bodies deteriorate with the victimization of time. All you've known comes to a slow and painful end. When I became what I am, I tried to live among the living. I tried to be like I once was. I hated the curse of bloodlust and the need to steal human souls to live on. I failed and became a beast. I fed on man and animal alike, without prejudice or regard. All of my humanity was lost. I vowed never to condemn another to this eternal death sentence. Then I saw, in the memories of one of my victims, an angelic face that demanded my attention. Once I looked upon this face in the flesh, I was captivated by its aura. A new desire was born within. A desire to live again. To thrive again. To love again. It was you, Pandora, who gave me back my way. Through our courtship, I came to regain what was stolen from me. My soul. My love for you has never changed. I love you now as I loved you then.'

"I looked into his eyes and knew this to be true. Not because I wanted it to be true or because I needed it to be. It just was. It just is. He never stopped loving me. He hates his endless existence. Only after living for centuries have I come to fully understand this notion. We all begin to question our immortality and begin to discover an alternative to life—living through the lives of mortals. For over two weeks it was just as it was before. For the first time in decades, we hunted together, four, sometimes five victims a night. We were again happy in our bloodlust, yet he still was distant at times. I tried to probe his mind, but it was completely blocked. Whatever it was, he didn't want me to know. It didn't matter much, for I knew whatever it was it would be discovered as an eventuality of time. That time came exactly twenty nights from the night I killed her.

"I awoke to a strange and unfamiliar scent within the walls of Castle Bran. It wasn't of a mortal, and it wasn't of Vlad. Though he was in the castle, he wasn't in my bedchamber. I left the room in search of this strange scent and came to the door of another room where Vlad would often allow traveling aristocratic members of society to slumber. The door was slightly open, and I heard his voice. I opened the door and walked in. Vlad was kneeling at the bedside. There was another lying in the bed. Another immortal.

"I came closer, and in a moment of surreal reality, I saw my mortal twin, once slain by my hatred, in the body of a vampire. I tried to move forward, but something was holding me perfectly still. It was Vlad. This was a power I'd not witnessed until that moment. He had complete control of my body, without even looking at me. He continued talking to Mynea, while I struggled to free myself from his paralyzing hold. It was futile. I couldn't break his grasp."

The sharpness of diction that accompanies rage returned to Pandora's voice. I could see the anger in her eyes. Clearly she was reliving the moments she spoke of.

"Vlad stood and turned to me. 'Be still, my love,' he tenderly commanded. 'Calm yourself. You have no enemy in me or in Mynea. She's your immortal sister, same as you are hers. You'll bring no harm to her as she'll bring no harm to you. In time your anger will subside as you'll find necessary companionship in her as she will in you. You'll come to rely on her as she'll rely on you, as I now rely on you both.' His chest rose before he continued in a commanding tone, 'I'm the master of this home and everywhere your travels will take you. You will do as I command, lest you suffer my ire. This has been explained to her as well. She won't try to harm you, for I forbid it.'

"Mynea rose to her feet in the form you now know her to be. It was the first time I had laid eyes on an immortal woman without the help of a mirror. Though we were still similar, twins we were no longer. Beautiful we both remained.

"She walked toward me. Instantly I was able to move. Vlad had released his supernatural hold on me. Mynea stood in front of me with her arms outstretched and palms facing the ceiling, searching for acceptance. I looked at her, and the fury returned in me. I was totally enraged and utterly confused, so I did the only thing I could think of doing. I left. Right before their eyes, I vanished.

"I reappeared in my bedchamber and, to my surprise, Vlad was already there, standing facing the window, as if he were expecting me.

"'How could you?' I screamed. 'How dare you follow your betrayal with this blasphemy. You told me it was forbidden to make another. To condemn another. To tear the soul from the living and condemn them to a life of death!'

"He remained utterly silent. His face showed very little emotion. He was a statue.

"'Say something!' I demanded.

"I rushed at him with all of my vampire speed and strength and struck him. This would have easily crushed the skull of another immortal. It would have turned the cranium of a human into dust, yet he didn't even blink. He didn't move. His face was misshapen for only an instant. It began to regain its supernatural form a thousand times faster than mine had when I was thrown against the wall. I struck him again and again, using all of my might, vanishing and reappearing where I thought I might have been able to provoke him, hoping to anger him, hoping to draw some emotion out of him. Nothing. I couldn't hurt him. With this realization I swiftly ran to the one I knew I could hurt and possibly destroy.

"I lunged at Mynea as she walked through the corridor, and before my claws reached her, he had me. I was in excruciating pain. With both arms outstretched and legs subdued by his, I felt his powerful grip begin to crush my bone. None of the pain compared to what seeing her was doing to my heart. I didn't care about his fury. I didn't care about his rules. I wanted her dead, and he soon realized this. We broke free from the confines of the castle through the window in the corridor. Far from the castle we traveled into the mountains. I struggled to get free, but it was to no avail. Finally he let me go.

"'Why?' I begged for understanding. 'Why?'

"'You will learn your place, Pandora!' His voice overwhelmed mine. 'My wrath will be far beyond what you've witnessed thus far if disobedience is your cure. If death befalls Mynea, the same fate will befall you. I alone command this house. You're now a part of my coven. My children! Everything you are belongs to me and me alone.'

"'How dare you?' I cried. 'You steal my life with your trickery! You arrest my soul with your lies! You killed my family to have me as your own, and now you aim at my heart? You mean to destroy me as you destroyed my brothers? My father went mad and my mother withered away in death. You're a monster, no better than the beast man fears in the night. No better than the murderers who plague mankind and on whom you have taught me to dine, though you yourself kill without concern. A fool I've been to believe such love exists. You love no one but yourself.'

"'Silence!'

"Words left me. I've never heard such a voice directed at me. Vlad's eyes grew large and black. His face became slightly more boorish, resembling the creature we had seen at the door of his innermost chamber that fateful day. The wind seemed to awaken, and a chill filled the air around us. My hair began to ride the wind as he walked toward me.

"Vlad extended his arm and hand and pointed a stern finger toward my face. The nail of his index finger was almost as long as the finger itself. The hair covering his palm made this gesture ever more horrid. 'You'll do as I've commanded and without question!'

"Vlad towered over me, and I felt a feeling that had long ago abandoned me—fear. I felt mortality once more. I knew then Vlad would indeed kill me if I disobeyed his order. I knew then what fate would bring if I harmed Mynea. The same fate of anyone who would harm me. An unspeakably painful death.

"The menacing fiend before me withdrew and resembled my Vlad once again. The wind's fury fell. The chill in the air disappeared. My master possessed powers I've yet to understand nor comprehend the rapacity they beheld. Calmer, I spoke. *Do you not love me as you once did? Do I not do your will as you expect? Why must I be forced to share what is mine with another?*'

"'My child, you are loved as you have always been. You will always remain in my favor, for you're the first. Go into the night and drink. Return, and we'll lie as we always have.'

"Vlad loved me as well as Mynea. He revealed this to me, and though I wanted to go, I also knew he would never let that happen. We would be his forever."

# CHAPTER 18

I closed my eyes and took a deep breath in order to take in all that Pandora had shared. The smell of the coming rain paralleled the bleeding inside my chest. My heart was devastated.

I opened my eyes as the sky began to weep. Cool against my hair and cheeks, the rain fell light and steady, just enough to drown the crimson tears that flowed slowly from the crevices of my eyes. I turned away from the vampire who had wounded my soul, for weeping was unbecoming a prince of darkness. It was not the way of the hunter. Yet the hunter fell victim to the stinging words of the most beautiful messenger.

The scurrying of human feet could no longer be heard. Hundreds of lights from the town flickered off, then on, then off again, until they too slept. Pandora and I were not alone. The wolves growled and snarled and howled as they hunted. But the two of us were the only two immortal creatures within the surrounding thick blanket of trees, shrubs, and dead leaves. We were all that mattered. The rain began to fall hard against us, but it didn't disturb us. We welcomed it. God was washing me, cleansing me of the filth of weakness, cooling the fire that burst within, allowing logic and reason to return. My focus turned back to Pandora.

Pandora could feel the sorrow within me. The thought of Mynea loving another. The confusion of why she kept Vlad's existence from me. The betrayal of leaving my side, her powerful fledgling. *Did she really and truly love me?*

"Could she really and truly love you?" Pandora replied after listening to my thoughts.

I knew what she meant by this; however, the notion of a charade from my princess was blasphemy to my ears.

"You must understand, Aleron, we have a powerful and undeniable love for our maker. It's a natural and sacrificing protection from the origin of us all. Think of it. You know you would give your very life for Mynea. You know you would protect her at any and all cost, from any and everything that could cause harm to her. Well, my dear, we all have that affection for our maker and, since Vlad is the first of us, he's protected by the most powerful of his children, the ones who have a direct bloodline to him. And since he's the first of us, his strength and abilities are unmeasurable. To my vast knowledge, there's nothing that can break him or the bond that exists."

I needed for Pandora to continue, and so she did along with the wild howls of the night beasts who stalked much less powerful prey.

"Years had passed, and Mynea and I learned to live together under one master and lover. We were more than just family. We became the instruments of death for Vlad. He would send us to seduce anyone who could possibly hinder his quest for dominance and power. We would love them at sunset, then feed on them before sunrise. We became masters at disposing of the bodies. Entire families would be our victims some nights. Mynea became a skillful hunter, whose appetite sometimes rivaled my unquenchable thirst.

"The closer we became, the more Vlad loved us. He showered us with gifts. Precious stones, luxurious clothes, exotic and rare herbs and flowers. We were his princesses. His royal and loyal concubines. A personification of Persephone's two halves. We both belonged to Hades. We both loved our King of the Dead. And, though I learned to live with Mynea, I never forgave Vlad for his betrayal.

"Many nights I withdrew into myself and needed to be alone, to hunt alone. I still felt Mynea to be an impostor and an unsuitable substitute. Whatever I felt didn't matter in the slightest to Vlad's will. He knew my feelings and would often speak to my mind with these simple and suggestive words: 'With time, my love. With time.'

"It wasn't long before Vlad's quest for more power led him to encourage us not only to feed among the aristocrats of society but to violate his rule of never condemning another to the life of the damned. His thirst for domination persuaded him to duplicate in others what he had in us, devotion to the death.

"He would begin to tell us what drew us to him more and more, which was his way of teaching us selection. Vlad wanted us to make two become many. We were to make more vampires. Mynea was reluctant. I, however, welcomed it. If it would please him, I was quick to oblige.

"Soon our threesome became many. I selected the most beautiful mortal specimens to receive the dark gift of immortality. Calisto was the first of my brood. She was followed by Amaltheia, Cymone, and Danae. And once I began, I, too, thirsted for more. My daughters were all extraordinary in life. Like myself, they, too, became exceptional in death. Together my brood and I would target the outlying towns throughout southern Romania and drink its inhabitants dry. Before long I was bestowing the thirst unto many others as my daughters began to multiply themselves, and before the turning frenzy ended, twenty-seven immortals filled my succession. We all served Vlad. He loved all of us, and none of us simultaneously. My daughters loved him because I loved him. We remained in his love because we loved him. In loving him, we willingly gave our souls to him to command.

"Mynea was different from me in fulfilling our duty. Mynea had just learned to stomach Vlad's love for me and was crushed by the love he apportioned to my daughters. Mynea chose mortal women who were defiant in life and thus less loyal in death.

"Despite Mynea's daughters' inherent flaws, we still grew as a whole. Many female vampires spread across Vlad's vast growing empire, the most loyal lieutenants a general and commander could ever ask for. We were all devoted to our beloved prince. As for me and Mynea, we had the absolute devotion of those we made. Vlad was truly a ruler among a sea of princesses, yet he took no favorites among them. Vlad would frequent many and any of our bedchambers. Each and every immortal would be pleasured by our master, for his lust was insatiable, his hunger, unmatched. Some of our fledglings would bring him victims, and he would sometimes share. Sometimes he invited all of us to Budapest where he would host an aristocratic ball. Of course, the true purpose was to expand his wealth and indulge all of our lustful desires to feed. He was masterful in his execution, never leaving the slightest detail to question. Truly a ruler. Truly our king.

"However, the confession Vlad revealed to me the night I was forced to accept another woman into our life, an immortal, would prove to be everlasting in his psyche. Our immortal father and master was still a slave to the lives of the living. He was still trapped by his lust for life through a mortal vessel. It is a prison the elders of our kind all come to know. Unexpectedly, we came face to face with another of his bloodline, Natasha."

Pandora stopped for a moment, though I never took my eyes off her. I could see her smile with the introduction of Natasha, but it was not a smile of happiness. It was more a smile of satisfaction, the feeling she must have felt during that time. She reveled in the existence of Natasha. And though Vlad repeated his betrayal, Pandora was content.

"Natasha was from the land north of the Euphrates, where the women grew tall, slender, and beautiful. Men traveled from all over those vast lands to capture a bride in exchange for their wealth. Natasha typified a red-haired society of unusually flawless females. True royalty from the depths of common birth, Natasha epitomized a princess, though her parents were common. Knowing Vlad, she had to be the absolute best among her peers. Not as young as Mynea and I, but equally radiant— some might say even more beautiful, or exotic, given the color of her eyes and hair. She had the height of a male and the grace of a lynx. Truly, she was an alluring specimen, an enticing vampiress.

"I had never before felt such hatred emanating from Mynea."

Pandora's voice had retreated to a mere whisper, as if in opposition to the thought of any woman, mortal and immortal alike, being compared to and exceeding her own beauty.

"Natasha's presence was a shock. However, I somehow felt relieved in this new situation. It confirmed that Vlad saw no difference between me and Mynea. However, Mynea didn't take in Natasha with open arms. Instead, your vampire mother withdrew into herself, writing in the journal you now carry with you. I can never mistake the stench of it. And though its contents are a mystery to you, I know the day will come when all is made clear.

"Mynea also, for the first time in her existence, began to defy Vlad openly. Her disgust with Natasha, and Vlad's affection for her, led her to set a plot into motion. For the next several years, there grew a blood feud between the two. I myself enjoyed the new element of excitement to an existence that often seemed lifeless.

"The resentment between my immortal sisters became less important to Vlad, for there was another matter that drew his attention entirely. One of the fledgling vampires of Mynea's bloodline did something unspeakable.

"You see, Aleron, until that moment, there were only female vampires, save Vlad. Creating another male was never considered. Many of us thought of it, but we never dared to try, for our master was all we desired and needed. Apparently, Sasha desired more exclusive companionship. Mynea knew of this, yet she allowed it to happen. Stranger still was Vlad's inability to read the thoughts of all those who were born from Mynea. It seems our master's gifts had limitations."

# CHAPTER 19

"Sasha was the first vampire Mynea ever made; thus she was very powerful, more powerful than all others in Mynea's bloodline. Not because she was the first, but due to Mynea's inexperience in making another. The feeling we get when we make another is equaled to the feeling we get when we drink. Without knowing how to control it, we overindulge. Thus, Mynea infused Sasha with much more blood than she did with all others. However, I suspect you're an exception in this respect also.

"There are ancient techniques vampires use when deciding on a mortal to give birth to. The mortal is watched and studied for whatever amount of time it takes for the vampire to decide. Mynea didn't find Sasha on her own. She saw Sasha in the memories of Vlad while sharing a blood kiss. And although Vlad ultimately showed no interest in the mortal woman, Mynea gave birth to her to ensure that Sasha's allegiance would ultimately be with her.

"Mynea was made powerful, for Vlad feared that if she were weak, I would undoubtedly be the instrument of her destruction. I admit he was right. If the source is powerful and unskilled at passing on the gift of darkness, the result would be a fledgling vampire with enhanced immortal abilities. Sasha was no exception. Her strength rivaled Natasha's. However, she would be no match for her maker or myself. As for our young sister, Natasha, Mynea loathed her, and with that knowledge I made sure no harm came to Vlad's youngest fledgling.

"Vlad lavished affection on Sasha as he did on all within his harem. However, Sasha wasn't deeply in love with our master like the rest of us. She found solace in the company of mortal men. And before many moons had passed, Sasha took particular interest in one man, who carried the name Seth, and she decided he would be worthy. She made Seth into an immortal."

Pandora smiled again while speaking about this male fledgling, a sinister and calculating smile. I was captivated by every word she spoke. She knew she had my undivided attention, my reasons being a combination of curiosity and mesmerism. She reminded me so of my princess. It had been a long time since I had encountered beauty for the likes of which nations would go to war. I continued to listen.

"Sasha kept her immortal lover at Carfax, in England. Vlad hadn't set his eyes on England at the time, and it proved to be a fitting abode. It was in a vision from one of Sasha's sisters that Vlad came to realize Seth's existence. A male had penetrated where no other male had ever existed. I remember as if it were happening moments ago.

"Vlad invited a plethora of souls for us to devour just after midnight in Bran. The feast quickly became a blood orgy of screams and death. It was pure ecstasy. Vlad often loved to watch his children play. It excited him. Everyone was present whenever our father brought such a gift. However, this night, Sasha was nowhere to be found. Vlad's expression suddenly changed as he called to Mynea. He spoke to Mynea's mind, and she replied in kind. Mynea silently called out to Sasha, and Sasha answered. Mynea returned to the main hall, and Sasha entered moments later. She wasn't alone.

"Silence gripped the hall. Whispers began to muffle the sound of Vlad's beating heart. Sasha took Seth's hand and walked with him through the bloodbath and scattered dismembered human remains. His eyes were astonished, fueled by the awe of Bran's grand room, which was adorned with marble statues, ancient pagan mosaics, and an elaborately painted ceiling depicting a war between the Ottoman Turks and Christendom, a massacre in which the artist included the eventuality of the Turks who were captured alive: impalement. The picture characterized on the ceiling was similar to the blood-soaked floor below.

"The other vampires parted as she passed and regrouped behind her. She turned and acknowledged Mynea as she led her new vampire lover to Vlad, seeking his approval.

"Vlad's children stared as he stood up from his enormous throne of carved wood, gold, bronze, and silk. The candles became torches. The winds were awakened and could easily be heard beyond the castle walls. Clouds filled the sky as the moon was blanketed. The young male knelt in submission on one knee before his master. Sasha stepped back and stood beside Mynea. Silence returned as Vlad approached the male.

"Vlad looked at him carefully. He began to walk slowly around the fledgling. His mortal age was no more than twenty-four years, which could be easily deduced by his naturally muscular stature and strong chin. His eyes were as dark as dried blood, his hair long and dark, magnificently groomed. Seth's clothing consisted of black trousers, overshadowed by a flowing cloak covering his massive and hairless bare chest. He was truly a specimen to be envied and desired. The others were intrigued by this new male. Surely, this newfound infatuation accentuated what was to come next.

"Vlad told Seth to stand as he continued to walk around him, examining him from head to toe. Seth was slightly shorter than Vlad, though it was difficult to tell. Sasha was concerned yet proud of her choice. Vlad's face changed from one of inquisition to disgust. He was visibly unpleased. He was sickened and offended at the very sight of this foreign male. It was an insult to his house and coven.

"Seth attempted to speak. But without warning, Vlad captured his words by grabbing the young vampire by the throat and lifting him into the air. Sasha tried desperately to rush to his aid, but Mynea grasped her arm, making it impossible. Seth struggled and fell to the floor as he broke free from Vlad. He quickly recovered. They began to stalk each other in circles while displaying ferocious teeth, deathly sharp talons, and beastly groans. The fledgling's arms outstretched as did his fingers and elongated nails. His face became more menacing than that of a wild animal.

"The skin surrounding Vlad's eyes retreated as they grew wide and black. His face, too, became something extraordinary, resembling the monster that chased my brothers and me the night I was born to darkness. Vlad's hands no longer were those of a graceful and elegant vampire. They had become those of a wolf man, full of tangled brown hair, fingers long and thick, nails sharp as chiseled bone. His cloak began to move on its own, much to the surprise of the rest of us, willed by a seemingly independent invisible force.

"The fledgling lunged toward Vlad as a cheetah would pounce on prey. However, this cheetah didn't realize his prey was a lion. Our king's cloak wrapped Seth's body completely as Vlad leapt over him. Before Vlad landed squarely afoot, he grabbed Seth's head and ripped it off. Blood erupted from the neck poking out of the apex of the living cloak before the garment unraveled and released the headless body. Vlad held Seth's torn head over his as the body remained animated, crawling in search for its head. The vampire's eyes still moved, mouth outstretched, exposing his vampire teeth. Vlad began to drink the dripping nectar gushing from the bottom of the severed head. While doing this, Vlad's eyes sought Sasha. The vampire concubines watched, some in disbelief. Some smiled at this night's offerings.

"Sasha's rage allowed her to break free of her mother's grip, and she appeared before Vlad. Before she could strike out or do whatever she meant to, two other immortals swiftly grabbed her and held her down to Vlad's feet. She struggled for her freedom, and without the strength to overcome her cousins' hold, she screamed. Mynea dared not move as Vlad looked right into her eyes. Mynea turned away, and her eyes found Natasha, who was standing next to me, smiling.

"Seth's body finally came to rest as Vlad tossed his head to the ground in front of Sasha, whose eyes were filled with tears of blood. She continued to struggle with the other immortals who held her.

"'Let her go!' Vlad said in a monstrous voice.

"The vampires released her and disappeared into the crowd of forty-two as swiftly as they had arrested her. She rose to her feet. Full of hatred and emotions, she raised her arm to strike her master. Vlad caught her arm and secured the other. He then bit down on her neck as the lion completed the assault on his prey. She gave out a cry, withdrew her hand, and reached for Mynea, who didn't move. Vlad continued to crush her throat as he drained her dry. Within seconds she was immortal no more. Vlad tore her throat with his enormous and unforgiving teeth and released her bloodless body to the stone floor below. She lay next to her fledgling male, headless and lifeless.

"The winds returned calm. The torches became candles. Vlad's cloak rested as his hands regained their preternatural beauty. And as Vlad retreated into his throne, his eyes became a deep blue. He raised his hand to address his coven and said, 'Continue.' And with these calmly spoken words from his blood-filled mouth, the feast resumed.

"Visibly shaken, Mynea left the main hall for her bedchamber. Sasha's remains were discarded into the moat. Her fate would be the same as the fate of all the delicacies of the evening.

"I've witnessed Vlad devour and dismember many mortals to quench his insatiable thirst. I've witnessed Vlad feed on many large horses, camels, and even bears, all of which he would leave unrecognizable to the human eye. This night, however, he seemed extraordinarily beastly. The very thought of a male immortal within his family was deeply troubling for some reason. I could sense something else in Vlad's thoughts that didn't involve this male. I sensed the pure contempt for this fledgling originated elsewhere, another distant and unknown event in Vlad's long life, one he would shield from our blood kisses for all eternity. I know something else exists. Perhaps someone else existed or still exists."

Pandora was implying the past or present existence of another male immortal. Mynea never revealed the existence of such a rule or the notion of my becoming having been an act of treason. I was still confused as to why she had left. I continued to listen to Pandora, leaning against a moss-covered elm for support during the remainder of her account.

"From that night forward, Vlad forbade the turning of any mortal men. We all feared ceasing to exist. Sasha's demise was a point well made. This blasphemous act was never to be repeated. Until now."

Pandora turned toward me. "Your existence will spell the end of you and Mynea once Vlad comes to know of you. If you want to live, then you must stay far from the Carpathians, far from your immortal womb. Mynea must become a forgotten memory, lest your thoughts betray you to another. Be forewarned, there are many of us. Some as ancient as I. Some as young as you. I fear there may even exist other immortals who are as ancient as Vlad. All are a danger to you."

"And what of Eliza? What have you done with her?"

"She's safe, Aleron. Under the protection of one of my loyal gypsies of this region. No harm will come to her. And I've provided what she needs to survive."

"Why would you protect that which is so precious to your first enemy?"

"Had it not been for your affection for Eliza, my mind would already be swimming in her thoughts, while her blood coursed through my veins."

"Why do you protect what is mine?"

"I've a particular interest in you, Aleron. You see, I am ancient. Life as an immortal can become quite uneventful. I rather enjoyed the death of Sasha and her fledgling prince. I rather enjoy seeing the fire in Vlad's eyes. I feel that fire will return once you disregard my warning and seek Mynea."

"How are you so sure I'll go to her? How do you know she won't return to me?"

"Oh, my dear young prince. I've lived for centuries and have come to know the irrational reflexes regarding matters of the heart. And besides, I've seen it."

"You've seen it? What do you mean?"

"What did Mynea teach you? Do you know some of us can see beyond the boundaries of time? It's one of my gifts that has grown stronger over the decades. I only need to be in somewhat close proximity to someone, and I can see his other life as if it were my own, a story revealed to me by mortals and immortals alike. Though I can see only a few months into anyone's path, it doesn't take any of my powers to know your intentions."

"What of my intentions with you? What does the future hold for you and me? Why are you telling me these things? Why have you come to me?"

"I'm here, Aleron, because I choose to be."

"There's more?" I became more agitated and forceful with my questions. Walking toward her, I asked, "Why have you left your lover and master?"

Pandora didn't retreat, yet she didn't stand firm. She welcomed me. Her eyes and the smirk on her face told me. "For an eternity, we all loved Vlad. We all wanted desperately to please him. And in doing that, we all have accepted each other as his concubines and means to increase his power. But this devotion comes at a price. And I've well paid and endured beyond what any other has. My birthright has been stripped from me.

"You want to know why your beloved Mynea has left you? It seems the immortal heart also desires what it cannot have.

"Vlad showed the same interest in all of us. Thus he showed interest in none of us. We were all special to him. Thus, none of us was special. Every one of us wanted to feel he loved us more than the others. None felt this as strongly as I did. And as the years passed in Mynea's absence, I noticed a subtle change in our master. Vlad began to miss her. For the first time since the days of Vlad and me, I saw emotion in him. No one else noticed. He longed for her as the years progressed. He began to see less of us, and he hunted more frequently. His hunts weren't only for his lust for blood; they included scanning the minds of hundreds of mortals a night for any sign of her. To him, Mynea was lost. To me, she simply left.

"She left to find you. Mynea left to make you. She left to love you. Mynea realized what I've come to know decades ago. None of us will ever truly remain in Vlad's favor for all eternity. In time, we want what mortals want—absolute, exclusive, and unconditional love. Vlad has always given unconditional love. However, with a harem, absolute exclusivity is impossible. In her absence, Vlad began to again feel love, but this time for an immortal—at least as close to love as Vlad can get with a vampire. It's truly a case of absence playing tricks on a longing heart."

Pandora's story was a window into our origin, into my origin. She revealed to me the reason why I existed. Vampires exist to bring death in order to live. We were God's balance, if not the bacterium or virus, or war or famine, or unforeseen chance, or the slow passing of time; the vampire was the last bringer of oblivion, the last souls to mimic those of angels in everlasting life as the chosen few. It was then that I knew Mynea never truly loved me.

There were no lies or deception in Pandora's words. She shared absolutely.

As for Vlad, I wouldn't make the mistake of my predecessor.

## CHAPTER 20

hat sunrise, Pandora and I slept together beneath the earth. She was familiar yet foreign to me, and the urge of desire burned within me. "Take me," her mind often said to mine. However, I didn't. She was indeed beautiful by mortal and immortal standards alike. She was graceful and angelic in her demeanor and countenance. Any mortal man would have fallen at her feet and answered her every demand without hesitancy. Her lush eyelashes fell softly over adolescent eyes that brilliantly shone. Her well-sculpted mouth was complemented by her nose and her full and succulently blushed cheeks. A worthy replacement she was, but Mynea she was not.

The next night would be the same as the previous ones. Pandora and I would talk, then hunt, then talk again. The coming of the sun would mark the time for our comfort. She wanted desperately to be held by my noticeably harder body. And I wanted to continue feeling her hair beneath my chin as we lay. I needed to smell her scent while I slept. I needed her blood to calm my heart. I longed for her touch to remind me of what once belonged to me, two solitary creatures living together to soothe the other.

I knew then Pandora also sought what Vlad couldn't provide. She needed me to love her. It would complete her betrayal of Mynea. The urge to share more than just a blood kiss grew as we continued to spend every waking moment together. Every dusk she would offer herself to me; I would refuse. As time passed, my refusals became a game to her, a challenge she welcomed.

Her passion began to awaken long-dormant feelings. Soon the very sight of her led to arousal. My dreams would be filled with visions of our embrace, my thoughts drowned by my desires and her persistence. And after several months, my lust took over me, and I was hers and she was mine.

Night after night we danced. And she loved with such intensity. Her lustful actions were fueled by her hatred of Mynea and magnified by the betrayal of her master. Our animalistic ritual became more and more frequent. We didn't wait until we were in the confines of our various resting places. Often we would find dark corners just out of sight. Rooftops became a favorite. Under some moons we would dispose of an entire family and embrace each other in every room throughout the humble abodes they had resided in.

On more than a few occasions, our lust would precede our meal, and we'd get caught by our victims. A man and his lady for the evening returned from a night on the town to his home where death danced in the shadows, dismantling the elegant furnishings within without regard. The woman screamed and interrupted our tango. We took this as a request to join us. And join us they did, victims that Charon ferried across the River Styx into Tarturus, though this pair had no coinage to pay the ferryman. And thus we delivered them both, bloodless and lifeless.

It was a game of love, lust, hunger, and life. With every waking moon, Pandora and I grew closer. And as we did, my remaining humanity drifted further and further away. I no longer sought only the guilty; I sought the good and evildoers alike. I also thought of Mynea less and less, though she would never leave my thoughts entirely. Pandora knew this. However, it didn't deter her lust for me. And my lust for her grew equally with hers for me.

She didn't lie in her desire to share all that she knew with me. "Aleron, you've yet to inquire about an important vampire ability. You've learned the basics of survival as an immortal and have come to respect your weaknesses while exploring your gifts. You've grown much stronger than I or Mynea could have imagined."

I already knew what she was going to say next. There was only one blatant vampire ability I hadn't inquired about. Until that moment, I had never cared about what she was referring to. I'd been perfectly fine with living with Mynea, then Eliza, and now Pandora. I felt no need to make another.

"My love, it's your inherent nature. You won't be truly fulfilled unless you make another, one with complete devotion to your life, one that will praise and protect you from all others. We vampires can be solitary creatures. However, we learn that survival calls for devoted companionship and protection from other immortals who may want to harm us. You know I won't be here forever, Aleron. Just as well, our passion and desire to be together won't be strong enough for an eternity. You know there'll be a time when you'll leave and claim what is yours. Before this can be done, you must embrace all of what you are. And you are a king! You are sovereign! Why else would you grow more powerful with every cycle of the moon? You have undeniable purpose, and to achieve its totality, you must protect yourself. You alone will not survive a millennium."

Pandora spoke with sincerity. She spoke what she knew and understood to be true. She was grooming me for a future I couldn't see at the time but one that she could see.

"There exists one such mortal who is already devoted to you, Aleron. You've already poisoned her thoughts and filled them with overwhelming feelings of lust and desire for you. You left her and promised to return to her. She still waits for you. Each day is agony for her. Every night she longs for her immortal prince to appear. You see, she was completely under Mynea's spell, but it was never love. You, my dear, didn't cast a spell over her. She simply fell deeply in love on first sight of you, despite being within the arms of her powerful and beautiful mistress. When you shared your blood with her, you filled a void created by your presence. You knew this when you let her suck your blood and couldn't stop the flow on your own. She did. She's proven her strength, and now you must go to her and complete her transformation."

"Where is she?"

"I'll take you to her. Let us go now."

Swiftly we left the wooded area and proceeded toward the Suez Canal. Pandora and I traveled so expeditiously that even the wind was undisturbed by our assault. People were but a blur. Voices were meshed sounds that resembled music. The water of the Suez felt cool beneath our feet, which barely grazed the surface of the majestic gulf.

I knew soon after our departure where we were going, to the Sinai Peninsula, the city of Sharm el-Sheikh. We closed in on a large home, which suffered from the passing of time and abandonment. The road leading to it had been overgrown with greenery, making it nearly impossible for humans to travel. It stood alone atop a badly eroded hill, a fitting place for a vampire. There was no need to use the front- or lower-level doors. Instead, we entered through one of the open windows on the second level. It wasn't long before I could feel her presence. She slept in the room adjacent to the one we entered. Her thoughts and dreams reflected visions of me. Her sweet, inviting, yet silent voice called out to me. Did she know I was near? Could she sense my return to her, even in slumber? Or was this her nightly ritual and daily desire?

Pandora took my face in both of her palms. On tiptoe, she lifted her lips to mine and took comfort in stealing a kiss.

"Go to her, Aleron. She's waited long enough."

Before I entered her room, I could sense the essence of another woman. She was no longer in the home, but it wasn't long ago that she had been standing in that very room.

"Pay no attention to your thoughts, Aleron. The one you sense is far away and was here under my command."

I could tell no malice or falsities escaped her lips. The mortal was to watch over Eliza for the weeks Pandora and I danced.

I thought the door to open, and it happened. I walked in. Eliza was still asleep, moaning in full captivity of her surrealistic dream. Her body moved as if being caressed by some invisible specter. I drew closer to her bedside and spoke to her mind. *Eliza.*

Her eyes slowly opened, and I came into focus. They grew wide and twinkled with reserved excitement. Her smile began to replace the expression of disbelief.

"Aleron," she said softly. "You came for me."

I said nothing. I simply marveled at her beauty, knowing this would be the last time I looked upon her in this form. The cover fell as she reached for me, her naked body partially exposed and warm with life. I embraced her. Though my eyes were now closed, I knew Pandora was moving away from us. Slowly she withdrew, retreating to the adjacent room.

Eliza's thoughts were full of questions, but she asked only a few. "Did you think of me, my prince? Did you think of me as I thought of you? I longed for you every moment. My dreams were consumed by your presence. I lived to slumber, for that was the only way you would come to me. And now you're here. Did you think of me, my love?"

"Yes, I thought of you," I replied while holding her to my chest. She broke free of my cradled hold and pulled herself up to my face. Her hands caressed the back of my neck as her eyes closed. She began kissing me, and I responded in kind. My frostbitten lips pressed ferociously against her warm mouth, her tongue frolicking within the confines of my chilled aperture, my tongue searching for her life. The hunger returned with voracity and focus. I could feel the heat pumping within her body. I lifted her completely off the bed and embraced her nakedness. She wanted me within her. She had waited and dreamt of this very moment every night since my departure. I could sense the moisture building between her legs. Desire and feelings for her never left my heart. They were simply passive until that night.

*Take her, Aleron,* Pandora spoke to me in silence. *She's yours.* I obliged her request and command.

I lifted Eliza and gently laid her on the soft fur on the floor next to the bed. Beds were for humans, and I was an animal. I knelt down and spread her legs. She gave a gasp and raised her chin and closed her eyes. I could smell the succulence of blood.

Her menstruation was a delicacy to me. However disgusting that may be to humans, the daughters of men were delicate during that time and thus feel more passion when embraced. It was ecstasy for her and necessity for me, the perfect appetizer to our fleshy lust. My chilled, hard body was warmed up by the heat I stole from Eliza, the heat that she gave freely. I ravished her with a vampire's insatiable appetency and beastly execution.

Eliza's hands clawed at the fur as her arms splayed out. I tossed her onto her stomach as her back climbed into an arch of our covenant. I took her. She lay completely helpless, yet her desire was for more, and so I gave her more. Her neck invited the hunger within, the burning sensation of anticipation. Her life, I wanted. A birth, I will offer as payment. If I began to drink, I wouldn't stop. She would surely die, and immortality would be but a dream for her. The orgasmic cry she gave fully awakened the monster within me. I bit into her neck and began extracting her soul. In full submission, she pressed her neck up toward my mouth. She wanted to feed me. I continued sucking and feverishly stroking her moist flesh. She was on fire, and I was quickly rekindling my own.

Her movements, suddenly, slowed to a crawl. She could no longer hold herself up to me. Her heart began to fade, and weakness replaced intensity. She was dying beneath me. I turned her over and looked at her. Her eyes were wide and fixed on me.

"Finish it, my love," she whispered as her eyes grew heavy.

"I will not end your life!"

It occurred to me that I didn't know how to accomplish what Pandora commanded.

"Kill her, Aleron! It's the only way for you to give her life!"

I knew what she meant and what I must do. In that moment it made sense to me. I began drinking again. Eliza's eyes rolled back into her head. Her hands no longer gripped my neck. Her mouth lost all its luster and color. Her heartbeat became faint. I brought her to the brink of death. Now I must give her life. My blood! My soul! She must have it all.

Instinctually, I tore open my wrist and placed the blood-filled wound on her open mouth. The blood dripped onto her tongue. Only a few moments passed before she began to suckle. With my blood flowing into her, her eyes opened again, her body reanimated with a single purpose—to drink more blood.

She clutched my forearm with both hands and gripped tighter than a vise. Something strange began to happen to me. I began to feel weak. This feeling was unlike any felt before. My fingertips began to tingle. My legs began to shake. My arms grew numb, and my eyes desperately wanted to close. I felt Eliza's pull on my soul. It became an unbearable and delicate balance between life and death. Immortal death!

*Give her more, Aleron. The more you give, the stronger she'll be.* Pandora's thoughts filled my head.

I felt paralysis taking me. It was as though the sun were rising, even though dusk was hours away. Eliza's entire body held onto mine, restricting my movements. We became a symbiotic pair. She was getting stronger; I was getting weaker. The memory of the darkness overtaking me in the water rushed back into my head. The feeling was similar in the sense of hopelessness and mortality. I broke free of Eliza's hold and tried to stand. Having failed at my attempt of rising, I stumbled like a drunken fool onto the foot of the bed, where I settled and, in a daze, watched what happened next.

Time stood still. Everything around us was frozen. Only Eliza and I were present. Sound was lost. Eliza's body began to contort unnaturally. She began to scream and shake uncontrollably. It was as if she were screaming inside my head, thunderously loud.

She stood and stumbled backward, breaking the small wooden table behind her. The glass of red wine that sat atop the table fell and broke against the floor, sending tiny shards of glass in every direction in slow motion. She continued to act as if her body was aflame, tossing and turning violently. Again she tried to stand, and again she was defeated. With her back against the wall, she used her legs to propel herself upward, her body possessed by some demonic spirit, desperately trying to awaken itself. Using the wall for balance, she tried to walk to me. I was much too weak to move. Her legs gave way, and she fell. Her head landed next to my knee. While she looked directly into my eyes, her screams ceased and became a cry, followed by a whimper. Her eyes begged me to help her, to somehow ease her pain.

I remembered the first time I consciously felt Mynea's blood within me, like acid. I was helpless to Eliza's cries. I could only watch, for I was also entangled between pain and pleasure.

Her body movements came to an end. Her eyes became a lifeless reminder of what was once mortal beauty. Now a gorgon. And in that moment, she died. I could almost see her soul escaping her breath. She was no more.

Pandora reentered the room. She looked at Eliza's body on the floor. "Gruesome, isn't it, my dear?"

"Yes," I replied. "Is she dead? Did I kill her?"

She looked at me with a smirk and uttered, "Watch."

I heard a noise from Eliza and turned to look at her once more. Waste began to escape her body. Her bowels were releasing onto the floor. I noticed urine had silently preceded this event. Moments later she took a breath, and life filled her lungs. Eyes still closed, her breathing began sporadically. I couldn't liken the rhythm to that of a mortal or immortal. Every few minutes her breast would rise and fall. She would continue in this manner for hours.

Pandora came to me and pressed my head to her breast. "Drink to regain your strength, Aleron. The sun is awakening, and you must take her to the bottom floor out of its harmful effects."

I did as she commanded. Pandora stayed behind and cleaned up Eliza's defecation.

I entered a stairway that led to a level deep within the bowels of the home. It was eerily similar to my cradle in Mynea's castle. We would be safe here, for no sunlight would ever find its way in. I laid Eliza on the stone floor and then struggled, in my almost paralyzed state, to get to the other side of the room, where I immediately lost consciousness.

❦

# CHAPTER 21

awoke just before dusk. I'd been waking earlier and earlier, with little to no effect from the remaining sunlight apart from a slight burning sensation that eventually became tolerable. I could taste Pandora's dried blood around my lips. The steady and unpredictable breathing of Eliza filled my mind, the stench of rotting flesh close by—her rotting flesh. My eyes focused on her. She was still lying in the very spot I had chosen. I recovered from the previous night, snapped to my feet, and walked over to inspect. She was still in a deep sleep.

Candles throughout the room were instantly lit, cued by my mind. The chamber was similar in luxury to Mynea's room in Cairo. The furnishings were so ornate as to have a life of their own. I saw deep, rich cherry wood that had been carved by a skilled sculptor in the style of Michelangelo. The portraits on the walls resembled Pandora, yet they were slightly different, and I wondered if they were portraits of her from when she was a mortal woman. The scene painted onto the ceiling was a bold parody of the Sistine Chapel, depicting, instead of the history of creation, two vampires reaching toward one another, separated by a winged angel with blood dripping from its feathers.

The furniture resembled the mental image I conjured when Pandora described how Mynea's bedroom had looked before her transformation. There were no windows in the room, but there was a second door, which was much smaller than the door we entered. This door was fit for a dwarf. Made of iron, it had hundreds of rivets displayed in a perfectly symmetrical matrix. There was a tiny opening for a key, which was large in proportion to the door. I turned my attention back to Eliza.

Though her shadow was full of life, thanks to the flickering candles, she didn't move. I knelt beside her and took her hand into mine. It was incredibly warm. I placed my hand on her forehead. It was an inferno. Every once in a while she would twitch and gasp, though her eyes remained tightly shut. Her mouth would open sporadically, the muscles in her jaw very pronounced as if to scream. However, no sound escaped her lips. The contrast of my bone-numbing coldness caused her to twitch even more as I ran my hands over her skin.

Eliza resembled herself except for the distinct skin blemishes characteristic of the dying or the dead. Her veins protruded beneath the skin, her lips cracked and dry. Death was at her door. Life eternal awaited on the other side.

"She's between life, death, and everlasting life," Pandora said as she appeared behind me. "Her body is dying, Aleron. It's the same process you went through. The same we all went through. You've started the process, but your work is not complete."

With my eyes still affixed on Eliza, I replied, "What else must I do?"

"If you leave her now she'll become vampire, but she won't be strong. She'll be easily defeated by other vampires, though no man will be a match. More blood is necessary to make her a powerful protector. You must do this now, while her body is still warm with what life is left. This is when our blood leaves its most powerful mark."

Again I punctured my lower arm and placed it over Eliza's gaping mouth. Like a reflex, her jaws closed tightly around my open wound. Her eyes remained closed, yet her pupils frolicked beneath the lids. I could feel tiny fangs biting harder and deeper into my arm. The pain was deliciously welcomed. Though I hadn't yet fed, I wanted to give almost every drop of my blood to Eliza. And as her thirst grew stronger, I grew weaker. Pandora stepped toward us and told me that was enough. It was difficult for me to release myself from Eliza's hold. Nevertheless, I managed to.

I fell back like a drunken vagabond as I tried to stand. Pandora made no attempt to catch me, though her eyes were fastened on my every movement. She was enjoying this. I felt excruciating pain and discomfort immediately following my collapse. My muscles were tense, my mouth was dry, and extreme hunger burned inside. Pandora finally came to me and again shared her blood. I felt strong enough to stand, but I was not yet my usually powerful self.

"Let us go into the night, Aleron. We need to feed."

We left to nourish our souls with that of a few unfortunate mortals. Driven by our ferocious appetite, magnified a hundred times by feeding Eliza, we devoured victims with ease. So many fell to our powerful and persuasive minds, I scarcely remember the number. Pandora's hunger was immense! She seemed to revel in the blood. Carelessly, she would pull her victims apart and allow the blood to purposely miss her mouth and drip down her face and chin, onto her sheer lavender gown. "It doesn't matter whether someone sees me," she said. "They would never live to tell a soul."

The males were as drawn to her beauty as the women were to mine. Though men weren't my preference, their blood offered more strength. Regardless the gender, the nectar was consistently sweet.

Our hunger satiated, we retreated to the shadows to talk. "Your work is done, my love. Eliza simply needs time. Time for her body to discard what it doesn't need and to strengthen what it does. When she wakes, she'll be a beautifully powerful specimen. You'll be proud."

"Why do I feel regret? Why do I feel I've condemned her to a life not meant for her? Eliza was good, and I feel she's now damned."

"She made up her mind to serve you the first night you shared your blood with her. You gave birth to a hunger in her, the likes of which you cannot imagine, for bloodlust pales in comparison to the infatuation of a mortal woman for a vampire man. She would go to the ends of the earth and blindly into destruction to please you. This is the quality your fledglings must have. This is why the master has always made females. The devotion is entirely different. It's unflinching. It's completely illogical and irrational; however, it is undeniable."

"And what of her love and devotion for Mynea, who shared her blood with Eliza before my existence? It was Mynea who gave her an unnaturally long life, almost as frozen in time as we."

"That's true, but it was you she fell deeply in love with. It was you who haunted her mortal dreams and whom she longed for in your and Mynea's absences. And now it's also you who's given her the gift of eternal life. Her devotion that will last an eternity. She'll be yours for all time."

I knew this to be true. I knew it to be true because of the love I felt and still feel for my immortal mother. I also knew that I would never love Eliza as I loved Mynea. Pandora knew this as well. However, she was right in her conclusion of Eliza's transformation. She was right about our love affair coming to an end. Pandora was the center of my affection, yet she was only a substitute for Mynea. Often, when in Pandora's arms, I could smell my princess. If even for a moment, my complete bliss returned and then faded into unrelenting reality.

Pandora and I returned to our estate to find Eliza still lying on the floor. Her breathing was now steady, and her open mouth revealed fangs larger than those that pierced my skin just hours before. Pandora left the room as I continued to examine my fledgling becoming.

Eliza was again lying in filth. Defecation wasn't the culprit; it was fleshy filth this time. True to Pandora's words and the memory of my first day as an immortal, Eliza began discarding her useless organs. The heap of organs resembled a fleshy soup. I recognized them in an instant, though it would be nearly impossible for a mortal to label them, save a doctor or the like. The liver, large and small intestines, kidneys, gallbladder, stomach, etc., were all ingredients in this soup du jour. Absent were the organs necessary to sustain life as a vampire. The stench was toxic and the rodents had already found their way in. I moved Eliza's cooling body away from the mess and allowed the rats to dine undisturbed.

This would save me the trouble of cleaning up. And besides, rats were a delicacy of sorts. I could feed on them after they fed on her. And indeed I did.

† † † †

Pandora and I filled the next two nights hunting, talking, and caring for Eliza, who remained comatose. Her appearance began to change, and I could see her breathing slow to a crawl each time the sun began to rise.

The stench had become intolerable, so Pandora drew a bath and washed Eliza's body of the rotting remains and filth. When her body was submerged in the water, Eliza flinched and twitched fiercely before settling back into a calm state, allowing Pandora to wash her.

I carried her back to the room where she could slumber peacefully. I could see more distinctly the changes to her appearance. Her hair was more radiant, her face slightly longer, her lips fuller, having adjusted to compensate for what hid behind them. She was almost entirely pale, save a few freckles surrounding her nose and cheeks. Her stomach was perfectly flat with the passing of certain internal organs. Though closed, I could tell her eyes were larger than before, her lashes full and eyebrows shapely. Her finger and toenails had also grown. The puncture wounds I inflicted upon her had vanished. She was even better and more angelic than her mortal self.

It may seem ironic to think of one of us as angelic, but were demons not angels that fell? Just as they were angels to begin, they resembled what they were in the end. Eliza as well as all other vampires were angelic, perfect beings, in a physical sense. Unblemished, she lay waiting to open her vampire eyes for the first time.

† † † †

It would be another twelve days before the hunger would reanimate her body. I remember returning only to find the room Eliza was resting in empty. I quickly scanned the structure with my mind and located her on the upper level. When I entered the room, Pandora was standing directly in front of her, blocking her from my view. I stepped toward them as Pandora turned to face me.

"She's beautiful, Aleron."

Eliza walked around Pandora, and I saw her eyes! They had changed and were now a reddish pink, clear and bright as a blood moon, her transformation complete. I stretched out my arms and she came to me. My bare chest lay against her naked body, the warmth of my last meal transferring to her chilled skin. We embraced, and I looked up at Pandora, who was smiling as a proud parent would.

I could feel the hunger within Eliza. "We must go and feed your thirst, my love. The night has been waiting for you."

The three of us left in search of her first vampire meal. The search wasn't long. Pandora vanished, allowing Eliza and me to hunt as a pair. I led her to an alleyway that I used to frequent when I needed a quick meal. It was perfectly situated just south of the main square, where people from all walks of life gathered socially. Every so often I would lure my victim to the alley, and they would be seen no more. I could have lured Eliza's first meal in the same manner, but it wasn't necessary. The meal came voluntarily. It seems the man caught a glimpse of Eliza as he tried to relieve himself in the shadows. I remembered snickering to myself when the boorish man failed to put away his penis as he walked over to Eliza, who was wearing only the near-transparent gown. "You lost, girl?" He asked while fixing his trousers and hiding his manhood appropriately. In her preternatural voice she replied, "Yes, sir. I'm lost."

With her head down in a submissive manner, she raised her eyes slightly, knowing the color of her eyes would cause suspicion.

"What's wrong with your eyes, girl? Have you been crying?"

He took her hand into his. "You're freezing! Take my coat and cover yourself." The man placed his coat around her shoulders and intended to give her warmth. As he made this chivalrous gesture, she grabbed him by his neck and began kissing him. He couldn't resist her allure, so he joined her passion. The man thought she was thanking him with a kiss, but he couldn't have been more wrong. She was tasting him until her thirst reached its peak and could no longer be contained. She drew back his hair and exposed his neck. With a swift and calculated movement, her opened mouth fully covered his entire throat. The man's muffled cry was silenced by the puncturing of his vocal cords. Eliza's eyes became dark red, infused with his blood. She sucked furiously, not allowing any of the man's blood to escape. Within minutes he was completely drained of life. She withdrew from him and allowed his limp body to find its final resting place on the damp hollow ground of that dark alley.

Eliza turned and looked at me. It was as though she just discovered life itself, eyes wide and red, mouth covered in blood, tongue licking her teeth. She basked in his memories and his aged soul. With the closing and reopening of her eyes she smiled and said one word, "More!"

And more she had. We fed frequently that night. It was nearly impossible to quench Eliza's thirst. If there had been any mortal prepared to become one of us, it was she. She had studied us. She had even known which blood to avoid and how to kill before becoming a vampire. She loved us with all of her heart. She had wanted to become immortal since the day Mynea took her in and shared life with her. It had been agonizing for Eliza to be an immortal trapped within the confines of mortality. That was why she called out to me, why she wanted more. She had wanted more for decades. Her destiny as a mortal now fulfilled, her future as a vampire had just begun.

# CHAPTER 22

n the weeks and months following her birth, Eliza came to realize her natural vampire abilities. We lived as a family: I, the father; Pandora, our mother; and Eliza, our child—and what a brilliant child she was. Every lesson was executed with perfection. In a few months Eliza began to hunt on her own. Gender mattered not to her; men and women were equally her victims. There was no particular pattern to her killing. She reminded me of my immortal mother, for she bled anyone who had the misfortune of crossing her path while she was thirsty. Eliza was exceptionally beastly with the disposing of the bodies if she were lucky enough to dine on a criminal.

By chance, she came upon a murderer of children in the city of Tikrit. He was a former Iraqi doctor whose lust for death went unchecked and unknown for years. Eliza made him pay for his sins a thousand times over. She brought him back to our home and placed him in the scavenger's daughter, a torture device handpicked and modified by Pandora and used to demonstrate the will and boundless treachery Vlad expected from his beloved coven.

This device was prevalent in sixteenth-century London and was an especially cruel way of torture. The victim's head was pushed down and the knees forced up into a crouching position. As a result, severe muscular cramps in the guts would precede blood being forced through the nose and ears. In time, the victim went from a state of acute suffering to one of madness. To add to this state of agony, Eliza would slowly feed on him as long as fresh blood oozed from his nostrils and ears. His prayers became incoherent and garbled noises. For six nights he cried. All the while Pandora observed just how cruel Eliza could be to those who were damned. I often wondered what fate lay ahead for the hunter of immortals, or if we were truly the zenith of the proverbial food chain.

† † † †

Pandora continued to tell me stories of ancient times when she and I lay together. She would read my thoughts and answer questions before I asked them. The only thoughts that would remain unanswered would be those that concerned Mynea. This didn't bother or surprise me, for I knew full well the ill feelings Pandora kept for Mynea. Mynea had twice managed to win the affections of their master from Pandora. Mynea personified her first and most hurtful betrayal. She represented the death of undivided love and devotion once shared between the eldest of us, a division between our Adam and Eve.

The union of Vlad and Mynea cast Pandora into the abyss of loneliness and despair, the type of hurt one never recovers from. I knew Pandora would give her heart to me if she could; however, it had died long ago with the birth of the third immortal. Her heart only maintained functionality, an organ and muscle charged with circulating dying blood throughout a decaying undying body.

Pandora poured herself into Eliza. The two were inseparable, with the exception of the few times Eliza would hunt on her own. Pandora, a mother to many, found intrigue in Eliza's bloodlust, and Eliza found a suitable replacement for her lost mistress. From two completely different origins, these two immortal females became kindred spirits, twin souls with a newly established singular purpose. That purpose began the night Eliza brought a human woman into our home.

† † † †

Well into the night I dreamed. Pandora and Eliza had left and returned, and into where I lay, they came. Careful not to wake me, even though I was well aware of their presence in that state, they placed my meal, a mortal woman, in the far corner of the room. The woman turned out to be much more than just dinner.

My eyes fully opened, and I turned without delay in the direction of her heartbeat. The woman stood, as did I. Completely naked, she began to walk carefully in my direction. This human woman was an exquisite specimen—dark, shoulder-length hair, brown eyes slightly slanted as if she had more than a touch of Mongol blood coursing through her veins. Her nose was perfectly proportionate to her face and mouth, and her lips full with luster and life.

Her thoughts told me her name was Sinaa, and she had been brought for my pleasure. I was obliged. I opened my arms to embrace her. As she stepped into my grasp, her body instantly flinched at my shockingly cold and hard touch. She relaxed, resting her warm, succulent breast upon me. Her hands began to explore my body, seemingly warming with anticipation and sheer desire for what was to come. She caressed my chest in a slow downward motion, ultimately finding my stomach and, alas, a slightly erect penis.

"Mmmmm," she whispered to me. I see you're more alive than your cold touch would suggest, my lord. Allow me to warm your blood and grow your interest."

I knew she was under Pandora's spell when she spoke. She kept her hand on my penis, rubbing, pulling, wanting it to respond to her call. Her touch didn't interest me as much as her heartbeat. I began to kiss her neck, and I felt her pulse through my tongue. Her heartbeat intensified as my penis began to respond to the blood meal soon to come.

"Ahh, yes, my lord. There you are. How wonderful you'll feel—"

While she was in midsentence, I pierced her neck with surgical precision. I didn't want her dead, at least not at the moment. Her warm plasma flowed through my body as she continued to feverishly stroke me. I laid her on her back, without removing my lips from her neck. She inserted me inside her warm soul. I drank ever so slowly in an effort to prolong her inevitable fate. I wanted to give her pleasure before I took her last breath. And so we were bound. Surreal visions of my intimate encounters with Pandora and Eliza plagued my mind. On her back she curled her legs around my body, thrusting me farther inside while maintaining the rhythm of the carnal symphony. Her breathing was no longer steady; the warm nectar continued to escape her body. Her eyes were now wide open, as if the feeling of pleasure and pain was too much for her soul to bear. She gave a cry as I felt her vagina squeeze intensely. She gripped me tighter. Her body shook uncontrollably, and though she tried to push me away to ease the stimulation, I continued to drain her. Her heartbeat began to subside.

It was time for me to retreat from my meal and from her body. I withdrew myself from between her thighs, still pulsating from ecstasy. Intercourse was secondary. I stood to my feet as her arms now lay at her sides. She was still looking up at me, too weak to speak. Her breathing slowed to a crawl as her eyes lost their glow. They now stared into nothingness. I whispered, "You indeed kept your word, Sinaa. I'm warm." And with that I left the room, knowing her end would come soon after. This, however, was where I was misled, for when I left Sinaa as an offering for Hades, Eliza entered the room.

I sensed Eliza in the room. However, before I could turn around, Pandora took me into her arms and began kissing me. I returned her kiss.

"I can smell Sinaa's scent all over you. She served you well. She was just the beginning, my love," she whispered to me. "She must now prepare her gift for you as only she can give."

I knew what Pandora meant! I knew then what they had been conspiring to accomplish. With Pandora still in my arms, I returned to the room where I had left Sinaa to die. Sinaa was alive and sucking from Eliza's bosom.

The mortal corpse had come back for an offer of immortality from my child. I stood still as Eliza's eyes rolled in ecstasy until they found mine. They stayed affixed on me as she continued to allow Sinaa to drink.

"Careful, my dear," Pandora said to Eliza. "She'll drain you completely if you allow her to."

Eliza pulled Sinaa away from her breast and released her. Sinaa's head fell back against the floor as her body began to violently twitch. I walked to Eliza and picked her up.

"My child, what have you done?"

"She's for you, my love. She's for us."

# CHAPTER 23

he next several weeks came and went as Eliza tended to her fledgling. Pandora paid close attention to Sinaa's tutelage, while guiding Eliza as she always had. I remained intrigued yet withdrawn from the happenings within my own house. I was anguished by the thought of losing my mortal mother. How selfish of me, I thought, for she lost me long ago, and I cared nothing for her loss, until then. When I was near, I could feel the life force of my mother barely clinging to this world. I couldn't help but feel she was holding on for a reason. That reason would be Shani, my mortal sibling.

As Pandora and Eliza continued their assault on the innocent and wicked alike, I, again, journeyed to Alexandria, to my father's home in al-Montaza. The night was crisp and cool, with flurries of snow entangled with the wind. I stood behind my father's home just beyond the large oak several yards away. From this distance I could sense my father and mother sleeping—she in her bed, he, ever watchful, in a chair slumped over his shotgun, which lay across his knees. All was usual until

I felt the presence I hadn't felt in decades. There, approaching from the east toward Aknon's home, was his daughter, my sister, Shani.

It was early evening, yet on that chilly night the streets were barren. Shani struggled with a suitcase while her free hand held her wool coat tightly at the neck. I remained in the shadow resisting the urge to assist. Her mind invited me in without her acknowledgment. Worry and fatigue filled her thoughts: worry for our parents, for me, and for another young boy. Shani had a child. Her reflection of his whereabouts was distinctly unfamiliar to me, a home of foreign design, unlike any that surrounded us, different from any I've seen in Europe and Northern Africa. I concluded her son was in the Americas, a land distant and obscure, a continent I wouldn't come to witness until much later.

I heard Shani's key enter the lock and release its hold. Aknon sprung from the chair with shotgun in tow. I broke my promise at that moment and entered through the same window I had before. Shani called out, "Father? It's me."

The door closed behind her as she continued past the kitchen and into the narrow staircase. While she climbed the stairs, her eyes met the eyes of our father who stood at the top. Wearing only pants and holding the gun, now at his side, he reached out for Shani with his empty hand. She joined him at the top of the stairs and, with a sigh, they embraced.

"I am so glad it's you, Shani," Aknon said tearfully. He then dropped the shotgun onto the thick rug lying at the top of the stairs.

"Are you all right, Father?" asked Shani.

"Don't mind me, child. My knees are not as strong as they once were, and that shotgun has become awfully heavy."

"There, there, Father," Shani said softly. "What enemies do you still have that you would greet your daughter with your gun? One that's almost as old as she?" A smile played on her lips as she leaned back and looked into Aknon's face, her arms still around his waist.

"Shani," Aknon said lovingly. "Please come into the room. She wants to see you."

Aknon, led by my sister, entered the room. I remained perfectly still at the opposite end of the hallway. No one had the slightest intimation of my presence.

Shani gently assisted Aknon to his chair, which faced the bed. Then she walked over to her mother's bedside. Her pulse quickened as her eyes fell upon our mother. I could see my mother through her eyes. Shani and Aknon knew death was upon her. Shani sat on the bed, facing my mother, and took her hand into her own. With the back of her other hand, Shani caressed our mother's face. Sorrow enveloped my sister as my mother began to subtly move. My mother opened her eyes and stared at her daughter. A tear escaped its crevice. My mother opened her mouth and said weakly through badly cracked lips, "Where have you been, child?" Aknon's eyes opened wide in disbelief, for it had been months since my mother had spoken.

"I'm here, Mother," Shani replied as she raised our mother's hand and kissed it. "I'm here."

My mother tried to smile, but her face would only allow a strange and malformed smirk to surface. Her eyes were veiny and red, brimming with tears. Suddenly, her breath became frantic and short. Aknon swiftly lifted himself out of the chair, sat on the opposite side of the bed, and grabbed his wife's left hand. I left my post for a final glimpse at my mother's life.

Though I stood in the doorway of the room, Aknon and Shani were still unaware of me. A moment later my mother gasped for air and slowly blinked. When her eyes opened, they were affixed on me! She desperately tried to speak, but no words escaped her mouth. The air in her lungs faded, and her gaze lost focus. Shani covered her face with both hands and began to sob as Aknon burrowed his head into my mother's bosom. I stood still, watching her soul escape its fleshy prison and return to the memory of its origin. A muffled and torturous sound came from my father as he, too, cried into the quilt covering my mother's body. I also felt grief. It was strange. I didn't feel sorrow for my mother dying; I felt sadness for the affliction I had caused her. As quickly and silently as I entered, I departed.

In those days, it was customary to bury the dead within one day of the death, so I returned after two days to say what I hadn't said to my mother when I became lost to her. And as I stood over her grave within an empty graveyard, I gave my final word to the snow and wind to carry into her faded vital force: "Goodbye."

The hour was late and the townspeople had retreated into their respective homes, with the exception of a few who remained chatting in the square and one who meandered slowly alone along a path that I myself had frequented on many occasions as a boy. This lone dove was my sister, grieving for the loss of our mother. I fought with myself regarding whether to speak to her or to simply remain a dead memory from her childhood. With quick deliberation, the brother in me chose.

I waited until Shani was virtually alone. I then appeared around the next corner she would turn. Her footsteps grew louder and louder until I heard a startled gasp of fright caused by the unexpected realization of a stranger leaning against the wall.

"Excuse me, my lady," I said while avoiding direct eye contact. "I didn't mean to startle you."

"It's quite all right," she replied while catching her breath. Shani then began walking again. Suddenly she stopped as if she wanted to turn and speak. I remained still. I heard her think, *He seems familiar.* However, caution overruled her query, and she began walking again.

*I am familiar*, I replied back to her mind.

She abruptly stopped and swiftly turned. "What did you say?" she questioned while trying to recall whether I spoke aloud or if she'd imagined it.

This time I spoke aloud, "I am familiar to you."

"Who are you?" she asked with a tinge of curious aggravation in her voice.

I began walking toward her. "I must apologize to you as I did to Mother, though she was no longer alive to hear me."

Shani's limbs stiffened as her heartbeat began to race. "Who are you?" she demanded in a manner reserved for the women of the new world.

I drew slowly closer. Calmly, I continued to speak. "I made a promise to myself the day I caused you to fall from the ladder and hurt your arm." Her eyes squinted in an effort to get a better look at me.

"It can't be. Aleron!"

My name coming from her mouth sent a bolt through me. "Yes, dear sister."

"But how? Where have you been?"

It was then that I came to look upon her closely. Shani was beautiful. At the age of forty-seven, she resembled my mother in her prime, long silken hair, absent the youthful curls that I had grown to love. Her high cheekbones were much less pronounced than before, her eyebrows elegantly outlined, hovering above dark lashes, enclosing honey-brown eyes. Those I remembered. She was much taller than before, of course, yet taller than average for a woman of Egypt.

"Where I've been is a story I will tell you when the time is better. For now, I must return. Just know that I've not forgotten you."

And as she reached up to touch me I moved swiftly into the darkness, then into the air. She was left standing alone with only a single word echoing throughout her mind: *Impossible*.

I left that night, never to return to al-Montaza. Shani remained a few more days only to witness the passing of our father, who had been overcome with grief. I provided the means shortly thereafter to purchase the home in Shani's name, though of this she was unaware.

And though I would never renounce Shani as my former flesh and blood, I had a new family to tend to, one who would be with me indefinitely.

# CHAPTER 24

trength was measured by many variables when it came to my kind. Vampires often gauge their strength in their ability to live: the ability to remain alive forever and protect themselves from other vampires. A single vampire can dispose of hundreds of humans in a single night. Our innate strength fueled by lust and hunger with an unnaturally acute ability to heal makes us nearly impossible to kill. However, regardless of foe, one mistake can ultimately spell mortality for us.

Pandora believed my life would come to an end the moment Vlad laid his sights upon me, and she had great reason to deduce that. However, I, too, began to see the future in dreams and through our sensual blood exchanges. This stolen ability gave me a window into her mind and allowed me to better understand what her plan was.

Her plan was simple: strength in numbers. She desired to grow my coven and thus protect me in the same manner Vlad protected himself and his assets, through the unconditional love and devotion from immortal children, imperishable female children. For even though I

existed and was adored by Pandora, she felt and believed in the pro-
hibition against the creation of other males. I, however, didn't give it
much thought.

† † † †

Night after night, my dreams spilled into my reality. I dreamed of my
parents, my sister, and Vlad. The dreams always began in a subtle
manner. Stolen memories would lead, immediately followed by lustful
appearances by Pandora or Eliza or both. Mynea sometimes replaced
Pandora in the blink of an eye, bringing to conclusion any role Pandora
formerly played, followed by Aknon and Camilia. Then I would hear
him. I would see his eyes. I would see his mouth, his teeth protruding
from his elongated, well-defined jaw. He would be instructing and nurturing various vampires. Some would have familiar faces revealed to me
from sharing with Pandora. Some remained unknown and I would only
hear their voices, as they passed in a blur.

In my dreams, Vlad was no beast. Through Pandora's memories I
recall legends of a king, formerly a prince, who conquered many with his
vast and relentless army, an army he commanded for centuries through
his mortal lieutenants' hands, lieutenants selected by him and controlled
by his family of vampires. I began to hear word of his conquest.

His growing territory of political influence and power was communi-
cated all over Europe and Northern Africa. Entire countries had bent to
his will and cunning persuasion. He had conquered kingdoms in a single
siege, both with and without the use of his army, for what his army
couldn't do, his concubines could.

In the year 1853, Vlad used a small force to slaughter twenty thousand Macedonian rebels. This was prompted by his promise to Macedonian rulers to rid them of the bothersome rebels pushing for civil
war. In fulfilling his promise, Vlad would gain a stronghold in the center of four important and desirable countries: Bulgaria, Greece, Alba-
nia, and Serbia.

Shortly thereafter, the conqueror set his ambitions on Italy. And within a few years, his Ottoman army staged a war against the kingdom. He wasn't successful in this conflict, however. But shortly after the Italian ruler found a new mysterious wife in Tripolitania, he contracted a mysterious illness that resulted in fatal blood loss, an illness that swept throughout the country.

His new wife was rarely seen during the day and was known for her unyielding beauty and massive dinner parties, from which some guests would not return. This private and sensual victory was carefully orchestrated and relished by Vlad. The resulting headless country easily allowed him to have influence on both sides of the conflict. He even, unbeknownst to the general Italian population, used some of the Italian soldiers for Turkish conflicts. Vlad's empire had in centuries long past slaughtered hundreds of thousands of Assyrians and Greeks. His influence played a significant role in the near global conflict.

Vlad seemed unstoppable. Indeed he was, to mortals, in every country and territory he conquered or controlled. I began to see his many castles and villas in my dreams. I also continued to see visions of Mynea as the new mother of us all. In one, she and Vlad stood towering over a large coven of vampires, she by his side. It made my heart ache and my anger boil. I wasn't angry that she was with Vlad; I now understood the bond that couldn't be broken. I was angry that she had left me. She lacked the courage that her first fledgling, Sasha, possessed. She didn't perceive me worthy to bring before her master. She simply left me in the dark, alone. My feelings, innate or learned, were strong for her and riddled with anguish. I knew then she would never truly leave my thoughts, my dreams, or my undead heart. Despite Pandora's prophesies, I desired Mynea, but I was not interested in initiating a conflict with an invincible foe who was as old as time itself.

Eliza and Sinaa were becoming a dynamic pair. Sinaa was taught the basics we all were taught as well as the use and control of her own unique skills, most of which had remained dormant. An intimate kiss with Eliza revealed to me an ability well worth noting. Following Sinaa, Eliza came across a band of thieves in Giza, just southwest of Cairo near the Arabian Desert.

The men, armed with rifles, sat ready inside an abandoned homestead. Eliza began to pillage the men as their guns posed no threat. She moved too fast for their pathetically inaccurate aim. While disposing of the men in a ferocious manner, Sinaa made a costly mistake, which distracted Eliza. Sinaa was shot several times by some of the men. Eliza turned in their direction, and with her latest victim in her left hand, hanging limp and lifeless, she raised the palm of her right in the direction of the four assailants seemingly overpowering Sinaa. Within seconds, gurgled screams fled their mouths as blood began to stream from their ears, mouths, noses, and eyes. They fell to the ground, each gripping their stomachs and chests. Within seconds, they were dead. After bleeding the remainder dry, Eliza turned her attention to the wounded Sinaa, who had made the mistake of drinking from the vein. Eliza opened her wrist and allowed her weakened fledgling to drink. With the infusion of Eliza's blood, her wounds began to heal and were reduced to mere blemishes within minutes.

Upon their return, Eliza's blood told me all. She wanted me to know that she could subdue the internal organs of humans at her will. She was proud of her discovery and even more proud that she could use this ability for the protection of our young coven, my young coven.

In time, our family grew. Some nights Pandora and Eliza would hold their own "invitation only" dinner parties and invite women from all walks of life, transporting them to our hidden abode. The evening would begin with the arrival of their guests, ushered in from private carriage. This was followed by music created by the fingertips of vampires. The preternatural melodies and rhythm would captivate the guests, who, of course, had never heard harps and violins played in this manner. Food would be served, but my children would only pretend to dine. Those who feasted on the offerings wouldn't notice my children's abstinence, dulled as they were by the steady stream of brandy wine poured into their cups.

As the night progressed, Pandora, Eliza, and Sinaa would have their meals. Only one, if any, was saved for transformation. The rest would suffer a more tragic fate. Some who weren't chosen for immortality would be bled entirely while the remaining watched in terror, then were burned before dawn. Others not chosen would be kept beneath the ground in catacombs under our el-Sheikh home. Once the chosen completed their transformation, they would dine on the poor souls who remained beneath us.

Every once in a while, I would be obliged to visit with the mortals in waiting, some of whom were brought to me by Sinaa. I adored Sinaa for her offerings and her beauty. All of my children were beautiful. In life they were radiant. In death and rebirth, they were exquisite! I was often amused by their games. They were happy to bring a smile to my everlasting stoic face.

It wouldn't be long before the disappearances were noticed. Signs were posted for the missing, and there was a growing fear that a serial killer was targeting women in the cities of Cairo, Gizeh, Tanta, El Faiyum, and Alexandria.

One of my youngest fledglings, Sakina, along with the first of Sinaa's brood, Raya, were reportedly seen with a few of the missing women. A witch hunt began in Alexandria, where they both lived when they were mortal. Pandora instructed both of them to let themselves be captured. This would end suspicion and return some normalcy to our lives in Cairo. They were also to confess to the slayings from the surrounding cities as well. It wouldn't take much to convince the lawmakers of their guilt. Pandora simply put some of the remains of the missing women in the basement of one of the homes rented by us in the names of Raya's mortal husband, who also met a most untimely and gruesome death at the hands of Eliza.

Raya and Sakina were decapitated in front of hundreds of spectators just as the sun set in Alexandria. In their last moments, they were both dressed in sack-like cotton gowns, hands bound with twine behind their backs, bent over what resembled a large, much-used butcher's block, with their necks outstretched. Their knees were fastened to the elevated wooden platform that also served as a stage. The executioners wore all black, including a black hood with two eyeholes.

One of the lawmakers signaled the executioner and, with one mighty chop of the axe, Raya's head sprang toward the crowd, landing just short of the edge of the platform. Sakina, having witnessed the beheading of her sister, began to turn her neck to the side in an unnatural way, looked out into the crowd, and smirked. In that moment another thud was heard by the menacing crowd, and Sakina's head settled next to Raya's.

The blood spewed onto the closest onlookers as the putrid-smelling reaper reached down and grabbed the decapitated heads by the hair and tossed them into the mob. All the while, the bodies searched for their heads.

The swarm became fiendish at the sheer sight of the execution, dancing and yelling in perverted amusement. They were mad to revel in such practices, men, women, and children alike. Bloodthirsty fiends! Vampires!

Pandora and Eliza were there to recover the heads, and they did so with such speed that the heads never touched the ground, seemingly disappearing right before the grasping onlookers eager for a trophy. The bodies were removed by the executioners, who soon were executed themselves just beneath the blood-soaked platform. Pandora and Eliza placed the heads upon the bodies, tore open their own flesh, and allowed some of their own blood to drip onto the necks.

The brain stem began to reattach itself to the top of the spine. Before long, Raya's and Sakina's eyes opened. The four of them disposed of the male bodies and vanished into the night.

Suspicions rose as the executioners' families complained of missing fathers and husbands. Plus, the bodies of the evil twins were never found. In time the story became folklore, then legend. Some believed Raya and Sakina were still buried in Egypt. Some have dedicated their lives to telling the story of the sister serial killers. A motion picture was made in their infamy. Mortals love to be entertained by us—and we love to entertain.

☨ ☨ ☨ ☨

From time to time, I would dream of al-Montaza, my father's home. In the dreams, I would always find him reading and thinking in his study. He would occasionally look outside his window, searching for any trace of his once-mortal son, a son who he knew was no longer human. In the dream, no matter how close I came to his home and no matter how well he searched, he never saw me. My father knew nothing of my presence, except the lingering feeling when he entered my mother's room after I had visited. The visions would always depict my mother dying. There was a burning desire within me to give her the gift of life everlasting, but the thought of actually doing this sickened me.

My mother, a vampire? Camilia, who spent her entire life making disciples of God? A soul whose light shone brightly, even to the angels in heaven, condemned to an immortal afterlife in hell on earth? It would be despicable! And if I had turned my mother, my father would eventually have had to be turned, too. I couldn't bring myself to condemn my mortal parents to hell. I began to understand Pandora's words about immortality.

As we lived, unchanged and uninhibited by time, we died a little each day through the mortals we loved. We watched them grow old and wither. As time passed we loved them from afar, lest they begin to take notice of our seemingly perfect and unchanging features. My father noticed this when he finally saw me.

Still, thoughts of the death of my mortal mother and father grieved me. My sister and her son remained my only link to the living. I understood why so many drove themselves mad after they received the blood kiss of life everlasting. They weren't able to handle our timeless existence. And with time, even the strongest of us began to waver. The only way to live was attachment. I was attached to my sister and to Mynea, as well as to my coven. However, Pandora was attached to memories and the days of old. She was changing.

Pandora began to withdraw. It was easy to pick up on her change since I'd witnessed it before. Then, I said nothing, because I didn't know what to make of it. Perhaps I chose not to see it, as I had when Mynea decided to leave. This time, however, my intuition was keen. I carefully observed Pandora's dealings with our young coven, and after seventeen months in my presence, I could easily see the change.

Aside from purchasing real estate and occasional words of welcome and direction for the young ones, Pandora was seldom to be seen with any of our family. Her visits to my bed on the highest level of our enormous home became fewer and fewer, as those nights were filled with fledglings. She wasn't jealous, for, as I explained earlier, Pandora no longer had her heart to give. She was preparing to leave.

One evening I waited for her in the courtyard in front of our estate. She arrived just before sunrise, knowing she would be alone since the coming of the sun sent the young ones in our family into a vampiric slumber. Her thoughts were unknown to me as she took slow steps to and fro. I called out to her.

"How much longer will you remain with us?" Judging by her immediate alertness, I must have startled her.

She turned swiftly and saw me sitting atop a massive stone depiction of a beast with a lion's head and the body of a gargoyle. "The sun's paralyzing effects on you are subsiding, Aleron. You've truly surpassed many who were born before you." She walked over to me for the embrace I longed for. I knew that she longed for my touch and that she wanted to share a kiss with me, to give me a glimpse of why she was leaving us. I got off the gargoyle and stood next to her. I bit her neck and drank; it was pure ecstasy revisited. I withdrew my fangs and continued with my tongue around the base of her neck. I closed my eyes for a moment, basking in the eroticism. When I opened them, she was gone.

I turned around swiftly and saw nothing but an empty courtyard, her scent fading in the night breeze. All she left me with was a vivid memory, a vision forced into my mind by her will. I distinctly saw Mynea in the reflection of the abyss, in the reflection of the eyes that haunted me. Pandora wanted me to see this. She wanted me to remember. I looked into the night sky and saw those same eyes within the moon, looking at me. Then as quickly as she had gone, they, too, vanished.

# CHAPTER 25

y dreams grew dark. I was the reaper of souls, the bringer of death, yet my dreams were even darker, saturated with despair. I traveled pathways to a destiny that was obscure, yet somewhat familiar to me. I saw myself in the eyes of those who were of him. I was invisible and immune to their touch. I ascended to the highest tower of his lair, where only remnants of what was once living remained, enveloped in the unmistakable stench of the slow decay of human flesh. I awoke many evenings with the smell still lingering from the dream.

Besides my dark dreams, an unknown voice had entered my mind, speaking to me whether I was asleep or awake. It spoke to me in riddles and unfamiliar phrases: *Whatever in you that is black compares not, for what you seek is a thousand times darker.*

The perfect baritone diction, no doubt from early fourteenth century Eastern Europe. He was speaking Romani Kapachi.

*Long is the way, but the path is not of your knowledge.*

At first I thought it to be Vlad speaking to me. But though it was supernatural, certainly immortal, and absolutely vampiric, I came to realize it wasn't the voice of Vlad. But how could this be? How could there be another male vampire other than Vlad? Was the call simply part of my imagination compensating me for feeling lonely, loathing the thought of living an eternity without what was rightfully mine yet painfully his? Was I subconsciously cursing my coven for lacking the nourishment I truly desired?

The sound was internal, and I felt it was driving me mad. Was this the loneliness Pandora spoke of? A feeling of isolation so great that it could bring the strongest of us to the brink of suicide?

Suddenly it occurred to me that if this voice were of an internal origin, it would naturally sound familiar to me. If not my own voice, it would be the voice of someone in my past, the articulation of my father or uncle or any other male who had managed to influence my life. If not a mortal, then I realized what I was deducing. It couldn't have been my imagination. It came from elsewhere and forced itself upon my mind for me to consider. I deduced that it originated from the thoughts, lungs, and mouth of an ancient one, whose power was so immense that I would briefly see crimson whenever it spoke to me. I concluded Vlad must also know of him, since he knew of Vlad.

Vlad had shielded this ancient one's existence from all of his children. The ancient one was why Vlad enforced the law that there could never be male children. Sasha's fledgling male had nothing to do with it. This must have been what Pandora sensed when sharing a kiss with Vlad, knowing he shielded this from her.

*In the beginning, I was there, and so I shall be at the conclusion.*

Who was he? Where did he come from? Who made him? Where is he now? All of these questions rushed into my head the moment my eyes sprung open, all relevant, yet all irrelevant compared to the most glaring query of them all: Why was he speaking to me? I heard it in my dreams, spoken from the mouth of the ancient one. I grew familiar with this tongue.

† † † †

Many moons had come and gone since Pandora's departure. I alone mastered this young yet powerful brood, and though I was essentially alone, Eliza never left my side. The first of my children born to me, she had given birth to all of the others. All of us shared a deep connection of the mind and heart. I could speak to my children through their thoughts, and they could call out to me through distance and necessity. I learned my desires would never be denied by them. They existed for one purpose above all others, to do my will.

Their devotion to me was overshadowed by one thing and one thing only, the thirst. Raya was especially keen at luring her prey to her. She was able to control the minds of many at once. Sometimes she would control an entire dinner party as a master puppeteer would, pulling the strings, controlling the limbs and thoughts of all those who played their part in her ghastly theatrical performance. Sakina would often provide the climax and denouement to Raya's plays. The two of them seemed inseparable in death as they were in life. "Twin killers," Eliza called them.

Sinaa was an entirely different matter. Upon waking, Sinaa would immediately disappear into the darkness of the alleyways of Thebes. Her victims would never hear her footsteps. She would simply snatch them from life and thrust them into a world of succulent pain. A proficient solitary hunter she was. Eliza was often surprised by the sight of Sinaa when she returned to our home, naked and covered in gore, wearing fleshy souvenirs from her nightly encounter. Her once beautiful hair would drip with her victims' blood, her hands and feet painted in blush, as was her face, save her yellowish orange eyes. In mortal life, Sinaa had been a teacher of literature. In death, she taught only one thing: suffering.

Sinaa wouldn't immediately put her prey out of their misery, so she was often forced to slaughter everyone in sight in an effort to maintain our secret existence. Her brutality left a barbarous impression on anyone unfortunate enough to discover the result of her game. The reports would classify the deaths as a monstrous attack by some unknown animal.

The locals of Thebes and her surrounding townships were in an uproar, for innocence was lost as my daughter continued to plague them.

Whispers of a grizzly beast that attacked at night were on their quivering lips. Fear and paranoia gripped the region, and at sundown, nary a soul could be found. Yes, Sinaa was depraved, indeed.

One evening I followed her, staying just out of her psychic reach, for without solitude, she wouldn't hunt. Her movements were graceful, her speed of travel across the lands to Thebes, without detection. As she propelled herself by leap, the leaves on the ground found it hard to determine the rhythm of her steps.

She came to an abrupt stop just outside of the palace of Luxor, which was enclosed by acres of land where dozens of animals were housed. Four large wooden barns contained stables where the animals slept. One by one she would gorge herself with sheep and goats, sinking her teeth into their throats, suffocating them while draining them. Her mouth, neck, breast, torso, arms, all of her, down to her feet, would be covered in the animals' blood and hair.

Horses in the stable became restless, bucking and banging against the stalls' thick wooden doors and walls. My vampire ears could hear the cracking of the horses' bones while she relished in them. The clanging of the locks against their hooves woke the estate keeper.

A light came on from the small house in the back of the estate near the stable. I flew to a nearby tree and watched as the keeper crept over to the stable's rear entrance with a shotgun in his hand, carefully stepping over bloody carcasses of sheep and goats. The beast he sought was in the stable, and he meant to shoot it and rid the property of the monster.

He entered the stable and saw what appeared to be the back of a woman bending over a horse, whose back legs were awkwardly and sporadically flinching as it lay on its side at her feet. He heard the sound of ripping flesh and gnawing bone, though he didn't quite know what to make of it. The keeper took sure, quiet steps toward Sinaa and her meal. She knew he was there.

"What the hell are you doing?" he yelled.

The noise grew louder as the other horses tried desperately to flee their stables, some kicking powerfully with their hind legs, others banging against latches with their front legs. Sinaa stood slowly, the legs and neck of the fallen horse twitching with echoes of life it had once possessed.

The sight of her dripping in blood rapidly evaporated the keeper's confidence. He nervously raised his gun, fired a shot from the barrel, and a deafening boom trumped the noises made by the horses' agonizing protests. The buckshot hit its target square on her back.

Sinaa didn't flinch. She stood tall. With her back still to the keeper, she did something unexpected; she removed her garment. The gown slid down her shoulders and back, until it gathered around her feet. The buckshot had scattered into her skin, from shoulder to shoulder down her spine to her buttocks, creating a gruesome mess. Sinaa raised her head and stretched her neck and shoulders, rolling them forward. She looked like a blood goddess, covered in a thick, shiny, dark crimson that accentuated every muscle in her back. And after a deep breath, the buckshot began to resurface and fall to the ground. Then the wounds began to rapidly close and heal.

The keeper's mouth fell open as his eyes witnessed a scene that his mind refused to accept. Sinaa began to turn toward him, and the groundsman frantically reloaded his shotgun. He fired another shot. This time Sinaa didn't stick around to feel the annoyance. She moved swiftly, and the buckshot penetrated the dead horse's hide in several places. Suddenly Sinaa appeared in front of the hired hand's smoking, ultimately useless weapon. The man stood frozen.

Looking like a beautiful crazed woman, she grabbed him by the neck and slung him onto a waiting three-pronged garden fork mounted on the wall. The metal tool pierced his skin without challenge, leaving a bloody mess protruding from his chest.

Before he could comprehend his imminent death, Sinaa was on him again. He stared down at her with open mouth and pleading child eyes. His eyes filled with tears as he witnessed Sinaa wipe the end of the fork, smear the blood over her face, and then tongue her fingers clean. The keeper's arms jerked in reflex to his brain telling him to act. When Sinaa ripped his right arm off completely, the gun slipped out of his left hand, crashing to the barn floor. After allowing the blood to drip into her mouth, Sinaa tossed the arm toward the dead horse and ripped off the keeper's other arm. He desperately hoped for death, and finally he was granted his wish. Sinaa tore into his throat and drained what life remained. She offered an ungodly shriek of satisfaction as she surveyed the carnage caused by her own hand. She exited the stable, leaving the spared animals still in their heightened state of agitation, the only witnesses aside from me.

† † † †

Once back in the courtyard of our home, I spoke aloud, surprising her. "You're of grace, but you choose not to use it."

She turned and walked toward me, her arms out. For an instant, I remembered her beauty as an immortal angel. I was drawn to her as I was drawn to all of my children. Her naked body was painted in rouge. I took her arms and led her to the stone fountain nestled in the center of the courtyard. She stepped in and began washing her arms and legs. Then she fully submerged herself.

After a few moments, she reemerged, hair slick and wet, face absent of all traces of her encounter with the animals and the groundsman. How arousing she was.

"It's been too long since I've come to you, my lord."

I accepted her passionate offering and began to kiss her, but only for a moment. I pulled her lips from mine, and I held her by her shoulders with a force she couldn't break from.

"You would jeopardize us all for your uncontrollable thirst. Your sloppy encounters are raising suspicion about the existence of our kind. Pandora forbade you to hunt in this manner. In her absence you'll remain faithful to her commands, for her commands are mine and the same, and you will do my bidding or suffer my ire in your resistance!"

"I leave no witnesses, my lord. Stealth remains on my side."

"You approach in stealth, yet you leave a trail of destruction and carnage that suggests the work of a monster! How long will it be before someone sees you?"

Her eyes widened as the moonlight reflected black on her still bloodied teeth.

"You're not immune to death. If you continue, you'll bring death to us all!"

"Why must I hunt in the manner that pleases you?" Her tone was elevated. "We are killers! The lioness leaves tales of fleshy lust everywhere she feeds."

"We are not animals. We are vampire! There exists no other being on this earth that should remain in stealth as we must. Darkness is our life. Exposure is our death. And they will bring that exposure to us."

I sensed Eliza was watching us from my room window. I loosened my grip. She seized this opportunity to set herself free. She stepped back and regained herself.

"You'll do as I command, Sinaa. I won't ask twice."

Sinaa then stepped toward me and softly kissed me on the side of my mouth, an act of submission. She then turned and walked into our home.

I felt anger that night, more than I'd felt for a long time. Eliza sensed this anger and waited for me. When I entered, she immediately took me into her arms and sat with me.

"She's young, my lord. She knows not what she's doing. She knows not the price of immortality."

"She must change her ways! Too long has she hunted alone, without your watchful eye. Sinaa is a danger to herself and the coven. She's a wanderer who will not survive in this manner. Before long she'll bring mortals into our realm and expose our existence."

"I will speak with her tomorrow, my lord. She'll have your grace again. Now, don't let the antics of a fledgling dissuade our passion. Lie with me. Love me."

And so I did.

† † † †

Dawn approached, and though my slumber wasn't necessary for still a few hours, my dreams called my presence to order. I answered.

Again I was visited by Mynea, Vlad, and the voice of the unknown ancient one. In my earlier encounters with this dialect, I was a child student without a guide. Over time and through a way unknown to me, I began to understand this forgotten language. It was more akin to memory than knowledge.

The deep, rich voice exclaimed, *Eu sint cu voi, tinerii unul. Acolo este mult trebuie sa stii. Mai mult! In timp veti descoperi mine si invata o putere care este cu mult dincolo de orice iti poti imagina.* "I'm with you, young one. There's much to know. Much! In time you'll discover me and learn a power far beyond any you can imagine."

The words "young one" confirmed my belief that the originator of the voice was old, very old. This unknown vampire knew of our master. He knew of me, and thus Mynea and Pandora. In my dreams I could not see his face or his eyes, mouth, or body. I could only feel his hot breath. I could only hear words. The touch of death in him was ancient and forgotten long ago. Perhaps he was banished for being feared! But feared by whom?

The voice would come and go quickly, and my dream sequence would change instantly. Unlike most humans, we remember every detail of our slumber tales. Our dreams are doorways to ancient shared memories at times. At other times, they serve as windows into what is to come. Only a skilled vampire can arrange the visions in such a way as to reveal their true meaning. The dreams served as a guide to our existence and also often as paths to our destruction. My dreams concluded with visions of Sinaa holding Mynea's journal. I didn't know why she had it, nor what purpose it served with her.

† † † †

Sinaa was beauty beyond measure; I hadn't met her equal. She was of average stature for a female of her age. Her beauty had been well known in the town of Tikrit, her slender delicate face accented by eyes of a ripe pear hue. Her brows and lashes were full and thick, nose small and petite, followed by full lips that were truly edible, a neck slightly longer than the average, giving her an innate grace and queenlike profile.

She was born into luxury, the brat of a politician. Though an often unruly child, she never realized the true power of her beauty, likened to Helen of Troy. She didn't realize men would go to the ends of the earth just to gaze upon her, and once there, they would murder to be with her intimately. She remained oblivious to the power she possessed over men. Her beauty was what attracted Eliza and Pandora to her doorstep.

Sinaa was a mere nineteen years old when Eliza granted her immortality. She was watched for weeks, studied even. Pandora approved of Eliza's choice in her first immortal child. Eliza wanted Sinaa for our family, for she yearned to please her master with her selection. She knew me. She loved me. I was more than delighted to see her first child.

My next dream revealed more. Sinaa was lost to us. She had wandered into a territory that was unfamiliar to her, unfamiliar even to me, far beyond the boundaries of my coven's influence.

She was following the travels of a woman of particular interest to her. Sinaa sought the carriage of her mortal mother, who was searching for her only daughter. Her mother had heard of women missing in the central and southern regions of Romania, that is, Transylvania and the city of Bucharest. Sinaa had tracked her mortal mother into the Carpathian Mountains, a place I've only glimpsed in the memories of Pandora, and as a consequence of our intimate kisses, also in my dreams.

The carriage came to a stop at a poor weather-beaten home deep within the mountains. The horses were in desperate need of water and the mortals in desperate need of sleep. Sinaa watched from afar as her mother entered the home. As the door shut, the clouds in the night sky erupted suddenly into a great storm. Lightning and thunder startled Sinaa. She was more frightened than I'd ever seen one as powerful as she.

The horses also became frightened, and they struggled violently until they had freed themselves from their leather straps. In every direction they ran, some falling off the narrow path that served as the road they traveled, tumbling hundreds of feet, ricocheting against the jagged rock of the mountainside. Their blood spilled into the darkness as screams began to fill the air.

Sinaa dropped the journal and swiftly ran toward the home, only to be completely arrested by some unknown and unseen powerful force. Her movements slammed to a halt. Her eyes became a fiery red orange, her hair blowing wildly across her face and into the air.

The door of the home was thrown outward off its hinges in an explosion. Sinaa's mortal mother dangled in the shadowy doorway. Something was holding her by her neck from behind, hoisting her bloodied body from the ground. Though barely alive, her arms reached for Sinaa, who was suspended in front of her very eyes. And then, I saw Vlad's eyes peering from the darkness surrounding the doorframe—the abyss!

I awoke abruptly from my slumber. I used my mind to scan the house for Sinaa. There was no trace of her heartbeat within my realm, nor her distinguishing scent. I looked frantically for the one translucent window Mynea had left in my possession, her journal. But I could find it nowhere. Eliza was startled by my hasty movements. I ran to Sinaa's quarters knowing full well they would be empty, and they were.

# CHAPTER 26

inaa never truly embraced her immortality. She was a vampire with a confused human soul. Thus, she hated herself. She hated our coven. She hated Eliza. She hated me. This madness led her to leave the protection of my territory. Though our home was rich with luxury, she needed more. She needed to return to what was most familiar to her. She wanted to ease the suffering of her mother. She wanted to undo the rumors of the suicide of her father, a result of her abduction and his assumed failure to find her. Into the darkness she went.

Pandora confirmed the foreshadowing of my dream when she revealed the following to me: Vlad had left Bran at dusk. Mynea was in Budapest securing a bank under Vlad's current alias, Vittorio Sange Fiara. Pandora assumed charge of Vlad's affairs in the absence of the king and queen. She hated this charge, but to remain in his grace, she obeyed.

Vlad had gone to the Carpathian Mountains for a meal, during which time he heard the stampeding of horses in the distance. Carriage wheels whistled, complementing the heavy breathing of the exhausted mares. Vlad could smell the blood coursing through the veins of the woman. The scent called to him, but her thoughts intrigued him even more. The woman was stricken with grief, for her countrymen long ago had abandoned her, leaving her to travel the most treacherous and least-known corner of Europe alone. Under such circumstances, any rational person would have returned home; however, her grief ran deep for a missing daughter, whom she believed to be in Romania.

Visions of her daughter remained vividly in her mind. One look into these thoughts inspired desire in Vlad for the beauty that was Sinaa.

He knew they would stop at the home on his land at the apex of the lower region, for everyone who attempted passage did.

The keeper was a partially blind old man, hired long ago by Natasha to mind the house. Perhaps she felt pity for him, for the abnormal twist within his spine and oversized forehead caused him to be shunned by the villagers from the town he came from. Forced to live as an outcast no more, here he could remain in solitude, save the passing of a wanderer every now and then.

The home had two extra rooms for travelers in need of food and lodging, for a nominal fee. The old man would warn them of traveling by night, completely unaware of the services he provided his immortal employer. Vlad often visited the home when he knew there was fresh blood residing there.

Vlad arrived only moments before the carriage. He put the old man to sleep with only a thought. There he would wait for the arrival of the winded mares pulling a grieving widowed mother in search of her lost child.

Vlad's power over the winds created a terrible storm, which further persuaded the woman to seek shelter. He met her at the door and offered to anchor the horses and provide them with wheat and water. There was little water along the path, so she welcomed the hospitality of the fiend.

The moonlight added a glow to his appearance, helping to disguise his ghastly features. She was initially startled by Vlad, for he towered over her. But with his kind offering of a place for her horses and a bed, she felt more at ease. She followed him into the home, and the door slammed shut behind them.

The steeds suddenly became troubled and began kicking to free themselves. Sinaa had seen her mother leave the horses and enter the home, so she took steps forward to get a closer encounter and a better look at the keeper of the path. *This man is no human. He is more*, she said to herself.

Vlad also knew of her presence. "You are not alone," he said to the woman. "I can feel your precious daughter near. I can hear her every breath. I smell her. She is immortal, and yet you are not aware of her deception."

Sinaa discerned something was wrong by the change in her mother's thoughts. She saw Vlad through mortal eyes. She perceived this to be no mere keeper of the path. He was a vampire! She instantly barged into the home, crushing the front door. She found her mother in the arms of the beast that had revealed himself the night Pandora lost mortal breath. Her mother's neck was ripped open, blood dripping from her chest down her dress and onto the floor. She looked at Sinaa for the first time in months, yet for the last time in life.

The beast continued to drain the mother of all of her memories of the beauty standing before him. His eyes were closed for a moment, though aware of everything around him. Her mother's eyes lost focus and purpose. Then they fell halfway closed, as his opened ever wider. Dark and black his eyes were, large and fierce. He dropped the middle-aged woman onto the floor to join the blood that had escaped his thirst.

Sinaa, in complete shock and rage, leapt toward them and was abruptly stopped in midair by an invisible force. She strained desperately with all her power to reach her mother, but much to her dismay, she couldn't move a single muscle.

The furniture was slammed into the walls by his force and broken into pieces, littering the floor with wood and iron. The shattering of the window enhanced the howl of the wind. The curtains billowed as the flames of the candles exploded with fury. Vlad began to walk slowly and methodically in the direction of Sinaa, his right foot nonchalantly crushing the hand of her mother, who lay dead on the floor.

He examined Sinaa from head to toe, as a father admiring his new-born child might. Vlad was intrigued and completely captivated by her appearance, yet he was enraged by the mystery of her birth. He threw his head back, raised and flared his nostrils into the air, and took in her essence. Her scent was unfamiliar.

"You are powerful, young one." He stroked her hair and sniffed at her, as a beast exploring something new might. His hands caressed her entire body, admiring the immortal specimen, until he settled on her eyes. He raised her to his eye level with a simple raise of his left palm. Sinaa could smell his terrible breath assaulting her. She was as furious as she was ter-rified. Vlad wanted this vampire woman and all the secrets she beheld. He took her into his arms, and in an instant, the vampires vanished.

# CHAPTER 27

here I stood within the empty room once occupied by Sinaa. Eliza knelt by her bed and caressed its satin sheets. She then closed her eyes and began searching for her, for she, too, became alarmed. It wasn't unusual for Sinaa to disappear and not return until just before sunrise. However, we both suspected this was no mere disappearance.

Seven nights had passed, and there was no sign of her. Eliza would wait in Sinaa's room after countless hours of searching the nearby towns for her or her corpse. I slowly came to realize the true meaning of my dream. She wasn't coming back. She indeed left for the company of whom she'd loved and had come to miss, her human mother.

Raya and Sakina searched for her every waking moment, save the time they took to hunt along the way, each night returning without the slightest inclination of her whereabouts.

I finally spoke to Eliza about the dreams that haunted me. I told her of the fate of Sinaa in one of them. After a blood kiss, she knew my words to be true. Frantic with the thoughts of losing one she loved so dear, Eliza began to stay out longer and longer. For three days, she didn't return to our home. Instead, she would rest in a cemetery vault or the various ancient ruins surrounding Egypt.

Then, shortly after awakening together, we both sensed something strange, Eliza more so than I. It was the faint voice of Sinaa calling out to Eliza, and though I couldn't hear the voice, I could feel it. Eliza looked at me with pools of blood surfacing in her eyes. I'd never seen such despair in her. She began to grit her teeth in response to the call of her child.

"We must go to her, Aleron! She's in grave danger, and I fear if we wait, she'll meet her demise by the hands of the one who haunts you without regard."

"Fear not, my love, for I'll go. You shall stay here."

"You cannot defeat this Vlad alone, Aleron. He's ancient. He's the first of us. He'll kill you upon sight! You need me." Eliza began caressing my face. Her gaze was calming yet full of concern. She wanted Sinaa back but not at the expense of her king.

"I won't go alone," I said to comfort her. "Raya will go with me. She and I will return with Sinaa or destroy the one who ended her life!"

"You're strong, my lord, but you know not of the power you face."

"I know of my power!" I responded boldly. "I forbid you to seek Sinaa. You're to stay behind with Sakina and look after the youngest and least powerful of our family."

Eliza knew it was futile to continue, for my words were uncompromising, my decision final. She put her head to my chest. Somewhere in my cold embrace, she found warmth and solace. She found salvation. I kissed the top of her head as I'd always done, and I held her tightly, the kind of hold one gives when it may be the last one ever given.

Raya, Sakina, and three fledglings were standing in the doorway watching me put on my black clothing.

Raya and Sakina had overheard my decision, and Raya was ready to join me. Sakina took my place cuddling Eliza. Raya looked into my eyes, and with a slight movement of her head, she gestured for our departure.

Raya and I left for the northwest, Eliza's thoughts not far behind. Raya, young yet powerful, possessed necessary abilities I would need once a violent confrontation ensued. Sakina, though strong in her own right, didn't bear the ferociousness needed to defeat whatever lay ahead.

We continued near the city of Saida on the westernmost border of Syria. I knew Raya was too young to take the long journey from Cairo to the Isle of Cyprus, though it was the most direct route. The travel over the vast sea would slow us down a great bit. Therefore, we took rest in Saida until sundown.

We entered the city as thieves, using the cloak of the waning shadows as our cover, for the sun was rising. Raya cried out as her young immortal body began to stiffen with the coming of the early sun. She dropped like a stone, for her energy had been exhausted during our long journey. Before she hit the ground, I caught her.

I desperately sought cover, for her body temperature began to rapidly rise. Her hair began to smolder. I saw a structure in the distance near the coast. I had very little time, so I took flight. The effects of the sun were upon me, although our flight lasted but a moment. Gravity hurled us downward, and instead of landing gracefully, I lethargically fell, purposefully protecting Raya from the ground and covering her body with my cloak. I then dashed toward the structure with her limp in my arms, barely beating the rays of the renewed sun.

There was a cellar entrance on the side of the house. Though the place was not vacant, I had no time to enter quietly. Instead, I kicked the double cellar doors open, breaking the wooden boards that kept intruders out of the cellar. Wood and nails littered the air, then the dirt floor. I threw Raya down onto the dirt at a distance from the entrance, then hurried back to close the doors. I crushed them together, creating a barrier that provided much more protection than had the wood alone.

I hastily broke through the compacted earth to make a resting place suitable for Raya. I laid her within the trench, wrapped in my cloak, and proceeded to cover her with the removed earth. I sat up against a stair post and drifted in and out of sleep, awakened periodically by footsteps of the mortals whose home we haunted.

Cast into another dream filled with darkness and voices, I could distinguish only two. One was of Eliza calling to me. She feared Sinaa was near her end. The other was my familiar specter. His powerful awe-inspiring voice took hold of me once more. *Pericolul te arunca pisica moarta, Aleron. Danger awaits!*

I was awakened by a robust man descending the worn wooden stairs leading into the cellar. Deeper into obscurity I retreated. Raya was already out of direct sight. The man lit a flame, and for an instant I was before him; with barely a thought, I caused the fire to dwindle, leaving him unaware of our presence. I spoke to his mind and persuaded him that whatever he sought wasn't there. He turned around and went back up the stairs. I returned to my resting position. The time for hunting would be later. The family would never know our infectious bite.

The day came and went as the coming of the new moon and stars began to call out to the creatures of the night. The earth began to move as Raya's limbs awakened. She broke free from the gritty grave I provided, and we were again off, leaving behind a scene that would generate much speculation, though no mortal would ever know what happened there.

We fed on two unfortunate vagabonds on our way to Turkey. Able to cover hundreds of kilometers in a single night, we pressed forward. We flew through the trees and brush as swift as the wind, until suddenly I felt a deep feeling of sadness and loss. My heart stopped for moments at a time.

We came to rest in the city of Mersin, still with several thousand kilometers to go. Though this sensation was the first of its kind, I knew what it was. It was the feeling of tragedy. Something tragic had happened to one of mine. Sinaa! I didn't know the exact state she was in; I just knew something significant had suddenly occurred that awakened a numbing feeling of loss and sorrow. Eliza also felt it, and she called to me in pain.

Raya's sense of awareness was also heightened. Following my lead, she stopped. We looked at each other in silence, for words were not needed. The muscles in Raya's jaws tightened as her hands became fists at her sides. Hers was fierce determination, while mine was vengeance. We took flight in pursuit of the Carpathians, this time even faster, with a renewed sense of urgency.

The climate became thick with death. Immortals frequented the land of Istanbul. Raya and I read the minds of the many townspeople searching for the source of an unknown plague draining the life force of both women and men, leaving their bodies to rot. Several people were reported missing only to be discovered dismembered, some found without hands and feet, some without heads, nothing removed with regard or care. The missing body parts were never found, and the vampires had been purposefully savage in their removal to hide the puncture and bite wounds of victims.

Many of the dead, however, were found intact, each bloodless, with small holes either beneath the jaw or above the wrist. An immortal was feeding and leaving plenty behind for speculation, myth, and legend.

The vampire folklore continued to flourish as empty graves were discovered and those who were said to be dead walked freely among the living as glowing specters of the night, ghastly creatures needing blood to survive—creatures said to be impossible to kill.

We settled in a town in Macedonia, where the murders screamed loudly from the minds of nearly all of its inhabitants. Young and old alike dreaded the night, and a curfew had been enforced to keep people indoors from dusk till dawn.

Raya took interest in a man closing his butcher shop for the evening in accordance with the newly established ordinances. We watched as the man locked the doors of his store and began cleaning the floors of entrails that had spewed from the various animals he had slaughtered and sold throughout that day. He was a rather robust and hairy man, who apparently hadn't been acquainted with a bath in quite some time. The aroma was of spoiled and rotted flesh—a cologne the butcher wore daily. I couldn't understand what drew Raya to this smelly specimen, but her choice proved to serve our thirst well.

When the time came to feed, we advanced on the house. We heard him curse and yell as we entered his butcher shop through a rear door. The place was covered in filth. From roaches to rats, vermin openly dined on the discarded remains of cows, pigs, and horses. To our surprise, the butcher was already bleeding profusely from the neck. One of his arms was missing, and a scent that didn't belong to the living was present. Raya and I stayed in the darkness as the butcher began to cry out again. "No! No! Please don't kill me. Please!" And with those words being his last, we saw a vampire descend upon him.

# CHAPTER 28

he vampire in the butcher shop was unfamiliar. I didn't know if it was instinctual or by choice that Raya instantly pounced upon this immortal woman and tore her from her prey. The vampire threw Raya into a wooden pillar, which shattered on impact. The ceiling of the store began to collapse on top of Raya, and using nothing but my thoughts, I kept the ceiling intact, remaining out of the sight and awareness of the unfamiliar vampire.

She leapt out and grabbed Raya again, throwing her across the room. Raya landed on her feet, and after an instant recovery, launched herself into the woman as a cheetah would her target, biting and clawing at the neck. The nails of Raya pierced the skin of the vampire, shredding her silk garment and her flesh. A terrible screech escaped the vampire's mouth as she fell to the ground. Raya pounced on her again, ripping her hair from her head while holding her neck with the other hand. The vampire managed to throw Raya off and regain the upper hand. She broke one of Raya's arms in the toss, then bit flesh from her leg. Raya fell to the ground.

As the vampire leapt into the air, I released my hold on the ceiling above her. It fell directly on her, driving her hard into the ground. I then reached into the rubble before the dust settled and ripped her from the broken wood, iron, and other debris. I held her in the air from behind, clasping the back of her throat. She was facing away from me, watching Raya recovering on the floor. She could see that Raya wasn't holding her. I turned her around so she could face her captor.

Her eyes grew large, and amazement and fright filled her thoughts. I drew her closer to me. Her blood spilled from the wounds inflicted by Raya; her eyes, of a pinkish hue, stared at me, unblinking. I spoke to her before her thoughts translated into speech.

"I'll ask you this only once. I seek a female vampire. She would be unknown to you. Have you seen her?"

Struggling to speak, she managed to utter, "You're the one the master speaks of! It's true. There exists another."

I tightened my grip on her neck. I could feel her bones cracking, her voice wavering with the blood gurgling beneath the skin.

"I know of whom you seek. But it's too late. She's no more. Death is her companion now. She sleeps for all eternity."

Anger filled me. She was lying. Sinaa couldn't be dead! "You lie!" I growled, bringing her nose inches from mine.

"Believe what you will, but know that upon my return, the master will know where you are."

"Indeed, he will!" I replied as I brought her neck to my waiting thirst. She struggled, but she was a mere child in the grasp of a parent. She hit me with a force that damaged my face, but her attempt to harm me was futile. As soon as she retracted her hand, my face would reveal no wound. I bit down feverishly upon her neck and exposed her throat. I drank of her immortal blood. Her searing nectar provided warmth from the butcher to my body. Memories came rushing into existence, a journey on a path unfit for mortal feet. Through brush dirt and stone she had traveled from the Carpathians through Varna until our encounter with the keeper of the land, each resting place visited by her and her sisters. Owned by her master, her memories played for my entertainment!

I continued to drink and drain this vampire of all. She became weak and I, invigorated, until I saw visions of what had occurred the previous night. From her blood into my mind came Vlad! He stood in a great room surrounded by many, all of whom were his own. He ranted and bellowed his contempt for the plot that he had detected. The faces of the female vampires told me that none of them knew by what outrage their master was consumed.

And suddenly, the vision changed. I saw Sinaa. She was defeated in body and spirit, and my heart broke upon seeing her like this. Her eyes no longer glowed, her angelic body had been reduced to a mere mockery of itself. I observed no restraints; however, she floated above the coven, for all to see. Then a blue inferno she became. She burned until there was nothing left. In a rage, I sucked more fiercely on the life essence of this vampire trapped within my jaws.

Then I saw Mynea, ensconced as Vlad's high counsel, overseeing this unfolding tragedy. My heart pounded as it did the first time I saw her, as it always had every moment she was with me, as it did every moment I was alone and thought of her. Her eyes found the vampire who now nourished me, seemingly looking directly at me through my prey's eyes. I wondered if it was possible for Mynea to see me as I suckled. No, only Pandora possessed such a power to see into time at will.

I sucked furiously. I sucked until there was no more. I dropped her body. She'd be among those who were missing in Bulgaria. She'd be found, lifeless and bloodless. She'd be burned as the others were. And she'd be headless!

I ripped her head from her neck and took to the night, with Raya following close. Our pace hastened, our newfound desire for death guiding us to life. The journey continued to a place revealed by the vampire woman's blood. It was a place seen many times by her, visited by her during the many decades of her life. To Varna we went.

# CHAPTER 29

ust before daybreak, Pandora witnessed Vlad entering the castle just below the main floor. She seldom visited the dungeon beneath the castle. Even as an immortal, the memories were too painful to bear. It was there that Vlad kept humans for feasting. He wouldn't feed them nor bathe them. They would literally rot within its dank, cold walls. A tomb it served for many, for once a mortal entered, he would never leave alive. Pandora would be the sole survivor, save Mordekai, who met his fate shortly after his escape.

Pandora sought the dungeon again and arrived unnoticed. Retreating into the darkness, she witnessed Vlad awakening Sinaa's senses and sensuality. Sinaa was deep within his power, for had she not been, she would have surely tried to kill him for killing her mother, whom she cherished.

Sinaa's eyes were tamed. Her breath was steady. Vlad tore off her gown, exposing her naked body. He caressed her, though he wasn't gentle. Fueled by the anger of being deceived, he wanted to ravage her, and so he did.

Sinaa's eyes widened and reclaimed focus as his spell over her weakened. She wanted his death. However, she knew not the demon beholding her. Sinaa lunged at him.

"You shall pay for your treachery, vampire!" Every word dripped with hatred and served as the catalyst of loathing for her own immortality. She wanted his death as she wanted her own.

"At your hands, my mother suffered a cruel fate. Yours will be the same!" She knew nothing of the presence she now graced. She knew nothing of the power that rested within the beast who was our creator. She knew nothing!

Sinaa powerfully struck Vlad with her hands and scratched deeply into his flesh. He stood still as she witnessed the wounds she inflicted instantly disappear. She struck him again with more force than before, and again while anticipating her next strike, his wounds were gone!

"Who are you?" she screamed. "Where do you come from? Answer me!" She stood ready to attack again as Vlad finally spoke. "You're unknown to me, vampire girl. However, the mystery won't be long lived. I shall partake of you and all of your beauty, leaving part for the rats' and wolves' delight."

"Hold your tongue—"

Before Sinaa could complete her thought, Vlad plundered her with contempt and beastly disregard for her. Sinaa fought with all of her strength and immortal gifts, but she was completely defeated by the fiend.

He bit her repeatedly, tearing and eating the flesh from her back, legs, arms, breast, and neck. Preparing for the blood meal to come, he began suckling her throat, tormenting her, until the blood began to flow into him. And onto him came a vision that stopped his feasting completely.

He tore himself away from her. Sinaa fell back and quickly began to recover. Vlad's eyes became enraged. The entire castle shook.

The hair on Vlad's back raised, his nails elongated and became ghastly sharp, and his mouth dripped with blood. Vlad saw for the first time another vampire within the blood memories of this fledgling girl, a vision of a powerful male. "Where do you come from?" he snarled in animalistic, near incoherent speech.

Sinaa, confined to the floor, nursing her wounds, simply smiled with a blood-filled mouth and cunningly vacant eyes. She said nothing.

Invisible hands grabbed Sinaa and slung her the length of the dungeon, into a wall where her bones gave, as did the stone boundary that she had been thrown into. She plummeted to the floor as Vlad pounced on her, biting down again into her flesh, drawing out the truth of her origin.

He released his toothy grip on her when he realized her memoirs would not reveal the location of this male. Vlad knew of his existence but knew nothing of his whereabouts, a fact that enraged him. His mouth displayed large ungodly teeth stained with Sinaa's blood.

"You shall tell me where he is or you shall die!"

"I'm already dead, beast! I'm waiting for you to finish this!"

Vlad grabbed Sinaa's arm and slowly pulled it completely from her body as he spoke. "I'll tear you apart, limb by limb, until you tell me where he is. I'll leave you to rot for all eternity beneath my castle as my wounded pet. I'll deprive you of what you seek the most, as well as what you need to survive. Tell me where!"

"I'm waiting for you," Sinaa gurgled while choking on her own blood. "I'm waiting for death." She writhed in pain, lying on her back holding the bloody stump that used to be her arm.

"Then death you shall not have." Vlad straightened himself and began walking around Sinaa's beaten and broken body. "You shall have weakness. You shall be fed on by my daughters. You shall be forgotten by your precious secrets. You shall know my wrath. But you will not have death!"

Vlad exited with such speed that the walls cracked. Sinaa crawled around in search of her arm, but Vlad had taken it with him, assured to keep his promise. Broken from her fight, Sinaa lay on the floor of the dungeon. As she fell into a deep sleep, a familiar voice filled her head. *You were lucky, my young one. Call out to them, and they'll seek you. Call out.*

And so she did. With all of her remaining strength, Sinaa called out to Eliza.

† † † †

Pandora returned to the main floor to find Vlad in a fury. He called all of his children, demanding their presence immediately. All business dealings came to a swift conclusion as the main floor began to fill with immortals. Natasha entered, followed by the fledglings she created in the name of her master. Her brood was younger and not as powerful as the rest. Then Pandora made herself visible for all to see, as her children waited.

A thick grey cloud surrounded the castle. Rain pounded into the moat. The howl of the wolves and the sounds of the beating wings and screeches of hundreds of bats joined the wind and thunder in a surreal symphony of darkness. Vampires poured into Bran. Hell had called upon all its demons resembling the angels depicted in heaven. Some arrived with dark blood caked on their mouths, some with muddy feet, some in gowns and dresses, both elegant and tattered. The eldest dressed with dignity; many of the fledglings cared only for the thirst, and everything else was a blur.

The candles in the hall were furiously awakened. Wax flowed heavily as the roaring blaze consumed the candle and brilliantly lit the walls of Bran, the walls of the underworld. Vlad was Hades. He paced in front of the elevated main floor, which served as a platform, and waited for all to arrive. He was the personification of anger and rage.

The open ballroom was hot and heavy with terrible spirits rustling about. Curtains feverishly flapped and fanned here and there. Vlad's cloak regained its own will. Dark shadows crept up from the floors along the walls and ceiling, screeching and erratically dancing, resembling frantic creatures called upon to witness his majesty's might and savagery. All the while Vlad's own shadow moved objects out of its way, a display eclipsing a hundred times the spectacle when Seth was born from Sasha's disobedience centuries before.

At long last Mynea entered the hall, her dealings in Budapest completed. She walked in with a queen's poise, Persephone in this world of the dead. The other vampires prostrated themselves upon her entrance. Her children loved her. All others adored her, except one. She made her way slowly to her throne beside Vlad's, which he refused to take.

"I have evidence of treachery," he began. "At least one of you has disobeyed my order! At least one of you has kept a secret full of deceit!"

The young vampires dared not speak, yet thoughts flooded the hall as they looked at one another in despair and disbelief. Mynea was impassive, as unflinching as stone, while a slight smirk arose on the lips of Pandora.

"*Tacerea este raspunsul meu?* Silence is my answer?" Vlad questioned. "This blasphemy will not go unpunished!" The door from the dungeon below swung open with such force the stone wall cracked. The captured and wounded Sinaa floated into the hall with Vlad's invisible force guiding her. She was bloodied and broken. Her eyes opened to a sea of vampires staring at her.

"Where did she come from?" Vlad spat, carefully examining the expression on his children's faces, searching for any signs of emotion, listening for any thoughts that might indicate the origin of this unfamiliar vampire. A young one from Natasha's brood screamed as she burst into flames, for Vlad targeted her as an example of his fury and power. Her screams filled the room to capacity, as she flailed and yelled for forgiveness of a crime she knew nothing of. It was a display of the utter disregard Vlad ultimately had for all of them, all of us. She burned in the very spot she stood, alongside her sisters, who did nothing except watch in horror.

Sinaa's living corpse was rotting on the bone; without the healing power of fresh blood, she had been reduced to a gorgon—the smell of decaying flesh with that of burnt flesh as the aroma du jour. Her eyes were partially open and cloudy as a wounded animal's might be.

Some of her less serious wounds had, in fact, healed, but most were much too deep. Wounds inflicted by a more powerful vampire aren't easily made sound, especially those inflicted by Vlad. She hung as if her entire body were clenched in the palm of Vlad's invisible force for all to see, for all to admire the wages of his rage, for all to cower in his unflinching vengeance. Her body was drained of its life force. The other vampires looked upon her in horror. Some had never known Vlad to be anything but endearing. Some had only seen Vlad through dreams and omens. This display served him as well as upheld his dominion.

Mynea was unmoved. She was a true queen—heartless, disconnected, merely present. She kept her eyes focused and her breathing steady. It was impossible to discern guilt on her stoic face.

"This immortal came not from the dust as Adam. She's not flesh of my flesh, nor bone of my bone. She's not born of me! She's spawn of someone else, something else. I saw this being in her blood. I sense I'm not the only one in this room with knowledge of this."

A blue flame engulfed the head of Sinaa. Then the blaze spread until her entire body was an inferno. The fire came from within her body, for her screams were heard before the flame became visible. Fire poured from her mouth and eyes. Her fingertips and toes glowed just before the flame broke free from them. Still suspended in air, her melting flesh began to drip. Some of her flaming tissue landed on the vampires beneath her. As we were at birth, she became at death— a foul soup. The remains of her once perfect body soggily slammed against the floor. She drew breath no more, her pain extinguished. She wouldn't join her mother, for her destination was Sheol, the gateway to Gehenna, damned forever!

Vlad suddenly disappeared, and the vampires looked to Mynea for counsel. However, this time, she offered none. The wind howled along-side the wolves no more. The curtains stood still, the candles defeated. His presence was no longer felt.

Mynea emptied the entire hall with one silent command. Pandora remained close by. Mynea walked over to the burnt body of Sinaa and took a piece of her flesh into her hand. She raised it to her nose and smelled it, taking in its essence beneath the acrid burnt odor. Had there been anything left for her to taste she would have put the flesh into her mouth and searched for an answer, searched for the smallest droplet of blood, for, of course, this deceased vampire's origin was of particular interest to her as well.

She let her mind wonder since Vlad couldn't read her thoughts or the thoughts of any who were in her direct bloodline. However, it would take some effort to shield her thoughts from one as powerful as Pandora, and without Mynea realizing it, Pandora easily captured them.

Mynea dropped the flesh back onto the burnt mass. "No. It cannot be. She's not of him! He knows not the power to make another." And with this, she walked away, leaving the rats to a feast.

Pandora made herself appear in Mynea's pathway just before she retreated into the hall. She simply smiled as Mynea walked by so closely that their shoulders brushed. The putrid smell of the night clung tight to Mynea's gown, detailing her close encounter with the corpse. Their eyes locked before Pandora vanished.

† † † †

To the east Mynea traveled across the Arges River. There she found Vlad beneath the ruins at Poenari. These ruins were once part of a fortress built by the Turks and seized by Vlad's father. Even the most powerful of us needed solitude at times. Vlad's solitude would be short-lived, for Mynea was never far from him since her return. This time would be no exception.

Mynea entered the dungeon beneath the ground. This place received no benefit from Vlad's vast fortune. It lacked the silk from Asia and the marble and stone from the west. No furs lined the ground, only dirt and ash. Vlad preserved these grounds for another reason, known only to him.

As she approached the doorway, Mynea found Vlad standing with his back to the entrance. Before she took her first step, he was behind her, his hot breath assaulting her ear.

"You've come to offer me comfort, my dear, or have you answers?"

Softly Mynea replied, "I've come to soothe you, love, as I've always comforted you."

She reached her hand back to caress his neck as he looked down upon her from behind, so close that her hair moved with his steady breath.

Her eyes closed as he kissed her neck softly. His eyes, too, were closed, yet his mind wasn't in the moment. Neither was hers. Suddenly, his eyes snapped open, wide and black as they stared into air; hers remained closed. In an instant he left her for the original spot where he stood when she first spied him.

Her reaction to his absence was delayed. Her body still felt him, yet he was no longer touching her flesh with his, her hair momentarily swaying, pushed by his last breath. Realizing she was alone in the embrace, her eyes opened and she collected herself.

"What do you know of her, Mynea? You smell of her stench. I take it that you took particular interest in her death."

"I know nothing, my lord. She's of unknown origin to me as well. I wanted to touch her flesh to see if I could feel her. I thought there may have been something left behind to tell me where she came from. I wanted to smell her scent, but through the ash I could not. For you, my love, to help settle your weariness."

"Lies! All lies! I saw another. In the blood of the foreign one, I saw another. It has been outlawed for centuries to make a male vampire. I alone am sovereign. I am totem. I have made all of us. All that is of us is through me. It is my blood that flows through the veins of all who are truly immortal. Yet the fledgling showed me signs of someone I have no knowledge of. Hidden from me for how long? Answers I must have, and answers I shall have!"

Mynea remained quiet, trying desperately to keep her mind sharp and strong as Vlad continued to confide in his queen

"How could this happen? Could I have been blind for decades to the existence of another? Who was his maker? Where is he now?"

Vlad focused his gaze upon Mynea. "I demand answers to these questions, Mynea. If I have to destroy all that I've created, I will have answers. Send out your scouts and bring me what I seek!"

"Yes, my lord." Mynea left the ruins of Poenari.

Vlad, settled in his charge to his queen, found the scent of another, a familiar scent, a welcome aroma, the aroma of his first love, his immortal Eve. She appeared within the walls of this very dungeon as she did long ago. She came bearing gifts.

"Pandora. You bring me sustenance. You're here to nourish me? To caress the one you loved as a mortal girl? To love the one who killed your family and brought you to a life of death? To me you return over and over, as I know I've crushed your heart many times over. You still care for me. You still love me."

Pandora stepped out from the shadows with two men, fast asleep, one slung on each shoulder. "These men have offered their lives so that you can live, my love. I merely accepted and became the vessel of deliverance."

She placed both at his feet. "What did she bring you, my love? More empty kisses?"

"Respect your queen, Pandora. I've chosen her with reason."

"Oh, I know, my lord. I know your reason for choosing her. You want what is most distant from you. And for all of your children and concubines, she remains alone and aloof at a distance. Your cold ancient heart desires for nothing that desires you."

"This hurts you. This is why you hate her so."

"I hate her because of your blind love for her. I knew this from the beginning."

"You know nothing of my love! You know nothing of her heart!"

"More than you, my king. Better still, I know yours. I've known since you stole me from my family and kept me at Bran as its mistress in waiting. I didn't know waiting would eclipse centuries. For now, drink from the offering I've brought you."

Vlad was able to control his thirst, but when presented with such a succulent offering, it would have been difficult for any immortal to resist. Vlad lifted his hand into the air, and one of the men's bodies began to rise. Pandora's spell wavering, the man came to. He opened his eyes wide and began to struggle against the invisible hold that was impossible to break. He screamed as the skin surrounding his throat began to tear open without as much as a touch. He tried to cover his progressing wound with his hands, but his arms were outstretched, as though he were being crucified. The man cried out louder as Vlad turned his palm in a calling gesture, summoning the blood within. A spate of blood appeared in the air and then followed the path drawn by Vlad. Gravity failed in its attempt to draw the life force downward.

Vlad opened his mouth as the blood flowed into it. The cries from the man reduced to a whimper as his body continued to shake from the assault. Once completely drained of blood, his body lay empty of its spirit and was engulfed in a blue inferno as Vlad released him.

The second man witnessed the burning of his brother from the ground, looking upward in awe. He scurried to his feet and ran for what he thought was a pathway. His exit became the entrance to hell as he was caught by Vlad's cloak. Dragged backward by the neck, kicking and screaming, he fought for his freedom. His eyes found Pandora and reached for her. Instead of salvation, she offered only a smile. His incredulous, moon-round eyes screamed silently as he screamed aloud. His hands clawed at the unrelenting cloak strangling him; his feet flailed about, trying to find footing.

Vlad's cloak lifted the man off the ground and presented him. Vlad opened his mouth, and the cloak fiercely stretched and offered the man's neck. With a loud and final cry, the man went limp as his body dangled from Vlad's hold. It crushed his neck until his voice called out no more, his eyes, nose, and mouth dripping blood to Vlad's delight. The blood flowing down the man's neck to his arms, then down his side, prompted Pandora to join the feast.

As the man dangled in the air, Pandora licked at the blood, hysterically accepting its nourishment, enjoying the production of his memories until the very last drop. He, too, met his demise within the fires of hell. Ash and stench were all that remained.

The blood on Vlad's mouth and cloak seemed to be absorbed directly into the garment and skin, providing the beast with his dessert. Pandora licked the remaining blood from his cheek before it, too, disappeared as they finished the embrace with a passion-filled kiss. Though she was enjoying the ecstasy of the embrace, Vlad was elsewhere, thoughts completely consumed by another. Pandora seized the moment.

"You'll come to know her origin, my king. You only need to look nearest and you'll find your enemy."

"Tell me all, Pandora."

"You already know I keep nothing from you. My thoughts have always been open to you. There's only one whose thoughts are closed.

There's only one bloodline that you can't read. The rest of us are an open scroll."

With this, Vlad realized the implication of Pandora's warning. And then he was gone, and Pandora was left in the ruins alone. She let out a loud and wicked laugh, then she, too, vanished.

# CHAPTER 30

ust before dawn the wolves outside the castle howled, announcing Vlad's arrival. Seconds later a mist filled the room where Mynea slept, surrounding her. She knew her master was present. She began to moan as the mist transformed into flesh within the bed. Vlad's cold, hard touch was one Mynea longed for. His lips appeared before her, and she kissed them.

Rage and rapture alike shared the same beat of Mynea's heart as they continued to kiss. He caressed her as he always had, and she quickly grew accustomed to his embrace, which was completely and totally enchanting. He held her close, as a father holds a child, inseparable, her flesh and his, indistinguishable. He opened his mouth, and she opened hers to taste his tongue. Suddenly her eyes sprang open.

That unmistakable aroma, the taste of life. There was blood on the lips and surrounding the mouth of her king. His teeth and tongue were swimming in it. Ordinarily, this would be a delicacy. For a kiss laced with blood is paramount between immortal lovers. However, this time it wasn't. The blood was eerily familiar to Mynea. It was the blood of not one but many. Not mortal but vampire.

She began to see the last memories of his latest victims, victims she knew well, victims she had given birth to. Her precious immortal children's blood filled the veins of her fiend. His beastly appetite for grotesque atrocities persuaded him to forcefully read the minds of most of her children.

She saw Cosmina first. It was a swift and painful death for her. As she slept within the walls of the Sighisoara citadel, he awakened her with his grip around her waist. She arose, stiff, into instant death. Her blood spilled from the vicious deep rending of her neck by his hand, his nails and fingers gripping her jugular and opening it for his liking.

He then searched for another. In the bottom of the adjacent castle, Vlad found Violeta and Stefania. He descended upon them both simultaneously while they were in the midst of a succulent moment. They welcomed his seemingly sensual advance. However, they, too, met with grave consequences as he held Violeta down with one arm and ripped the head off Stefania with the other. He allowed blood to fall from the severed head into his mouth, and within moments, his hand penetrated the bones protecting the heart of Violeta.

Mynea flew to her feet as the visions flooded her head. Vlad simply smiled, as he marveled in her despair. She tried desperately to stop the visual assault but couldn't. She raised her hands and cupped both ears shaking her head to and fro, as if to frantically answer no to a question yet to be asked.

Anca would be the next, followed in short order by Crina—both accosted while hunting together. Vlad killed them and their prey as well, leaving only smoldering ash in their place.

"Why?" Mynea screamed. "Why have you done this?"

"It's of your blood that I've no sight, my queen." Vlad's voice was a scolding whisper. "All others knew nothing of this treachery," he continued, his voice projected and infused with anger. "I've examined their minds many times over to find nothing. It's only your bloodline that could have kept such a secret from me!"

"No, my lord. My children are innocent of this charge. I've sent Alina and Daciana to the east to answer your question. Please spare the lives of all who remain. I beg you!"

"And why should you ask this of me? Your children know full well the consequences of disobedience. I would kill every last one of them to discover where the interloper is."

The sun began to rise, and Mynea grew weaker by the moment. She braced herself against the back of a wooden chair next to her bed to keep from falling, eyes full of tears the color of roses streaming down her face and dripping onto her white gown.

"Sleep now, my queen, for you have much to do. Tomorrow night you'll call out to the rest of your brood and summon them to me. I won't ask questions. I only need to feed for answers. This is my wish, my command."

"Please, Vlad, please," Mynea replied as her muscles began to tighten as if she were slipping into rigor mortis. "My children are your children. You're killing your own coven!"

"Then give me what I require of them, what I demand of you."

And with that, Mynea's eyes closed as the slumber took her. In his last request, he gave her an opportunity to save the rest of her children, whom he now hated.

Vlad retreated to the Chindia Tower in the Royal Court of Targoviste. It was within this court that Vlad had spent many days and nights as a young mortal prince of Wallachia. This tower had been long forgotten by humans—ruins to them, but protection to us.

Outside the tower was a bust of Vlad as a celebrated man, a crude depiction of flesh carved in stone—stone that ironically resembled more his current countenance than that of his former self.

There he would remain alone, his mind wandering as the sun seared the sky, illuminating the clouds. Vlad looked over the horizon shadowed by the tower wall and spoke in his ancient tongue, *Lupul. Venit la mine copiii mei.* Wolves. Come to me, my children.

The shadows of the room closed in as the sun rose and began to move on their own. A low and agonizing moan from the ink-black shadows filled the tower. The wolves gathered below. These beasts weren't ordinary. They had tasted Vlad's blood and now served his bidding as protection during the day. They were vile, filthy, and wicked-looking demonic beasts. Nearly double the size of an ordinary wolf, they were made in Vlad's image. Their backs were humped with muscle and mangy, matted fur that was bare in spots. Their teeth rivaled the butcher's blade and were just as sharp. They proudly displayed them as they were called to duty, circling the perimeter of the tower.

Though Vlad needed no rest from the sun, he was still weakened by it, his immortal abilities limited, his strength questioned, an immortal sovereign enervated by the source of mortal life. There he would remain until just before dusk, protected by ravenous beasts whose only wish was to kill for him.

† † † †

Dusk collapsed upon Romania, and as darkness crept in, the undead awakened. Within the walls of Bran, Mynea's eyes opened, and she searched the room for her king and found not him but another standing a few feet from her bedside.

"Pandora, it's been too long since you've visited my chamber. All of my children have come to me, some more often than others. Even Natasha has sought my counsel. It's truly a delight to have you in my company, particularly more now than ever." Mynea gestured for Pandora to sit close to her. Although the inherent insult in Mynea's implication of Pandora being her child enraged her, Pandora maintained a cunning calmness and stepped toward the queen; however, she didn't sit.

"You wish not to sit with me?" asked Mynea, for in her presence all others remained in submission.

Pandora glared down at Mynea and spoke in a condescending manner.

"My concern is for the master."

"I know, my dear Pandora. Your concern has always been for my king," Mynea replied as she stood face-to-face with her subject. "But I'm afraid your concern should be with me."

"Oh, but it is, my queen. The matter at hand involves you." Pandora replied contemptuously.

Mynea turned her back to Pandora. "What matter do you speak of?"

"I speak of a matter of particular interest to my love. Such knowledge that will spell the end of your short, undeserved reign."

Mynea swiftly turned around. "How dare you speak to me in such a manner! How dare you come to my chambers and insult me to my very face!"

Knowing Pandora's power and ability, Mynea silently called out to two of her remaining children. Though it would take only moments for them to arrive, it would seem an eternity to Mynea.

"It was no insult, Mynea. You've insulted yourself. You've disgraced your lordship. You have a role in this ordeal," Pandora said, pointing her right index finger at her adversary.

"You know nothing of what you speak."

"I know much more than you'll ever know, my dear. As for the true origin of the female fledgling, I have intimate knowledge."

Upon saying those words, Mynea lunged at Pandora in utter desperation unfit for a queen—her sovereignty in question, challenged even. And as Mynea reached for the throat of her older and more powerful sister, she found nothing but air.

Pandora appeared on the other side of the room near the window, which shattered at that very instant, announcing Iliana and Madalina, daughters of the queen. They grabbed Pandora's arms, pinning her against the wall. She chose not to struggle with them.

Mynea then found her target; her hand gripped the neck of the first female immortal, her children's teeth glaring sharp and white at the anticipation of a meal more satisfying than any other they would have known.

"You know nothing of what you speak," Mynea repeated with renewed confidence. "I've watched you for centuries. You have always tried to bring disorder to our coven. Your jealousy of Vlad's love for me has made you rotten. A true demon you are! You're a beast of a woman. You sicken me. The very sight of you is a mockery."

Confined to the wall, Pandora replied, "Jealous of you. Yes, my queen, but not in the way you think me to be. Vlad never loved you. He doesn't love anyone, save himself. This should have been apparent to you when he gave birth to Natasha. Our master has no heart. So your boasts are inherently flawed."

The nails on Mynea's free hand began to grow. Saliva dripped from the opened mouths of her children. Unflinching, Pandora continued: "As for my heart, Mynea, passion has resided here before. Passion that will live here again. For your time as queen will soon come to an end. Your pitiful and ill-gotten reign at our master's side is over!"

Mynea instantly clawed Pandora's face. The assault, accompanied by a screech from Mynea, won smiles of approval from her daughters.

Pandora threw Iliana into the opposite wall with a tug of her left arm. She then leapt across the room with Madalina still holding on to the other. Upon landing, Pandora regained her footing and appeared behind Madalina. She held one of Madalina's arms behind her back while plunging her nails deep within her neck. Blood began to flow from Madalina's throat. Looking directly into Mynea's eyes, Pandora ripped her head off as easily as a child would a rag doll. Iliana tried to avenge her sister, but Mynea prevented her attack by holding her arm out and blocking her advance. Madalina's headless body hit the floor. Thick, dark blood spilled out of the ragged stump, spreading and filling the imperfections in the stone floor.

Mynea's eyes were wide and wild, affixed on Pandora's every move. And even with her powerful vampire sight, it was impossible to keep Pandora in sight, for she simply disappeared and reappeared across the room, taunting Mynea. With each sighting of Pandora, Mynea could see that the shallow scratches she had made had already begun to heal.

"Fare thee well, queen, fare thee well." With this, Pandora backed away from Mynea and Iliana. She swiftly moved to the opposite corner of the room near the closed door. Untouched, it opened, and Pandora exited, a thud echoing as something fell onto the floor. Mynea and Iliana looked at the object that had struck the floor. It was a book! Mynea's eyes grew large. Iliana walked over and picked it up. She examined it for only a moment, then brought it to Mynea.

Mynea hesitated before her hands reached out to receive the offering. "I've never seen this book, my queen. Do you know of it?"

She snatched it from Iliana. "Go away from me at once!"

Iliana exited her queen's chambers.

It was her journal, where she kept all of her secrets, in which she wrote tirelessly while away from Castle Bran. It was the journal she had left in Cairo, which her secret prince had come upon once she left him. The book hadn't been here before dawn or during the fight with Pandora. Mynea knew Pandora had dropped the journal purposely. Pandora wanted Mynea to know that she knew of Mynea's prince.

"She knows of Aleron," the queen whispered to herself as her hand caressed her naked neck; the necklace given to her by Vlad when she was mortal was missing, likely stolen by Pandora.

# CHAPTER 31

he journey proved to be exhausting. Raya and I crossed the Black Sea, and with daylight only minutes away and Varna beneath our feet, we took refuge in an abandoned manor, which once served as a Russian military stronghold, just south of the Theotokos Cathedral.

The manor was built in the late eighteen hundreds, and its halls and rooms were rank with the smell of mold and rust, which is common in structures that have been neglected for a long time. It was foul and musty, an odor that attacked our keen sense of smell, leaving us in utter disgust. The layers of dust and multitudes of cobwebs told the story. Children's footprints in the dust created patterns among the weathered and worn outdated furnishings that were scattered about.

We hadn't stopped to feed along the way, and Raya could feel the effects. In mere seconds after our arrival, she caught the scent of the human responsible for the nearby cathedral's maintenance. Raya left the abandoned house in pursuit. I stayed behind.

She returned weary from the approaching sun, yet as I embraced her, the warmth from the caretaker told me she wouldn't go hungry into her slumber. She retreated into one of the dark spaces within the house. A large closet served her well. I settled in the lower part of the old manor, for I, too, felt weary from our travels.

I dreamed of a time nearly forgotten, the passing of my parents into the afterlife. My near transparent body floated above my mother, who lay next to my father as his strong heart finally gave in to the depleted sands of the hourglass. She wept for him, while his lifeless body still caressed and comforted her. She continued to lay cradled within his cooling body. I felt her tremendous pain and loneliness. She had lost all that she knew—a son who vanished, a daughter whom she would only see for a brief time before dying, and alas, following her, the man who made up the rest of her. Now even he was gone. My mother embraced me that night—not my flesh, for she embraced death, and death I was.

I felt myself awakening before dusk. My mind was fully aware, yet my body was still asleep. Someone was near! *Perhaps a child come to play*, I first thought. No, this was no child. I sensed an inhuman soul residing within this visitor. Play was not the motive. Its movements were erratic and swift, feline, too fast and soft for a human, heavier than a rodent. My eyes opened, answering my will.

The transient was still present, though the movements ceased. I could smell her. A fragrance worn by a woman pierced through the awful smell of our resting place. I sensed Raya remained undisturbed. This creature was another vampire.

"How fortunate I am to have encountered you." The female vampire spoke from a dark corner shielded from the remaining evening sunlight. I said nothing, in an effort to use her voice to locate her. And so I did. The words became louder.

"Tell me, prince, who was your mother? Which of our sisters gave you the gift? To whom did you give your blood in exchange for theirs? And though I sense you are powerful, you will answer me!"

I felt a desire to test her power. I wanted to shut her mouth entirely. The very sound of her words sent me into a vengeful frenzy. Rage passed from Eliza through me to avenge her first. This vampire would offer me more information as well as quench a newly developed burning desire. I could not contain the desire to repeat the assault I levied on the first female vampire, for her immortal blood invigorated me far beyond any mortal's. I had to have hers. I needed to deliver her into the memory of her maker by sending her into Gehenna.

I slowly stood and paused for just a moment. Then I boldly leapt out of the shadows in the direction of the voice. So swift were my movements that nothing could have evaded my attack. The dust disturbed by my flight thickened the air and was illuminated by the sun's evening rays. But as I swung my powerful hands, I hit only air!

Snickering, the vampire continued, "My voice won't reveal to you where I am within this wretched place. The stench of the blood clinging to the face of the female who travels with you called out to me, just as loud as a child would."

Her voice came from an entirely different direction. This irritated me. Was she even there? I began to question my senses. I turned, and for just an instant I saw the reflection of silver eyes just beyond the shadows cast by the tall wooden bookshelf. I took this opportunity to lunge at the intruder, this trickster of a vampire, and again my attempt failed, leaving only an echoing crash and a crushed bookshelf.

"You've awakened the young one," she said with sarcasm.

The door to the closet where Raya slept broke open, and out of the dust flew an animalistic Raya. She spoke to my mind, *Where is she, my lord? I will destroy her.*

*No*, I replied in our silent manner. *She's more than a challenge for you. Remain alert and still.* She did as I commanded.

"You're not as pitiful as I suspected, young girl," the vampire shrieked yet again, her voice coming from elsewhere. "It is wise to listen to your master."

I knew to find her I must block out her voice and pay attention to the movement of the dust. As she spoke, I looked for disturbed particles that rustled about to the rhythm of her speech. And once I found such a place, I raised the rubble on the floor without the aid of my hands and forced the debris to attack the spot where I anticipated her next destination to be. I flew to where I thought she would flee to, and my hands caught hold of her. She dug her claws into my arm that held hers. It caused an excruciating pain, one I had never felt as an immortal. Her fingernails were acid and my skin was mortal to her touch, for there was no immediate healing afterwards. Despite the pain, I held fast and managed to collect her entire body into mine, squeezing her tightly from behind, eliminating any opportunity for escape.

"Clever girl," I whispered into her ear. She struggled and kicked for freedom, only to have her legs held by Raya, as I held her arms and torso. Her movements settled soon after her defeated attempts.

"I've plenty for you to answer, and you will give me what I desire, what I need." I swiftly bit down into her neck and began to suck her blood. Her life's force flowed into mine as if it were damned and my teeth freed it. Rushing and unwavering, it continued.

"Drain her dry, my lord. Kill this demon!"

Suddenly the euphoric feeling was interrupted by the burning sensation underneath the skin that had been exposed by her claws. Somehow the fire was rekindled beneath my skin and burned unabated. This distracted me as she tore her neck from my mouth and then kicked Raya into the opened closet. She then opened her palms and pushed the air toward me. A great force threw me back some twenty feet, sending me crashing through the door and into the hallway. The vampire also fell back into the table and chair, obliterating them.

I found my footing and immediately charged her. With my adversary before me, I unleashed a powerful strike against her, hitting nothing once again. She was gone.

I charged outside and to the top of the roof, but there was no sign of her. Raya burst through the front door, startling the single wolf that was patrolling the front of the house. Before she could take in her surroundings, the large ferocious wolf jumped at her throat, its mouth open wide and salivating violently. Killing was its only reason for existing. With blinding speed, Raya simultaneously sidestepped and ducked under the airborne beast. She then struck the wolf in midair, sending it into the shattered doorframe. It was ultimately impaled through its ribcage by protruding pieces of wood. The beast let out a sharp cry and bled right at her feet.

I returned to the ground next to Raya.

"He'll know we are coming, my lord!"

"No, he won't, my love, for I tasted her blood, and I know exactly where she's going. We must leave posthaste."

I gathered Raya into my arms, and together we flew to Constanta, on the coast where Romania meets the Black Sea.

The vampire's scent was carried by the wind. We were getting close to her. I knew that I would have no chance of entering Bran if its defenses were alerted prior to my arrival. I had to catch her. I had to continue and complete what I had already started. Her blood was shouting out to me.

I released Raya close to the ground and continued in my pursuit. She tried desperately to keep up, but she simply couldn't. To the treetops I went. Raya was running fiercely below, reading my thoughts to maintain proper direction.

I looked down as the scent grew stronger, and I spotted the vampire moving rapidly through the brush. A pack of those ungodly beasts followed her closely, charged with protecting her. Her movements were swifter than a fleeing feline. Even the leaves and branches were barely disturbed during her escape, while the wolves slipped farther and farther behind. I kept my eyes on my target.

Swiftly catching up to the snarling angry pack, Raya saw them maneuvering through the dense forest and undauntedly continued her pursuit. To her mind I spoke, *There are many of those wretched beasts this time. Are you up for the challenge?*

*I am pursuing them, my lord. They are the ones running for their lives.*

After receiving her silent confident answer, I looked to complete my own task at hand.

The fleeing vampire moved with incalculable speed, but I moved faster. Ahead I recognized the Carpathians. Dark and ghastly they were under the moonlight. She was trying to return to her master's bosom. She sensed me and looked up over her shoulder slightly. She didn't catch my eye, but her vampire instincts told her to be evasive. This proved to be futile as I threw my will at her, and though I failed to knock her off her feet, I managed to push her out of her stride just long enough to grab her.

"You'll feed me life!" I growled, slamming my shoulder into her torso, ramming her to the ground. The impact sent us into the dirt, and several yards of earth were displaced, rustling the leaves and breaking the small branches along the ground.

On top of her, I grabbed a handful of her hair, yanked her head forward, and ripped her immortal locks from their resting place. With my paws no longer on her, she threw me off, and I landed squarely on my feet. She crouched down, accepting of my challenge. Dirt and leaves clung to her disheveled hair, and the bald spot began to fill in before my eyes.

To my surprise, she smirked. "Your young one seems to have met her fate at the fangs of the master's pets. Only fitting since my sister's blood is within you. I felt it when I wounded you—anguish that you'll find hard to dismiss!"

She was right. It was as if the recognition of the wounds reawakened its fury. The fire was reignited upon my arm. However, this time, it did little to distract me, nor did the thought of Raya and the wolves. I was focused on one thing. My very life depended on the blood I'd already savored—her blood. I wanted all of it. I needed all of it.

My anticipation quickened my reflexes and vampire senses. I could feel the blood I'd already consumed rise and boil within me.

She ran on hand and foot, as a true animal would, toward the trunk of a tree, leaped onto it, then rebounded off, hands outstretched and reaching for my throat, her teeth finally making their grand entrance to the stage to join the opera finale that would end in my death! I took flight seconds before her talons met their mark. The force I exerted on her descending body knocked her backward and into the tree of her flight's origin, but she returned.

Injured, she hit the ground. The leaves scattered upon impact. I landed again on my feet. Without a second to delay, she was attacking me again, over and over a series of clawing, scraping, and scratching, her arms flailing, driving me back. She managed to rip my cloak on the left side. Pity she didn't see my hand leave my side for her face. And with one single powerful blow, I heard a loud crack as her head whipped back and to the side. This, of course, wasn't enough to kill her; it merely slowed her down.

I was amazed at her resilience. Her head was twisted abnormally, eyes nearly facing her back, the bones beneath her head slightly protruding, stretching the skin on one side of her throat, pulling her mouth and chin crooked.

She needed both hands to attempt rescue as she began choking on her own blood. I didn't allow her to fully recover. I pounced on her as a lion would another after a vicious fight and display of might. Her blood was waiting for me. It called to me, and I answered it. Her hands left her neck as I drew blood from it. She tried to tear my teeth from her throat and nearly succeeded. Nearly. But it was far too late.

Her blood nourished me, and her heart of fire began to cool, her eyes no longer staring at me with intent, replaced by helplessness and desire. I saw a longing in her eyes, and in that moment, I realized we vampire all want death in the end. She gave into me. She welcomed death with open arms. She was my mother lying almost breathless next to Aknon, hopeless and at peace. As my mother was delivered, so was she.

Her heart stopped as her eyelids began to close. The silver glow was reduced to a dim grey. In her very last moments, I saw a woman who in a different life may have served as a mate instead of a meal.

"How touching, my lord," Raya said as she approached, witnessing me in a moment of passion. For it must have looked to her as two immortals embracing each other, despite one being completely limp. Her fight with the pack of wolves yielded a face full of dirt, blood, and ripped clothing. She wore a wolf's head and skin atop her own, with its bottom jaw completely severed. A bold statement!

"What took you so long?" I replied in sarcasm as I dropped the body.

"Had to walk the dog," she said with a tinge of laughter. "Was her blood as sweet as the last?"

"Sweeter."

"As sweet as mine?"

"Sweeter still, my child." My vampire teeth were unmistakable in this moonlight, offering up a quick smile. "We must go." We gathered ourselves, and with one last glance at the lifeless vampire lying on the ground, we were gone.

# CHAPTER 32

t was November twenty-third in the year 1886. Mynea was now frantic and consumed with worry. Pandora had returned to her a mirror of her life: the journal—a memoir of the life and death of Mynea. A reflection of the adulterous kiss she had given to me. Mynea had only to look in it to discover herself again. She would see the night Vlad delivered her to the devil. She would see her embrace of the fallen angel with only a title and without the importance or significance of a name. She saw her life immortal, living as a maiden among many others, fighting for the affection of the supreme. She witnessed betrayal, deception, and death, all at the hands of her master and lover, at the hands of her sisters, even of her own hands, and bloody they were.

In her jealousy, she did what Sasha couldn't. She had created the nemesis of her king. From her rage spawned one more powerful and deadly than any of the others. And through her own deceit and longing, she gave birth in him a desire to break free of her impossible hold.

The blood-stained record now told only of death, terrible reflections of her children being targeted and slaughtered, her own actions and will turned against her. She was full of dismay and confusion when her journal revealed her to herself!

Mynea swiftly left the castle in fear of Vlad's return and what Pandora would tell him before his arrival. She didn't know where they were, but she had a place she often visited where she could remain in absolute solitude. On Lake Snagov there stood a single structure situated in the middle of the black water, the Snagov Monastery.

The night air held much more than a chill, thus the streets were completely empty of mortals. The local townspeople kept their pets and animals inside, for the brutality of the bitter cold was unforgiving and knew nothing of discrimination. The rain that fell early that day became snow before resting on the ground. Continuously falling, it completely blanketed the entire region.

All was dark, perfect cover for a vampire as swift as Mynea. She fled Bran, feet barely gracing the snow below them, the white blanket undisturbed for hundreds of yards at a time, a specter in the night if witnessed by anything other than an immortal. She called out to her children, and the remaining ones answered. They knew where to meet her.

Mynea arrived at the bank of the lake, barely panting from her journey. She felt vulnerable for the first time in centuries; mortality was at her doorstep. Through a second-story window she entered the monastery. She scanned the island and sensed nothing immortal. She felt a moment of peace as she let her children know she awaited their arrival.

Waiting in the main hall, she nervously paced and thought. She had seen what Vlad's rage could bring. Time and time again she bore witness to pain and suffering, ending in death and dismemberment followed by total consumption in fire. He was no ordinary vampire. There had been none other known to have his thirst for blood, and to my knowledge that is still true.

She heard a sound coming from beneath the main hall. Frantically she scanned the entire monastery. Her keen vampire sense failed to reveal a threat, so she dismissed the sound as that of an animal crawling around beneath the building. Then she heard yet another faint sound. She scanned the area prior to going down the staircase to the basement. Though completely unaided by light, her vampire eyes and senses searched and found nothing out of the ordinary. She went back up the stairs, and before she reached the top, something snatched her in midstep.

It threw her back down the stairs into the darkness, catching her by surprise and using such force that she couldn't recover before her body hit the ground hard. Whatever it was, she still couldn't see it. It grabbed her again and threw her into the center. With a roar and magnificent display, fire erupted, surrounding the room entirely. The stone walls burned as if doused with an incendiary catalyst. Mynea regained her control and sat up in the room, which still contained no life, save hers.

She looked around frantically as the flames illuminated the room, and what she saw brought terror to her heart: the heads of the three remaining daughters strewn about on the floor. The horror on their faces told of an excruciating demise. Crimson tears welled in her eyes. Then she heard his slow and steady heartbeat. It was menacing, simultaneously soothing and terrifying. Methodically she turned around and saw, sitting in an old wooden chair, Vlad.

The look of disgust on his face and blood thirst within his eyes spoke volumes to his intent. For just an instant she saw the eyes of a once mortal Vlad, rich and brilliantly blue. Slowly the white surrounding the blue blackened.

Mynea finally sensed others were near, and soon, one by one, the immortal children filled the basement. The flames continued to burn. The shadows screeched and rustled about. The wolves began to sing, and Mynea's heart began to bleed.

"My dear, there isn't any need for sorrow," Vlad commanded from the wooden throne. "For this is a great event, grand in all its splendor." He stood enormous before his coven, before his council of elders: Pandora, Natasha, and, lying on the floor, Mynea. "For hundreds of years an event like this has never occurred. We're blessed with immortality, yet it comes at a price that's maddening to our existence."

He walked slowly through the crowd of his children, all of whom were from Pandora and Natasha. He made eye contact with each of them. "A great betrayal occurred decades ago, and the present offers its resolution!"

Mynea, broken-spirited, lifted her head and stood firm in the center of the room surrounded by the bloodless heads of her daughters, accusing eyes prancing upon her from all directions. She wasn't their queen tonight, nor would she ever be again. She was their enemy, for Vlad required absolute devotion. Any wavering meant death!

Mynea looked around only to find the evidence of her blasphemy written on the faces of all who witnessed her rise. They would all witness her fall and ultimately her demise. Those who had loved her, hated her now even more. She felt totally alone in that moment, and she was.

Vlad walked slowly to her, and she called out to the only one who loved her unconditionally. If vampires gave in to prayer at times of certain death, this would have been hers. However, she prayed not for God, nor for salvation of her soul. She prayed for me!

Calmly he spoke, "I need not your blood to know. I need not your blood to see. For I've already seen this Aleron. And when I'm finished with you, my queen, this abomination will endure my unbridled wrath!" As Vlad sternly made his declaration, the flame roared louder and burned brighter, punctuating his promise.

Mynea ran for the entrance, and in an instant the vampire children blocked it by their numbers, forcing her back to the center of the room. Vlad commanded the others to tear her apart, and so the carnage began.

One vampire pounced onto Mynea's back and bit into her neck. And just as fast as she sank her teeth in, she was flung inches deep into the shattered stone floor, her body broken completely. Mynea finished her with a mighty blow to her chest, crushing her heart.

Another flew and knocked Mynea into the crowd, who all began to bite flesh from her. Vlad stood still as Pandora smiled, enjoying her position next to her love.

One by one the vampires were thrown about. But as soon as they hit the ground, they were back on her, clawing fiercely at their sovereign mother, completely destroying her gown.

A vampire bit her wrist and nearly severed her hand. Though wounded, the queen proved to be more than capable of destroying the vampires. Some burst into flames, and screams escaped the mouths of the unfortunate burning few.

Mynea moved like a lioness protecting herself against an unruly and hungry pack of hyenas. But as the fight progressed, they wore her down, for there were still many more waiting to taste the blood of an elder. With a great cry, Mynea pushed forth a force similar to Vlad's and sent the vampires into the surrounding marble statues and stone walls. Some were crushed, others merely wounded. Some even regained their footing instantly.

"Enough!" announced Vlad, and with this the surviving vampires retreated immediately.

And there in the center of the floor lay a weary and bloodied Mynea, trying desperately to keep herself from crossing the River Styx. Exhausted she was, yet she knew she mustn't give in, for her death wouldn't be swift.

Vlad knelt and lifted Mynea back onto her feet. Staring at her eyes, he remembered her. "You were beautiful the first night I came to you. You held beauty beyond my imagination. From that night forward, you were mine to have and to hold."

Pandora continued to smirk in full anticipation of Vlad's wrath and the death of her bane.

For moments their eyes met. King and queen together once more, Mynea bent and bleeding from her assault, Vlad standing tall, cloak bending to its own will, chest pressed into the air, chin as hard as stone, eyes black, teeth white, thirst enormous!

Mynea looked upon him in disgust. If she ever loved him at all, she loved him no more. Her hand tried to reattach itself, hair began to grow in where it had been ripped out, and her face, horribly scarred from countless claws, slowly began to heal as her strength returned.

Mynea stretched her neck and engaged his thirst for death. She knew he would never let her go until her heart was no more. With the knowledge of Pandora knowing Aleron, coupled with his failure to come to her aid, and with the loss of her children, she welcomed death. And death would answer!

Vlad's mouth opened, and saliva traced his great canines. His nose was sharp, and with his mighty bite, she let out a low cry. He began to drain her. The wounds on her face stopped healing and reopened, re-exposing blood and bone. All others watched as Vlad dined.

But Vlad wasn't enjoying this meal. He was disturbed by a sense that something was coming—fast! The other vampires became aware of it as well. They began to spread about, looking for its origin. They could hear the wolves scattering about beyond the monastery walls and above the basement. The howls were interrupted abruptly by sharp canine cries, and then silence gripped the hall.

Suddenly wind whipped into the basement, and Vlad's meal came to an end. Snow rushed in behind something that no one could see. The flames struggled for life; most were darkened instantly.

Suddenly, Vlad was knocked into a statue that resembled him, which was reduced to dust upon impact. As the dust and snow settled, Vlad regained his feet and turned around. Full of rage, he turned to see me!

I stood in the center of the room, Mynea in my arms. She was cling-ing to life, yet her eyes still found me. All present looked upon me in utter shock! My eyes focused on Vlad as the others began to circle me. He looked around to see the faces of his angels. He wanted to see how they saw me.

Was it awe he noticed from his coven? Was it envy? Was it lust? I also examined them; however, I wasn't interested in their faces. I was inter-ested in their fear. They had seen their master knocked completely off his feet and unabashedly disrespected. Their master needn't know how they saw me; he only needed to smell the fear that permeated his daughters' thoughts and feelings. It seemed the room's breath slowed to a crawl. Mine was steady. I laid Mynea gently down at my feet.

Vlad studied me for only moments before he spoke. "You have found your way, Aleron. Now you must perish with your maker."

One of the vampires leapt out of the crowd and sought my throat. She mattered little as I caught her and bit through her neck. She fell next to Mynea. The blood oozed onto the floor, drawn to the living corpse that was my maker, and she began to lick it up.

Another young and unsure vampire ran at me, and I simply moved out of her way, and into the crowd she went. Regaining her dignity proved to be fatal, for she tried to leap yet again and found herself in excruciating pain. She doubled over and grabbed at her chest. Raya walked in with hands outstretched in the direction of the misfortunate vampire. And with the closing of her palm, the vampire's heart burst. Blood escaped her eyes and ears, then her nose and mouth. She emitted a ghastly scream as her body fell lifeless.

Natasha flew to the aid of her fallen daughter. She grabbed Raya by the wrists and slung her into the ceiling. Raya failed to adhere to the laws of gravity as she simply traversed the ceiling until she reached the other side. When she landed, as a cat, onto the floor, the others began to surround her.

"Be still, my children." The voice wasn't of their king. It was Pandora. "This will be settled this night by the master and not any of you."

The vampires stayed in formation, but they didn't attack. A ravenous fiend, Raya stood, looking upon her many foes as food. She also didn't move but stayed at the ready.

Vlad walked slowly to me and began to speak again. Before he could finish his first word, I flew at him, drawing my strength from my fury, and forced him back into the wall. The stone gave, but my hands did not.

I looked Vlad directly in his eyes, the same eyes that had haunted me for decades. Dark and ghastly they were, larger in the flesh than in any dream or blood memory. And though his eyes still captured my soul, I meant to destroy his.

"Your blood reign ended the moment you exacted your will upon Mynea." I pulled him out of the wall and threw him into the ceiling, following him and then kicking him to the floor, where he landed face-down. I took a single step back and grabbed him by his hair. With a great call upon my immortal strength, I twisted his head swiftly until I could feel his spine break.

Satisfied that I could detect no heartbeat, I turned my attention to my fallen queen. It seemed my victory would be denied in that moment for I felt Vlad's cloak grab my neck and sling me. My bones felt like broken glass as I hit the stone pillar, which crumbled as did I onto the floor.

When the dust cleared and my eyes focused, I found Vlad rising to his feet, his back to me. His cloak was still wrapped around my neck, and it lifted me up out of the rubble and brought me slowly to him. He turned around, his bones actively realigning themselves, the protruding neck bones disappearing and erasing the distortion within his face. He displayed both of us for all to see, a true testament to his will and might as king.

I dangled, suspended in air, as seconds passed that seemed like hours. His eyes reopened as air filled his lungs and his disgusting breath filled the air. No matter how much I struggled, I couldn't break free of his cloak. His powerful will began to hinder my movements. I could feel it pushing against my every attempt to free myself.

"Your feeble bid to destroy me only fueled my thirst to end your existence." He smiled as his own blood dried and dissolved before my eyes into his skin around his mouth.

His cloak released me, and I fell hard to the floor. My feet found the ground, allowing me to strike again. I wasted not a moment and flew into Vlad once more. This time he caught me and used my momentum against me. He swiftly turned the tide and allowed me to buffer his body. It felt as though time had slowed to a crawl as the wall gave slightly, welcoming my back and spine. Broken stones of all sizes littered the floor. I couldn't help thinking that, if Vlad had been the originator of the force, the bones in my spine might have been fractured.

My thoughts at the time implied that Vlad was stronger. Though I had no idea of my true strength, I was convinced that his at least matched my own, and with centuries of knowledge of our power, he wielded more than I.

Vlad lifted me from the shattered barrier and thrust me across the room. The vampires standing there dispersed as I hit the floor. This time I didn't capture my footing. My back was injured and my balance was off. However, my senses remained sharp and on alert. Before I was able to stand, I felt his hand around my neck. He pulled me up, and into the ceiling once more I flew.

He was powerful, his strength magnified by his living cloak. The ceiling gave, and gravity reclaimed me. I hit the ground showered by the chunks of stone debris. Silence took over. I could no longer hear the other vampires chattering. The various heartbeats ceased to exist. My vision became blurred, and I couldn't remember if I was standing or lying helplessly on the floor. Vlad wanted all to know I was no match for him as he again lifted me into the air and drew me in with his arms.

"You're powerful for such a fledgling. However, ultimately you're pathetic," he scolded. "You're unworthy of the life Mynea has given you."

When he said "Mynea," I remembered why I was there. Defeated and in his hands, I remembered the water and almost dying at the hands of my own ignorance and lust. I remembered waking in my mother's arms and the way she gazed upon me.

My eyes opened, the blood from within feeding upon itself, drawing a strength like none other I'd ever possessed. The flames stood still, every eye upon me, my queen unresponsive on the floor, Vlad in absolute control. I opened my mouth and did what none other before me had ever done without his grace. I bit him.

I sank my powerful teeth into his neck and tore open his flesh. He tried to free himself, but the more he struggled, the deeper I bit. His blood rushed into me, and all was lost, save the two of us. The room and the rest of the world vanished. Upon a pure white background, we stood alone. I could hear the others, but I could no longer see them. I could feel them, and I knew they could see me, but as his blood flowed into my body, I saw nothing but him and me. I sucked and drew his essence into me. I took what he didn't want me to have. I stole what he refused to give anyone. I stole his memories! Thieves, aren't we all?

Within me I bore witness to his life, mortal and immortal alike. The visions came crashing into my mind like thousands of tiny explosions within my brain. I could scarcely make out what I saw, and yet a familiar sound filled my thoughts. It was a sound I'd come to recognize time and time again: the voice of the ancient one warning me. A shape appeared, his face coming into existence, coming into focus. And just before his features became distinguishable, Vlad had freed himself of my theft.

He had lost flesh and blood in the process as a chunk of his neck ripped out upon our separation. He fell back onto one knee as he caught his breath. I, on the other hand, fell to both knees, not out of defeat or fatigue, but as an overwhelming feeling of power, too heavy for my legs to bear, overtook me. My arms propped my body up as my legs regained mastery. My breath was erratic.

Suddenly I heard his heartbeat from deep within. It was fast and desperate, while mine steadied. I stood straight, and my eyes rekindled their keenness. Sounds and voices came rushing back into my head, similar to the time long ago when I was just hours old and the melody of the forest was too much to control. Strength rushed back to me.

Vlad stumbled a bit as he stood and removed his hand to display the wound in his neck, which sputtered blood synchronized with every beat of his blackened heart. And his eyes changed yet again. They became even larger. His ears grew pointed, and the hair upon his head danced to a breeze that wasn't there. His nails became black and long, his mouth no longer resembling a beastly human, not even that of a vampire. His mouth became more than ghastly. It became grotesque! Sharp teeth began to protrude from the top and bottom of his jaw. He was becoming . . . what, I didn't care to know.

I took my newfound strength and charged him. Upon impact, the remaining statues shattered and pushed the others back. Satisfied in my attack, I stood firm and looked upon the damage I'd imposed, and to my surprise, he didn't budge when my body fell against his. His feet were planted into the stone floor. They resembled a beast's hind legs, his muscle tone distinctly different, his nose elongated. I thought of the hellion wolves.

He was the beast of Pandora's living nightmares! He was the animal that man was most afraid of! His enormous hands instantly had me. This thing took back from me what I had stolen. It plunged its mouth into my collarbone. I could feel the teeth tearing at the muscle in my neck. I was unable to move; my will was completely dissolved. In an instant I recalled what Pandora had revealed to me. Could she have been correct? Was I not prepared for this challenge? These types of questions flooded my mind as I stepped closer and closer into the blinding light of mortality.

I continued to feel my life drain away. Weakness befell me, and as

I stepped closer into death's abyss, he stopped. He dropped me to the floor next to Mynea.

I couldn't move, but I could see. The monster held his chest and neck as if he were in terrible pain. His arm reached out, and a blue inferno enveloped one of the vampires. Yet the flame was short-lived and dissipated before it began to roar.

I looked at the recovering vampire and, to my surprise, standing in the stairway of the basement of this wretched place was Eliza. She was crushing the organs of the beast, similar to what Raya had done but more powerfully. Though it wasn't enough to kill him, it was more than enough to stop him.

Eliza was accompanied by Sakina, who reached out for me and swiftly brought me to my feet. She began to lead me out, but I refused to leave without Mynea. Raya gathered Mynea and leapt for the door as all others focused on their king. And into the night we went, into the Carpathians, Eliza traveling close behind.

# CHAPTER 33

akina moved swiftly without my aid, footsteps scantily brushing the earth, trees and scenery becoming a blur and indistinct. My eyes toyed with cognizance as they remained half closed. Flakes of snow fell upon my face, but only for a moment, for the speed of our travel tossed the tiny stowaways into the distance. Visions of the pond returned to me. I could see myself sinking toward the bottom, lifeless and without hope. It had been just over one hundred years since I felt human, and now I could think of nothing else.

I remembered my parents wasting away alone in al-Montaza. Visions of my sister and me frolicking as children, then Shani becoming a young lady and following in my mortal mother's footsteps with the Christ in her head. Far removed from the land of the living and ostracized from the rest of the living dead, I toggled a fine line—a line between what was real and surreal, memories that may or may not have been my own. I had stolen so many, it was nearly impossible to distinguish whose I was

beholding. The one thing that remained without question was the gruesome pain that came rushing back to remind me of what had happened
just moments before. It had been a skillful and powerful attack by the
beast that mocked every forewarning I had received from Pandora as
well as the ancient one.

The bite from the beast was spreading like a bonfire, from the
wound to the rest of my body. The pain was unbearable! He had nearly
drained me of all the blood I'd stolen from him as well as my own. I
was certain this would be the end of me. I had clearly underestimated
his power. I was warned, yet blind rage forced me into his hands. I had
lost all self-control when my eyes found Mynea lying motionless on
the floor.

Until that moment, I had thought that the love I possessed for her had
been locked away within the confines of my heart and mind. I was there
to destroy and avenge what was taken from me. My dreams led me to
that wretched place, but it was the sight of her that fueled me. The rage
took over. I no longer cared for myself, nor for any other vampire, save
her. She was all that mattered. Despite the guise of our original intentions, I knew we hadn't come for Sinaa. We had come for Mynea!

Raya held Mynea and traveled just behind Sakina and me. Though
I was far too weak to feel her, I was able to see her through Raya's
thoughts. She was beaten, aged, almost lifeless. Her head dangled without purpose, jerking to and fro with every step, her gown nearly ripped
off and bloodied, her hair disheveled, resembling a peasant rather than
a queen.

We began to slow down just outside of the mountainous region,
where Eliza retook the lead and ordered Raya and Sakina to continue
south with Mynea. Sakina placed me on the ground and joined Raya. I
could feel Eliza gathering me into her arms and placing her exposed wrist
to my mouth. Her blood flowed, yet the wound continued as a cancer
within me. Eliza's blood did little to stop the infection She removed her
wrist from my mouth and squeezed it directly over the torn flesh at my
neck. This allowed the blood to drip directly onto my wound. Though
it did little to slow the illness within, her blood began to numb the pain.

As soon as I began to feel strength returning, Eliza's pace changed. She began moving to and fro as if avoiding something or someone.

*Quiet your thoughts, Aleron,* she said to my mind. *We are not alone.*

Though my senses were dulled, I began to hear treacherous voices in my head.

*You were unwise to come here with such a lowly brood. There's no way to flee our mountains, for these are not your lands and there's no home for you here. We will finish what the master evoked!*

The silent chatter continued undifferentiated. I knew there were five of them taunting us. Raya and Sakina were far ahead with Mynea, Eliza and I in grave danger from skillful and unforgiving vampires whose footsteps gained ground with each passing second while my abilities suffered to near ineptness. I relied on Eliza for my very life.

Eliza abruptly halted, then dashed to the west. She then placed me into the hollow of a huge tree.

"You're too weak to fight, my love. Remain perfectly still here, and I'll return. Sakina has been summoned. Raya is to continue with Mynea."

Eliza fled for position as the chatter grew thunderous in my head. *You can't hide from us. You stink of fear, and it's the fear that will lead us to you.*

Eliza purposely led them away from where she hid me. However, only three followed her. The others continued to search for the wounded male.

Eliza's blood allowed me to close my mind and seal my thoughts, for if I hadn't, I would have been found lame and unfit for battle. The two vampires continued in their search, swiftly moving about in the vicinity of my wooden cradle, which could very well serve as my tomb.

It was in those moments that I felt my insides begin to boil. This wasn't the feeling of Mynea's blood coursing through my veins for the first time. This was something completely different. My lungs and heart felt as if they were aflame. I was being burned from within! In reflex, I clinched my chest and used all the strength that remained within me to extinguish the assault. I accomplished this, but the relief lasted only seconds as a vampire hand grabbed my shoulder and yanked me out of the hollowed tree into the snow. I cleared my eyes as I lay on my back and saw one of them.

The vampire had long reddish blonde hair. Her eyes were completely pearl white with a tiny pupil in the center. She wore a billowing, silky red gown, which flowed like blood as the wind tossed it at will. She wore no shoes, yet she still stood over six feet. Her retreating lips made her deathly expression even more menacing. I wasn't afraid. If Death awaited me at her hands, then I would meet him with dignity.

I slowly raised myself to one knee. My heart and lungs recovered from their fiery possession. I smelled the other vampire just moments before she scored and tore open flesh on my face. As I was reduced to kneeling, both knees planted on the ground, I looked upon two completely identical vampires, not only identical in physical appearance but also in garment.

They began to speak. It was peculiar, for they spoke perfectly in sync with each other. The oneness in speech created an unnatural and lingering echoing effect, Vlad's sirens of death.

"It's futile to stand against us. Either of our powers could easily destroy you, for the master's bite has imprinted you with certain death."

I gripped the cold, wet mud and snow between my fingers. This allowed me to focus on the matter at hand, for it distracted my thoughts from the pain of Vlad's bite. They could have easily attacked me, but they allowed me to stand.

"What are you waiting for?" I questioned. "Am I not a fitting meal? Or has fear changed your miserable minds?"

They both giggled then suddenly lunged at me from opposite sides. From some unknown depth, I drew on strength that I hadn't felt since my deathly encounter moments before. I moved with such speed the two of them nearly collapsed into each other, narrowly escaping inevitable and momentarily crippling injury. They redirected and came for me again. This time one secured my legs as the other grabbed my arms. They had me. And I had them.

I forced myself backward, dragging one twin, who held onto my feet into unforgiving brush; it was a minor annoyance for the vampire but an annoyance nonetheless. The other's grip slightly loosened out of concern for her twin, whose screams echoed loudly from the discomfort of the tiny branches scraping her eyes. I threw the vampire holding my arms into the hollowed tree Eliza had previously picked for me. She landed squarely with a thump.

I then kicked the remaining vampire on her forehead with enough force to crack her spine, and she let go. It was only seconds before the fallen twin lunged from the tree and took hold of me from behind, biting and clawing at my flesh. It took all my remaining strength to pull her by her head and force her release from my back. I threw her over my head and dropped again to my knees. And like a feline, she landed squarely on her feet near her sister, who turned and contorted her neck until the spine resumed its function. She then, too, stood as they both began to smirk while looking at me.

"You'll be a scrumptious meal, Aleron. You must know your death is upon you."

"And what of my death? Will I be as tasty as my master?" Sakina swiftly descended upon them both from above the tree canopy and landed next to me. Shortly thereafter, Eliza returned. She was caked in blood, and the garment she wore hung about her in tatters. She tossed the heads of three vampires at the feet of the twins.

"They were but a minor delay," Eliza said, showing her crimson-soaked teeth. "You'll prove less worthy than they!"

The twins suddenly felt doubt, and in an instant, they were gone.

Sakina was preparing to give chase, but Eliza spoke before her feet left the earth. "Let them go, my child. We need to leave these lands now."

That night seemed to last an eternity, yet, like all others preceding it, it too came to an end.

We settled in a vessel, which had been previously readied for our voyage by Raya. The ship's crew had met an untimely death at her hands, save one who could guide us under Sakina's spell. Mynea lay beneath the main deck inside a coffin that was filled with earth that Raya had gathered from the ground surrounding the pier. There was another coffin next to hers, which lay empty. When it was offered to me, I accepted.

Eliza laid me in the wooden box and kissed my mouth before closing it. The earth within this coffin began to soothe me. It created a new cradle, one that would heal my wounds inside and out. Then I heard a familiar voice.

*La Noua lume trebuie sa te duci Aleron. Departe de el!*
*To the new world you must go, Aleron. Far from Him!*

# ACKNOWLEDGMENTS

Special thanks to Mr. And Mrs. C. Jones Jr. Thank you for your unwavering support. Your faith has allowed me to accomplish wonderful works that will forever be immortalized in the minds and thoughts of all those touched by this literary work for generations.

Special thanks to Kane and Kai. You two are what is pure within me. You are my very reason to keep going. I pray when it is your time, you, too, never stop. Be the best you can be in whatever you do.

Special thanks to my parents. Everything begins with you. You have encouraged me in all of my endeavors, from taking my first step to writing my first book, and everything in between. To make you proud has always been my goal; however, to make you smile is all that truly matters. Thank you.

Thank you A.R. Crown. Though we may not always agree on what should be captured by the pen, you make me think, and for that I am grateful.

Thank you Elaine Bell. Your influence on me began many years ago, and, still, it has a positive effect on me. Thank you for helping me achieve my dream.

Thank you L.A. Milton. It is your patience with me and understanding of my ways that has helped me reach out beyond my own boundaries. Thank you for your support.

Thank you Bert Fitts for setting a wonderful example of remaining chaste in business dealings and a great friend to everyone, including those who are less than great to you. You are truly inspiring.

Thank you Leonard Millsaps for listening to my imaginative ideas and for sound, constructive criticisms.

# ABOUT THE AUTHOR

Kane has been interested in fantastical creatures for as long as he can remember. His fascination with the paranormal grew as he studied witches, warlocks, and werewolves. Finally, he sank his teeth into the world of the vampire. *Aleron* is his first of five novels that detail the challenges of being immortal.